Praise for
Cole Alpaugh

DASH IN THE BLUE PACIFIC

"Surely Dash's run of bad luck must be winding down. He's lost his job and fiancée and finds himself alone on what should have been his honeymoon flight from Vermont to Australia. What else could possibly go wrong? Lots of things, as it turns out. In Cole Alpaugh's darkly comic and richly layered *Dash in the Blue Pacific*, the defeated Dash never makes it to Sydney but instead crashes in the South Pacific. What seems like a near-death experience at first is actually the beginning of a mind-bending, life-changing journey for a man at the end of his rope.

"The weird parts work because Alpaugh integrates them into a story that is physically raw and wickedly funny. Dash is as incredulous about all that is happening as anyone, and his self-conscious skepticism keeps the magical elements from seeming off-the-wall. Little by little, Dash's conversations with Willy reveal Dash's deeper emotional wounds, and offer another interpretation for his dreamlike visions.

"Taken simply as a comic adventure story, *Dash in the Blue Pacific* is thoroughly entertaining. When you consider the other elements— racial tensions, human grief, and spiritual redemption—it takes on new levels of meaning. Book clubs will be talking about this one."— Sheila M. Trask, *ForeWord Reviews*

THE SPY'S LITTLE ZONBI

Finalist, 2014 ForeWord Magazine Book of the Year Award

"Forget James Bond. I'd much rather spend my time with Chase Allen, the idealistic journalist-turned-government spook at the center of Cole Alpaugh's outlandishly entertaining new novel, *The Spy's Little Zonbi.*" —Josh McAuliffe, *The Scranton Times-Tribune*

"Imaginative. Funny. 3D Characters that come to life on the page and leave you wanting more. *The Spy's Little Zonbi* is Cole Alpaugh's best work to date!" —Michelle Fleece, Publisher, *The Wayne Independent*

"*The Spy's Little Zonbi* defied my expectations. It is at times gruesome. It is at times heartless. Cole Alpaugh's use of dark humor and timing is impeccable .... Part *The Girl with a Dragon Tattoo* and part *The World According to Garp*, Alpaugh's latest offering is an exhilarating read that I highly recommend." —Ann Schmidt, MLS, The Public Library of Cincinnati and Hamilton County

"*The Spy's Little Zonbi* is a clever and sometimes sad novel about the lunacy of the modern world. It is a vivid, emotional, and imaginative read." —Olivia Patel, Redbridge Central Library, London

THE TURTLE-GIRL FROM EAST PUKAPUKA

The book is playful and comic in its creation of ... misunderstandings and coincidences. As their stories unfold and intersect, one comes to believe the island is indeed paradise, as Jesus plays a heroic role and the cannibal, Albino Paul, the shark god, and the birds play out a finale resounding with echoes of myth." —*ForeWord Magazine*

"Dr. Doolittle meets LOST ... interesting and colorful cast of zany characters on a crash course with fate." —Michelle Fleece, Publisher, *The Wayne Independent*

"Teeming with outlandish scenarios and bizarre yet deeply compelling characters, *The Turtle-Girl from East Pukapuka* is a veritable feast for lovers of playfully absurd fiction. Who knew cannibalism could be this much fun?" —Josh McAuliffe, *The Scranton Times-Tribune*

"Would a god really eat his own boogers? He might in this wonderful, crazy, non-linear novel filled with a cast of characters floating in and out of a literary universe peopled with pirates, South Sea Islanders named Dante, Jesus, and Butter, and a Loggerhead turtle with cosmic consciousness. Controlled craziness at its best, this novel dazzles with its stylistic inventiveness. " —Jack Remick, author of *Blood* and *The California Quartet series*

"Lyrical and yet wonderfully warped, if *The Lord of the Flies* had been written by Kurt Vonnegut, you would have some idea of what to expect from Alpaugh's second novel. Heavily outfitted with wry humor and cutting sarcasm, this unique tale doesn't pause for a breath. You are swept into *The Turtle-Girl from East Pukapuka* with the same energy as the tsunami that sparks the critical events leading the reader across the vast South Pacific and at breakneck speeds along a downhill race course, all headed to a place in the afterlife known as Happa Now .... A highly entertaining read." —Hua Lin, MLS, Los Angeles Public Library

"Butter is a six-year-old Pacific Islander who cares for wounded creatures; Dante is a hot-shot downhill racer; Jesus Dobby runs a scavenging barge; Ratu & Jope are pirates and Abilone is a cannibal. All these characters meet and while it is not always pretty, it is pretty entertaining. I quite enjoyed the ride. Alpaugh reminds me of James Morrow with more gore and explosions. He has created a fairy tale with mythic figures and classic characters; and an assumptive logic to the cosmos that allows him to end the story without tying everything up with a bow. *The Turtle-Girl from East Pukapuka* made me laugh and made me cringe, but most importantly it made me think about the world order and how to spend the time we are here." —Uncle Barb's Blog

"Alpaugh's words dance in the mind and tug on the heart." —Regan Leigh, writer/blogger

THE BEAR IN A MUDDY TUTU

"There's a story inside, both charming and heartbreaking." —Alex Adams, author of *White Horse* (Atria Books/Simon & Schuster)

"If you enjoy fast-paced, quirky reads filled with offbeat, colorful characters and a touch of sorrow draped in the colorful striping of a circus tent, I think you'll enjoy *The Bear in a Muddy Tutu.*" — Damien Walters Grintalis, author of *Ink*

"Pick up *The Bear in a Muddy Tutu* if you enjoy taking a literary journey that is twisted, peopled by characters who are social misfits, caught up in events that range from bizarrely tragic to merely sad. Reminded me in a way of *A Confederacy of Dunces.*" —Molly Rodgers, Library Director, Wayne County Public Library

"I'd recommend it if you want a charming, bizarre tale with a satisfying, fate-driven ending. It reads a little like Christopher Moore but with more heart. It's fanciful, beautiful, and escapist to the core." —Mercedes M. Yardley, author of *Beautiful Sorrows*

"A delightful read full of wonderfully twisted characters trying to muddle through this thing we call life ... a must-read." —LK Gardner-Griffie, author of the two-time Pearson Prize Teen Choice Award-winning Misfit McCabe series

"If you are looking for a 'big top' read with lots of heart and laughs, and characters you can sit down with to listen to their story for a spell, magic, whimsy, and dancing bears, then look no further than Cole Alpaugh's *The Bear in a Muddy Tutu.*" —Shannon Yarbrough, author of *Stealing Wishes*

"From the first page to the last Cole Alpaugh had my attention. His zany and colorful characters and style of writing puts me in mind of one of my favorite authors, John Irving. I suspect that I have now found my next new favorite author." —Michelle Fleece, Publisher, *The Wayne Independent*

Walking
to
Candy Land

Walking
to
Candy Land

Cole Alpaugh

caleastupress

Los Angeles, CA

caleastupress

California East University Press
PO Box 1081
Los Angeles, CA 90017

For more info go to www.caleastupress.com and www.colealpaugh.com

Cover design by Ty Alpaugh

WALKING TO CANDY LAND

ISBN: 978-0-9982670-0-5 (Trade Paper)
ISBN: 978-0-9982670-1-2 (eBook)

10 9 8 7 6 5 4 3 2 1
Library of Congress Control Number: 2016957431
Printed in the United States of America

For Emilia, The Princess of Charleston.

ACKNOWLEDGMENTS

Thanks to my old pal Henry Rollins, whom I first met two decades ago while assigned to photograph his spoken word tour at a college somewhere in Jersey. We were in a faculty lounge, with a platter of Cheetos and onion dip, and a stunning coed in tears after spilling a water pitcher down Henry's back and on his beloved notepad. Henry, I said, thousands still want to bang into each other while you perform the most psychotic music ever conceived, why bother with this storytelling gig? Henry dipped one of the Cheetos and dropped it into the empty pitcher, then rinsed his fingers in my glass. Cole, don't underestimate the impact you can have on a quiet room, with Candy Land game pieces spread across the bed, and a pair of adorable kiddos dreaming about unicorns. That to me is a perfect stage for chaos.

Thanks for all the weird memories, my friend.

My deepest appreciation to Amy for making these books possible. I'm nothing without her. And my gratitude to Regan Leigh, my talented writing partner. You both rock like Rollins.

So now the room is quiet. The children are asleep. I'd like to welcome everyone to my Candy Land.

Also by Cole Alpaugh

Dash in the Blue Pacific

The Spy's Little Zonbi

The Turtle-Girl from East Pukapuka

The Bear in a Muddy Tutu

ONE

Lizzy feeds out string and lets the wind gobble away. The diamond-shaped kite soars, wild vibrations blurring its butterfly patterned skin, knotted tail an angry snake. Her burden grows as if the air is thicker near the clouds, and she frowns like she always does when juggling a thought. The kite bobs and tugs, the same as when Petey was a puppy and held on to his purple dinosaur for dear life. A squeaky snarl meant mine, mine, mine. Her frown twitches into a smile, and she glances back toward her mother. Lizzy opens her mouth to share the memory just as a powerful gust jerks the thin nylon fiber across her palm and slices tender flesh.

She wrestles for control as it dips and pinwheels. Green leaves tear free all around, join napkins chasing paper plates over bent grass. She digs in her heels, hips turned sideways, and twists the spool with both hands. The string is spotted red, but she isn't afraid of blood. Not anymore. Only babies cry when they see it, and she isn't a baby.

"I'm not a baby."

She frowns again, tries ignoring the heat from her wound as she turns and turns, wrists aching as the kite reels closer.

"Don't lose my kite, baby." Celia stalks up from behind, bumps her shoulder. "Gimme."

Her older sister snatches the spool even though she's maneuvered the kite clear of dangerous tree tops.

"I didn't hurt your stupid kite." She rubs a thumb across her palm, feels the bloody groove as proof of her competence. A baby would have let go. Or cried.

"Help Mom pick up trash. Dad's still trying to get dumb Petey to play fetch."

Lizzy eyes the scattered plates, the flying napkins that have

1

made it almost to the tree line at the meadow's edge. Daddy wanted this picnic, said the wind would make it even better. A perfect kite day, plus a storm is coming tonight and they might be stuck inside tomorrow. But she knows it isn't just the weather and the possibility of being home without TV or internet. God, she could picture Celia's Candy Land board spread out on the kitchen table, the camping lantern turning everything yellow. Worse than not being able to flush.

Daddy is making them do family things because Mommy is sick. Not throw up sick, or even blow your nose a hundred times sick. Lizzy has seen him hold her hand in the car, and any time they are close enough to touch. Like their hands are magnets. It made her smile at first. But he keeps asking Mommy if she's okay, and if she's taken her pills. He whispers so the girls can't hear. He started cooking, mostly spaghetti that is chewy because he doesn't read the instructions on the box that tells how long the noodles are supposed to boil. Even she knows not to stick them in when the water is still cold.

He promises that Mommy is fine. Everything is hunky-dory. She is afraid to ask again. Mommy isn't fine. He told a lie. She has to take pills. Celia doesn't know anything. She pinched her arm really bad for being stupid, and Lizzy was confused by the meanness.

Daddy is taking care of Mommy in a secret way, taking care of a secret sickness that Lizzy suspects he doesn't fully understand. His whispers are always questions. And Mommy has stopped jogging every day. Her pretty hair is greasy and flat even though she takes long showers.

Lizzy has stopped smiling when her parents hold hands. It feels like they are saying goodbye.

"Go!"

She is jolted back, her sister practically breaking her eardrum. Celia is her bossy self even though Lizzy knows her sister still does baby things, like worship her Candy Land game. And even though she talks to her friends about boys they want to kiss, Celia sometimes sucks her thumb when she's asleep. If only Lizzy had a camera. No boy would ever kiss a girl who did that.

Lizzy considers fighting back, but the litter is more important. They learned in Miss Shedd's class how it is everyone's duty to keep nature clean and not pollute. Miss Shedd held up a picture of a litterbug, which is a cartoon grasshopper with a cigar in his mouth who throws bottles and crumbled papers from all his hands. They learned China is the worst polluter in the world, a place where litterbugs own factories with gigantic smokestacks that make acid rain, which kills everything. But not people or dogs. She had raised her hand.

She ducks under the kite string without another word, heads in the same direction as the rushing clouds. She scoops the first plate of smeared ketchup and baked bean juice, folds it over so it isn't so gross. She does the same with the next, but the napkins are still on the move, probably a whole dozen. They look like birds that can't see very well, or aren't sure where their nests are hidden.

The wind whips hair across her face as she jogs the last stretch of grass, dandelion heads bumping off bare shins, her breath huffing. Maybe she hears Mommy's voice, or maybe it's Celia teasing some more. She doesn't turn, doesn't give her sister the satisfaction. Mommy says ignore your sister, but it's hard work. The wind makes the trees sway and rub together. They are tall, without limbs until way up high where the leaves turn them into giant lime or green apple lollipops. She finds two napkins pinned to the same tree, but all the rest have flown inside the dark place.

She stands with her black Converse sneakers far apart, hands on her hips, trash squeezed in sticky palms. "I'm not a baby," she tells the shadows that begin a few feet away. "I'm not afraid."

She steps over a low prickly bush and out of the daylight, shorts and Powerpuff Girls t-shirt offering little protection. The edge of the forest is cool, and light flickers as if someone is taking pictures. The sound is different. It's the kind of rumbling the ocean makes when they carry towels up over the dunes for a day at the beach. The noise is big but not loud, like thunder that's still far away. She nearly steps on a napkin, smiles, plucks it from a tangle of twigs and dead leaves. I'm not afraid, not a baby. She looks around for others here where the air is almost still. They wouldn't have gotten far.

A flash of white catches her eye, forces out a hiccup. She takes two quick steps behind a pine tree's rough bark, and stands frozen on a thick matt of brown needles. A man is crouching, bent over his hands that seem to be molding a chunk of clay. He is skinny, the curve of his backbone a bumpy row running up his droopy shirt. And not just skinny like Aunt Melissa who got cancer and had to wear a wig, but skinny like a Halloween skeleton. He wears funny sandals that show his dirty his feet and ankles.

She is close enough to see his crooked nose, the messy gray hair that's long, with some of it tucked behind an ear. When her eyes adjust even better, she sees it is a bird and not clay in his hands. It looks like one of the seagulls from the landfill on the other side of town, where the yellow bulldozers growl, and the giant trucks come and go all day. The man's fingernails are long, the same as the fake ones in the drug store aisle with the pretty bottles of polish. But his are also different, cut into points instead of half-moons. Weird.

A drop of sweat rolls down and stings her eye. She crumples the trash into her front pockets, leans into the tree and wipes the back of one hand across her face.

The bird makes a low squawk that doesn't sound like fear, so the man must not be bad. Animals can tell. It would have flown away if there was danger. Dogs always knew, even Petey who hardly knows how to fetch. Miss Shedd said that cows lie down on their bellies when an earthquake is about to happen. They know even before the really smart scientists. Cow scientists! Imagine a cow in science class, standing on its back legs and trying to use a microscope, a doctor's coat with a Professor Cow nametag. Lizzy smiles.

The man rocks on his heels, stroking the white feathers, and then leans forward like he's going to smell the bird. But instead of sniffing, his tongue pokes out from between his lips, and he does the most wrong thing she has ever seen. Even the cleanest bird can have bad germs. Mommy told her. You're supposed to wash your hands with soap after feeding Alice and Gus, even if you only touch the food tray latch.

She watches the man lick the bird, one hand across its chest and the other trapping both wings. He licks and licks. Like an ice cream cone! She has to cover her mouth to stop the giggles. The strange man thinks the bird is vanilla flavored. Blinking to concentrate, she decides it must be a motherly thing, at least an animal mother thing. She saw a newborn calf being cleaned, and mother cats do it to their kittens all the time. Maybe it's his bird, and not one he found here in the woods. Maybe he knows it doesn't have a mother.

Petey yelps out in the meadow, and she hears her mother beyond the ocean sound of the trees. Guilt washes over her for spying, which is a naughty thing to do. She turns her back, feels the jagged bark against her shoulder blades. The tree catches her hair, pulls out a few strands when she moves, like it doesn't want her to get away. If she marches slow and straight, the bright light and safety are only a few steps, almost close enough to touch. There's another napkin off to her left, snagged on a root and waving like a surrender flag in one of her school books. But she lets it stay because the bird's voice has changed, is asking to be set loose, and she can't risk it. She will have to be a litterbug.

There are wet sounds, and she knows without peeking that the man's tongue is sliding over the bird, wetter and wetter, lapping like when Petey drinks. It grows loud enough to drown out the ocean above, is even louder than her thumping heart. She would be caught for sure if she tried for the napkin, caught by something that might pin her arms down, lick her like a dirty bird.

She begins one step toward freedom and hears an awful crunch that is something like snapping twigs. The words *snapping bones* come to her lips. Her legs turn to stone as she listens hard and prays not to hear that sound again. The sweat on her arms is suddenly icy, her stomach jabbed by a cramp that makes her need a bathroom. She risks a backward glance, can't help herself, but what she sees doesn't make sense, isn't possible. Nobody would do such a thing. *Only a monster*, she whispers, rubbing at the groove made by the kite string.

In the wavering shadows, the man's long face is turned toward her hiding place to look at the naughty little spy. His lips are pulled wide, teeth clamped down on what she wants to believe is something else, anything else. A fat marshmallow, maybe, like the ones they were going to put on sticks and turn black over the fire. But Daddy said it was too windy, maybe next time.

Her legs come back to life and she runs until she can't breathe, until Celia is laughing and calling her a fraidy cat and a baby. *Fraidy cat, fraidy cat. Baby is a fraidy cat.*

She almost tells her big sister that monsters are real. But she won't. She's not a baby. She is slumped in the back seat when Daddy reaches for Mommy's hand. Her hand is pale. So pale it hurts. Daddy takes them away with only one hand on the steering wheel. Lizzy watches the trees, and then the telephone poles. She chews her bottom lip, squeezes her bear. Theodore makes it not so bad. Celia has headphones and hums all the way.

Hours later, she is all tucked in. There is distant lightning beyond the bedroom window. She knows the man bit off the bird's head, was eating something that had just been alive and making sounds. *A monster, not a man.* I saw a monster, but I'm not a baby.

Next to her bed, Alice and Gus come awake inside their hooded cage with a song she doesn't recognize. She rolls over, burrows under the pillow, wonders what her canaries know.

TWO

The front door of the tidy farmhouse explodes inward from a perfectly placed kick. The man wearing heavy work boots has made it through his fair share of dead bolts, and this one is cake. Some guys pick locks, others knew what all those goddamn alarm wires meant. A boot was good enough for him, the right tool, whether lacing them tight for a hard earned buck or stomping a random queer for a little Friday night fun. A good boot did the trick every motherfucking time.

The man's partner slips past and shows off his own special talent, popping the switchblade and quieting the homeowner's brave little pooch with a single quick slash. Not a cut meant to kill right away, no crippling disaster for the meat and bone. This is a surgeon's flick of the wrist that twists the old blood faucet to medium. It sends the mutt scurrying with a shiny liquid in its wake, blood that's nearly black on the hardwood floor. The intruder with the knife nudges his partner, points the blade down at the gory trail, smiles and shares a wink. The men begin following the dog, the one in front humming a song about a yellow brick road.

**

Miller is wrenched from a peculiar dream of flying monkeys when Petey leaps onto the bed and stumbles across his naked feet. Sharp nails dig into soft spots, and Miller curses under his breath. He stifles a yawn to make sense of the throaty slurps filling the dark room; a noise that competes with the downpour threatening to drown the old farmhouse. Petey is making his drinking from the toilet sound, messy gulps of water and air, done fast because he knows he'll catch holy hell if the light flicks on. The dog circles as though trying to get comfortable, but loses balance and splays over his master's legs. Petey never liked thunder, but this is ridiculous.

"Christ's sake." He shifts to get the dead weight off his knees, and Petey emits a sharp whimper that isn't right, buries the last real chance for sleep. The dog lurches forward on his belly, rough paw pads are sandpaper on his shins. Pain in the ass. He reaches for his wife's warm thigh under the blanket, but she's in her usual full-on hibernation mode. Lucky her, it'd take a crash landing by one his flying monkey to stir before the alarm.

Petey tries rolling over, hips and legs jerking. "It's a just a storm, you dopey dog."

He pushes up against the headboard, yawns, and then squints at his watch dial. The Indiglo says there's three more hours of night. He'd been drowsing in and out, listening to rain hammer the clogged gutters, one more lousy chore before there was a chance of ice.

Something heavy strikes the roof on the far side of the house, the vibration felt through the bed, and Petey is back on his feet. His bark is an old man's damp cough.

"Chill out, hero, or I'm sending you to investigate." He taps the mattress for the dog to lie back down.

Miller pulls his legs free from the comforter and is about to shove the dog off the bed when the room lights up for an instant. It leaves a crazy afterimage across his vision, and he blinks at the frozen snapshot. The half-terrier, half something else mix stands on three legs atop the messy covers. The dog's front right leg is cockeye, as if broken, pointing off into the dark corner by the closet. Blood surging from a deep slash across his throat's white fur is the wet racket source. A pink bubble on the side of the poor mutt's neck is about to burst in the image left on his owner's confused eyes.

Another flash and Petey is back on his belly, head lolling to one side. Miller grabs for the bedside lamp and twists the switch, but the room stays dark. He twists again and again, panic building as the wind has somehow gotten inside their cozy home. The ancient electric clock that's gently buzzed a foot from his pillow for as long as he can remember is silent. It takes a moment to comprehend the power has been knocked out. He maneuvers to his knees with low grunts and bends over the dog, the rain tapping the window as if asking to come in. Reaching blind except for the horrible picture that is now only a memory, his trembling hand finds the top of Petey's head.

"What happened to you?" He drops both feet over the edge and begins scooping the now lifeless animal into his bare arms. He wants to at least save Mary from the worst. She can deal with splinters and scraped knees, but he has to get Petey out of the room and wrapped up in something. Jesus, the girls can't see this.

As he begins sketching an immediate plan, wind slams the bedroom door open hard enough to crack drywall. Downstairs, there's the sound of breaking glass and blowing papers.

Then there is a voice. Three or four unintelligible words spoken in a manner that turns his stomach and makes his testicles draw up inside his abdomen. It is the voice of a man trying not to be heard. Miller stands frozen, straining to hear more, but there is only the rain and his own muffled heart beating deep inside his ears.

"Honey?" Mary's drowsy voice makes him nearly drop the dead dog. He looks down, considering if there's any chance she can see what he's holding. He prays the lightning doesn't repeat.

"A window broke." His throat is bone dry, a contrast to the deluge outside, and the warm trickle down his arms. Perhaps a broken window explains everything, and a glimmer of relief blooms. Petey had freaked out, had somehow run through one of the living room windows and been badly cut. It explains the wind, too, as he angles away from his wife and begins skulking around the bed with his terrible cargo.

What about the man's voice?

"Oh, shoot, the power must be out." She clicks the button of her own bedside lamp. "I'll get the flashlight."

"No!" He shuffles toward the door, sticky blood oozing down his belly flab, surely coating his boxers. Before he can reach the door, there are footsteps on the wood stairs. They are heavy, lumbering, and there's no possible chance it's one of the girls. He knows their sound on those old steps, whether it's bare feet, fuzzy slippers, or squeaky sneakers. This is marching, the robust thumping of determined evil. He bends to let Petey slide from his arms next to the door frame.

"Someone's in the house," he says to Mary. Intruder is the word that comes to mind, but the warm slime old Petey has left on his hands says something much worse. The voice comes again before his wife can respond, and he's deciding on some makeshift weapon when two dim figures cross the threshold. Mary cries out, and there

9

is laughter from one of the men that sounds more like one of poor dead Petey's barks.

Down the hall is the commotion of beating wings and distressed chirps. The girls' canaries must be darting from side to side in their cage, banging up against the bars, night cover a billowing fabric ghost. Sit and wait for them to calm, he had told his daughters each time the fragile birds became agitated. Stay back and talk to them in a low voice. They'll eventually settle for the night.

"Fucking bats," says one of the dark men.

"You got bats in your house, buddy," says the other, making a cluck with his tongue. "I hate them things."

Miller balls his bloody fists. "Get out of my house!" He spreads his feet on the wet carpet, preparing to fight. His night vision has adjusted well enough to see they are both about his height, in jeans and the dark shirts of people who break into other people's innocent lives.

There's quick motion, and it's Mary's bedside lamp that strikes his left cheek. The white flash isn't lightning, but an explosion inside his head. The porcelain lamp was one of the treasure finds from the weekly flea market down in Dalton. The rotted cord was an easy enough repair. On top of the four dollar fixture was a brand new thirty dollar shade.

Now the lamp is in a hundred pieces, some small chips embedded in his swelling face. My blood is getting all mixed up with Petey's, he thinks, and tries to reconstruct how he ended up on his back. His jaw aches, and then his hair is pulled hard, nearly torn from his scalp. Something snakes around his neck.

"Mary?" He tries to get a fix on exactly where he is in the dark room, but the noose is yanked tight and another internal flash stutters across his vision. He tries calling her name again, but there is no air for words. The noose is further cinched, as though his hangman isn't content with strangulation. No, this bastard wants a beheading.

He reaches for his neck to feel the texture of the lamp chord he'd so cleverly replaced. It is new and strong, slick and bone hard. Maybe I'd have half a chance if this monster was trying to kill me with the old cord. He is jerked up and back, and there's the sensation his hangman is tying the cord off on something, like a calf roping cowboy. Probably three looped swings around the closet door knob.

How long since my last breath? He pries two fingers under the cord, making it even tighter.

"Please, no!" Mary is screaming again, and he can see the outline of the man on top of her. There is tearing fabric and hard slaps, the dull thud of a punch. She stops screaming just as he's able to squeeze the tiniest hint of cold air down his throat. His temples pound from his drumming pulse. He pictures himself with a cartoon head being pumped full of air, a comically fat balloon near the point of bursting.

Mary is being hurt in the bed they picked out on a broiling Sunday afternoon. He remembers the air conditioning of Chucky's Sleep Paradise, and her silly mood. His shirt was clingy with sweat from the short walk across the lot, and she'd tried tickling him on each bed they sampled. He was embarrassed by the growing roll of blubber around his middle, and he snapped at her a few times. But she kept it up, and he relented to a ridiculously overpriced set after a few whispered naughty promises. To him a bed was a bed, but she saw it as something more. It was a special place for romance, and for the nightly routines of a husband and wife that were even more meaningful. He hated himself for being short tempered that hot day.

"Mommy?"

"Please, no … " The two words use the last bit of air. His eyes bulge as he strains against the cord when both girls step timidly into the room. Beautiful Celia is twelve, in her pink shorts and white pajama top. Little Lizzy is in her hand-me-down robe and footy pajamas, stuffed bear clutched to her chest. Somewhere near their feet, hidden in the darkest shadows, is their real pet, probably still oozing blood into the carpet.

"What's happening, Mommy?" Celia asks, and the man assaulting her mother stops his animal thrusting to look over his shoulder.

"We're here to fix the washing machine," says the man pinning Mary to the bed, and his partner snorts, then spits. Miller lunges against the impossibly tight cord, his neck muscles beginning to spasm.

"We're Maytag men!" shouts the other man from behind his girls, blocking their exit. Both scream and run toward the far corner. Lizzy falls across tangled bed linens and Celia tumbles on top of her. The girls grab at each other and hold on, crab walking on their butts away from the intruders.

The man in the doorway takes three steps toward the girls on slightly bent knees, arms held out as if herding chickens. He has black work boots with eyelets that suddenly shine silver, and Miller strains for a glimpse at the window. A truck is approaching from town, rumbling along the unlined blacktop, a yellow safety light turning circles. Inside would be two Pennsylvania Power & Light linemen with cell phones, or two-way radios at the very least. The diesel engine drowns out the pummeling rain, and the invaders pause.

Miller's mind begs the driver to stop. There must be some reason to pull into our driveway. Maybe check on a good, paying customer in the middle of a raging storm. They'd see the door has been jimmied, rain blowing across the welcome mat and soaking the wide plank floor of the mud room. Something is wrong here, and one of the linemen would remember reading a newspaper story from a few towns over. "Call the cops," he'd shout over the gusting wind to his coworker, and the two monsters would be scrambling back down the stairs to search for another way out of this family's still salvageable life. But the power company workers aren't out in this storm making folks answer doors. They are surely looking for a live wire dangling from a blown over tree. The wire that's too dangerous to wait and fix after the storm is dancing and arcing across the road, maybe catching small fires the rain keeps dousing.

"Stop," Miller pleads to the power company truck as well as the invaders. His mind pictures a red button and an imaginary finger pressing it over and over. A rewind button also appears, and he begins hammering it with his palm.

The spinning yellow light grows brighter, turns the eggshell white walls into a disco room, as distant lightning precedes the drumming base. He can hear the gears grind and a metal squeal that might be brakes. The invaders are still frozen, Miller's two girls whimpering in a flashing huddle, trying to be small, trying to be somewhere else.

"Help me." It is Mary. Miller has momentarily forgotten his wife is pinned under the weight of her rapist. In the turning light, Miller can see the man's bare rump.

"Mary," Miller tries, gasping, digging his fingers into the cord. Sucking in another painful breath, he lets go with his right hand and reaches blindly along the carpet at his side, until his fingertips brush a solid object. It is the remainders of the shattered lamp. He inches his fingers forward, raising his chin and choking himself more. Fingers scuttle across porcelain bits and moist carpet as his windpipe is nearly collapsed.

"Please," he hears his wife say, and he wills himself farther, the chord slicing into his throat that is blood-slick and hot. His fingers spider walk around the heavy lamp base and he uses the heel of his hand to push backward an instant before blacking out. I did it, he revels, and is surprised by the air filling his lungs. The chord loosened a fraction, and he takes deep breaths to recover some strength. The yellow light is approaching their driveway as he finds a solid grip on the round metal base. It will easily break the window, but what are its chances of reaching the road? It's another thirty feet beyond the front porch, but maybe the lineman riding shotgun will be looking at the small, well-kept house at just the right moment.

He slows his breathing and relaxes his muscles. Not too soon. Be patient. He pulls back his right arm as far as it will go. The dresser makes it difficult, but by leaning to his left and sacrificing his newly found air supply, he has a clear shot at the window facing the road. White light floods the room when the headlights splash over the house. Miller tenses, and then swings his arm with all his might. He lets go with a strangled, bear-like groan. The metal disc flies from his hand toward the brilliant light, a short tail following that he recognizes as a piece of the same chord wrapped around his neck. The storm window doesn't just break, but erupts outward in shimmering fragments. The truck noise invades the room as violently as the two men had only minutes before.

"You fucker," says the man looming over his girls. He turns on Miller, face pale and unshaven, hair wet or greasy. The man's eyes are baleful slits. Miller sees his teeth, brown in front from cigarettes or chew. And then the man is in silhouette, and it is probably the black boot with silver eyelets that squarely strikes Miller's face, mashing his nose and setting off a whole grand finale of blinding fireworks.

"Run, Celia," he tries to say, and maybe he does. "Take Lizzy's hand and run." Another kick snaps his head back hard enough to crack the surface behind, and he senses something has also broken inside him. The room goes black, but his hearing still functions because the noise of the truck engine remains, although its welcoming growl has lessened. It is now *outside* the room, is rumbling on down the road, leaving his family alone to fend against monsters.

"No!" Celia cries out, breaking his heart into more pieces than the lamp and window combined.

You could have made it, honey. It was your one chance. But I spent too much time teaching you that monsters weren't real, didn't I? Nothing in the closet, and absolutely nothing under the bed waiting to pull you down with it. The munching and crunching that woke you up was Petey working on a chew toy. The bump in the night was your wonderful imagination; the terrible shriek a lonely barn owl searching for a mate. I had it all explained for you. Nothing to worry about because Daddy would always be there to hold you tight and keep you safe.

"Leave her alone!" Lizzy shouts, and Miller knows the monster is devouring his oldest daughter. Above, the other monster is making the bedsprings come to life, the headboard drum the wall. A one man band performing a symphony from hell.

"Help me, Daddy." It is Celia's voice. And there are ripping clothes and more animal grunts.

She doesn't know about this kind of violence, is still only a little kid, really. She'd had the talk with her mom, but she'd been more interested in the abstract concept of love and commitment, and how you were supposed to know when the first kiss was okay. Mary kept him somewhat in the loop with an overview of a chat that included the mechanics, anatomy, and even condoms. There was no mention of brutality, of this kind of violation. Miller had sometimes imagined the boys he'd have to deal with, sniffing around his suddenly pretty oldest. That was supposed to be some other kind of tragedy, dealing with teenage boys with the same perpetual boners he once had. His 12-year-old still wore princess pajamas, bounded down the stairs on Christmas morning happily pretending Santa Claus was as real as Taylor Swift. She had her first babysitting job two months ago, carting her own Candy Land board game under one arm, the box taped in ten places. She called her mother a half-dozen times to check in.

"Where are you, Daddy?"

I'm right here, honey. Mommy's here, too. Even Petey's here, but he's hurt real bad, isn't breathing anymore. I'm so sorry,

14

sweetheart. I should have explained this was a possibility. I thought I was protecting you when I should have prepared you. I believed with all my heart this couldn't happen. I thought telling you and Lizzy would be too much, would make you afraid of the wrong things. And now I can't take it back. I can't undo any of this. I let you down so badly, only warning about the easy things. Look both ways before you cross the road. Brush twice a day, even more. Monsters are only in books and movies.

"Gloppy is a monster," Lizzy once said, shuffling the cards and resetting the colorful playing area of the game her sister introduced. But Lizzy never obsessed the same way, had been suspicious of the characters.

Candy Land had been Celia's favorite when she was little, and the box has resided on a shelf in the girls' room since she was three. For Lizzy it had been storybooks before sleep. For Celia, it had been two solid years of bedtime Candy Land, until it abruptly stopped mid-Kindergarten. Had some stone-hearted classmate made fun? Nobody still plays Candy Land. That's for little babies. She never said, and they didn't pry. She was navigating stages, had found something new. She took up colored pencils, drawing the world as she saw it, boldly discarding the familiar view of a game invented in another century by a teacher recovering from a virus now nearly extinct. He can picture the box on the neat shelf, feel the melancholy. How many times had they played? Hundreds, he was sure, and maybe a thousand.

He was guilty of not preparing Celia for evil. But guilt wasn't a new emotion. He'd learned to live with it over the years, spending too much time distracted by his job, hearing but not listening to the tiny, serious voice of his little girl navigating the colored spaces—she'd once proudly counted all 134—across Gumdrop Mountains and Peppermint Forest. He tuned her out too many times.

"Help me, Daddy!"

The man on top of his oldest daughter is naked except for a sleeveless undershirt. They're called wife-beaters, right? His body thin, but his shoulder and back muscles are well-defined from hard labor, maybe construction, or maybe prison push-ups. One black work boot filled with a dirty sock faces Miller, as if daring him. Lizzy is balled up beyond them, squeezed next to the trash basket, hard to distinguish with his damaged vision.

"Take a card, Sweetheart." Miller's voice is a croak, his throat an open wound. But nothing like what Celia is feeling. No sir, not even close. "What color did you get?"

"Make it stop!"

"You landed near Gramma Nutt, and we laughed about your grandma being a little nutty. Remember when she baked a pie with her reading glasses inside? Oh, heavens to Betsy, that's where they got to, she'd said when cutting a piece. She told you she loved getting old because she could hide her own Easter eggs and still have a whale of a time finding them."

His daughter answers with gurgling noises, as though she is drowning.

"I'm safe here next to Jolly, but have to make another trip past Lord Licorice and all those creepy bats," he tells his oldest daughter, who sounds as if she's dying. "Why does a lord have bats? Are they pets?"

He does a quick memory check for who recently spoke of bats, but nothing comes.

"The bats are just pictures on the game, Daddy. You aren't supposed to ask things like that," Celia had explained.

"My turn with the runt," Cowboy Boots announces, making the bed springs twang as he dismounts Miller's motionless wife. He is also naked from the waist down, shirt unbuttoned to show a filthy white t-shirt with a truck logo over the heart.

"Mary?" he tries, but the cord has come to life, is iron fingers and jagged nails, and now there's a low whistle with each push and pull of his lungs. He wryly decides he's also a musical instrument.

Cowboy Boots laughs when he steps over the man defiling Celia. "Giddy-up, Lone Ranger!" he says, and does a fast two-step, some sort of country line jig. Then he snatches Lizzy and her stuffed bear, hauls them to the bed. She's thrown face down, then rolled to her back. He pushes at her robe, rips open the footy pajamas bellow her belly, the worn seams giving easily. Her underpants tear as if made of paper. No, Miller thinks crazily, they are made of pink bunnies and blue flowers. I saw them folded on the hamper when I started her tub.

And while Celia is no longer making noise under Black Boots man, Lizzy begins screaming. It's an unimaginable sound, an almost unbroken shriek that lasts the entire time Cowboy Boots hovers, pumping his evil, a spastic drunk demon calling out words, maybe a song, or maybe he's encouraging Lizzy's screams that are the color orange on cobalt, the smell of ammonia. It is the same ear-splitting pandemonium as when she stepped on a nail where Miller had performed doghouse repairs, narrow metal shaft sliding through a sneaker to impale one full inch of tender flesh.

When Cowboy Boots nears finishing, Miller sees him lift his hands from the bloody sheets and grab her precious throat, brawny arms tensing as he squeezes the life out of an innocent baby girl. Miller hopes she is still holding her bear.

The room is quiet for the next few minutes, or maybe it's hours. The rain has let up, and the thunder has rolled off to distant places. The walls begin to flash red at some point, and Miller finally stirs for real. His head throbs and his eyes are dry from being open too long. It's the clock, he realizes, reborn with its electric buzz to flash twelve, twelve, twelve. The linemen have found the downed wire, have taken care of the danger and restored power. Everything is back to normal, despite Miller still hanging by the neck from a closet doorknob. He shuts his weary eyes, unaware that the evil men have left him alone with his dead family.

THREE

Miller wipes mint shave cream from his ear lobe, brushes it on the front of his jeans. He's fresh from showering away smeared lipstick deposited by a sobbing coven of women in black. A dozen shades cake in both corners of his mouth like dry spit. But it was the blood that came off the hardest. It stained his skin no matter how vigorously he scrubbed. It tattooed his forearms, left scarlet tears on his jaw, and a red ghost of Mary's face printed on his chest. There was so much of it. Even worse than wearing the blood was seeing it swirl down the drain. He shut his eyes and followed it through the narrow pipes to witness it spill into the dark septic tank.

His lovely, kind Mary. She had rubbed his fevered temples, always remembered to kiss him goodbye. She looked at him with unwavering love when he did something right, and forgave his short temper. She took care of him before she took care of herself. He got fat and she took up jogging. She didn't pressure him to come along, didn't make him feel the guilt he deserved. Her way was to present an opportunity. It was also her *modus operandi* with the girls. Allowed them their own choices, good or bad. And now he had spent most of the day rinsing the last bit of his wife to mix with foul dishwater, with urine and shit.

How many days since the police arrived with spiral notebooks and yellow tape to create a temporary crime scene? It used to be a home. It had two beautiful girls who rarely fought and almost always did their homework; girls with perfect skin despite all the candy. Girls who listened to silly music and danced in front of the television to video games he didn't understand. It was a home with girls who each had their own diary full of secrets. He stands facing out the open front door of what might still be a crime scene, fighting an urge to go find the diaries, not to read the words, but to smell the child-scented pages.

He had wandered into the girls' room hours earlier, hungry canaries making a fuss, zipping from side to side of their metal cage. Little feathers wafted to the cluttered carpet. He lifted the cage and sat with it on Celia's unmade bed. Wrapping his arms around it did nothing to settle the birds, but he was overwhelmed by an urge to make them know his sorrow. They had suffered, too, had lost the soft voices of comfort.

The window over the bed was ajar, probably to have allowed in night air but keep out the storm. Mary knew to do those little things. She understood harmony and balance. He let go of the cage with one arm and shoved up the window. He pushed out the screen that was always sticking from a bent frame, let it cascade into the backyard. He pried the delicate bars of the cage and lifted it to the wide sill.

"Go," he had told the birds, then dropped the empty cage and went back to his shower to scrub at another layer of blood.

Miller's hair is still damp. The heavy oak slab is pushed half open, fresh air and buzzing insects flooding past to explore the new shade. The door is inches thick, with three double panes of glass at eye level. The dead bolt extends like an accusing finger, but its wood and metal cradle is twisted and splintered. Locks are supposed to keep you safe. Close the windows, pull the curtains, and turn the locks. Alarms were only good for after the fact. Poking those little buttons and having the green LED wink was all for show. An alarm would sound after the intruder was inside, flashlight in one hand and maybe a knife in the other. Who might answer when the alarm company dialed your number?

A dead bolt was supposed to be different. It was supposed to keep your wife and daughters safe from the boogie man. Miller touches the splinters with the tip of a middle finger, presses the wood shards with the soft pad. Like a porcupine must feel. He presses harder, feels prickly numbness all the way to his toes. Was it some kind of pressure point? He knows the one behind his vaguely mint-smelling ear lobe, has rubbed it through sinus infections and occasional hangovers. Mary had shown him. He pushes hard enough to break the skin, and the strange numbness tingles at both shins and behind his pudgy kneecaps. Harder still and his nipples go erect. A tear fills his right eye. He would drive the wood slivers clean through to his fingernail if the truck doesn't distract him.

He closes his mouth, reaches with a bloody hand to wipe drool. A voice, probably inside his head, chuckles and calls him a village idiot. *Here you are, slack-jawed and slobbering down your shirt, with nowhere to go and feeling shot up with Novocaine, or maybe heroine. Speaking of drugs, isn't there a stash of Mary's brown prescription bottles with little typed-on labels? It's over the bathroom sink. Waddya say, sport? We can stop all this sad-sack, moping around bullshit and have us a party. I'll even help with those pesky childproof caps.*

"I can't die right now." He speaks to the truck's cloud of diesel exhaust slowly lifting in a bluish cloud, out where there are two monsters and three fresh graves. *Oh, make that four graves,* chimes the voice ... *can't forget the one out back by the big elm. Yes, sir, there are all sorts of unexpected things in this new world. It's a brand new place! You didn't really put old Petey in the grave. It was more like you* poured *him in. Light as a feather, too, and you know why? Petey leaked all his blood on your bed and into the carpet. Man's best friend was running on empty by the time you tucked him in all cozy with a topsoil blanket. Ha, well, running is definitely the wrong word.*

A brown sedan slows, the car perilously drifting toward the far side gulley as driver and passenger turn for a look at the crime scene. The woman in the passenger seat has neatly piled white hair. The man squints behind gold rimmed glasses. Miller sees his mouth move and her head nodding. *That's the husband,* Miller knows he's saying. *Poor bastard did nothing while his wife and daughters were violated right in front of him. He seemed to make it through just fine, though, barely a scratch. Makes you wonder what kind of man allows that to happen to his family.*

Miller tucks his bloody hand into the front pocket of his jeans, shouldering away from the heavy door and its broken lock. He begins to walk.

FOUR

The road is a faultless gray line, narrowed by perspective to cradle a dying sun. It is a landscape painting too ominous for a motel room. Perhaps a few horses bent over the alfalfa would dress it up. Or some other element of tension to make it Holiday Inn worthy. Me, whispers Miller, putting one foot in front of the other, marching into the gloaming. I am the element of tension in this landscape.

"You're so full of shit." It is a familiar taunting voice, had made itself known during long road trips when fatigue convinced him it would be okay to close his eyes for a few seconds. Sure, go ahead. No worries. It'll be refreshing, make you good as new for the next eighty miles. You know you want to.

The voice was in the bloody shower, and each time he woke from tortured sleep. The moment his mind wandered, it was there to remind him what was lost.

"It's pretty here," says the inner voice. "And while we're on the subject of motels, we should get a room in the next town and hang ourself in the closet. God, I love the smell of cedar."

"Shut up." His voice much weaker than the one inside his head, he tries concentrating on moving onward over the loose gravel.

His shoes are a gift from Mary, still new and cushiony. Hiking shoes, she told him, light and durable, ideal for the trails in the links she'd sent. They are the most expensive shoes he's ever owned, the price of a dinner for four at the Applebee's in Dickson City. Too expensive, he'd said, but understood the investment for an out of shape, 40-year-old man's heart. The shoes remained boxed on the dining room table for better than a week, before Mary put them up on his closet shelf. No pressure. They were there if he wanted them.

He doesn't remember taking them down. They felt right when he'd laced them while sitting on the stained mattress on which he'd never again dare sleep. He had flexed his toes against the nylon and leather, or whatever space-age material made them so light and yet rugged. They made him feel like he could walk forever.

Night takes over as the miles pass. Cars are a steady stream. And plenty of pickups with aluminum ladders and steel tool boxes. He picks out a star to follow, not knowing much about astronomy. There was a TV show about ancient sailors who used the pole stars for navigation because they never disappeared below the horizon. He imagines being adrift in a boat, a patchwork sail to catch the slight breeze, as his feet power him forward.

There are houses every few hundred yards, though some cluster behind dented mailboxes with flickering bare bulbs casting erratic shadows. Bullet riddled stop signs are intersection sentries.

The houses are barges and the surrounding fields are open ocean. On the knoll of a grassy pasture is a solitary mermaid eyeing his slow progress.

"Nice mermaid, sport. You and your fancy-pants Dali mind," his inner voice mocks. "Sometimes a cow is just a cow."

All around is the near silence that comes from huge empty spaces, where a distant bark is stifled like a blanket over a candle. There's an unseasonable chill for early fall that will sharpen in the coming hours. The recent storms have pulled air down from Canada, hinting of change. Clogged gutters will fill with ice and pull free. The first few inches of dirt will also freeze and create another barrier to what was his life.

From miles away comes the hushed sound of an army marching in step, which delivers comfort from loneliness. It is an hour before he recognizes the sound as his own feet, masked by all the numbness.

***

Miller is stirred from a dream by voices and reaches for the alarm clock. He stumbles along the gravel shoulder. Blinking and rubbing at his eyes, two men are playing a violent game of tag around a small pond in the side yard of a ramshackle house. The pond is a perfect circle, maybe 15 feet across, and rimmed with flat stones. The man giving chase has a metal baseball bat that reflects the glare from a garage flood light. The house is flanked by a rusty sedan up on blocks. In the chaser's right hand is a flashlight that projects a dancing beam.

"Goddamn sonofabitch!" The pursuer is barefoot, naked except for boxer shorts and the great hairy mat over his chest and potbelly.

The other is tall, with a shock of white hair that bounds off his shoulders as he turns clockwise loops. He runs hunched over a clutched package. His gate is spastic, heels kicking up behind too high, almost comical. He's wearing sandals that provide miserable traction on the grass.

"You put them fish back 'fore I crack your skull!"

Miller leans at a mailbox with peeling paint, its surface cold under his arm. His legs tingle and his lower back is caught in an aching knot.

"They were sick, sick, sick," the tall man calls over his shoulder. He maintains a half lap advantage until the armed man performs an unexpectedly graceful pirouette and reverses direction. The move gets him close enough to take a swing that barely misses, and the motion causes him to lose ground. He drops back, chest heaving, but keeps his beefy legs pumping.

"We should let these loons sort it out for themselves," chimes the inner voice. "The road beckons."

Miller kneads his lower back. "In a minute."

"I'm gonna kill your ass!"

"It was animal cruelty," says the tall one, his voice high, almost delirious, and it begins to appear he's purposely staying just out of reach to tease the fat man.

But the fish thief's feet slide and the gap again closes for another swing. This time the bat's sweet spot glances off a skinny thigh, although the blow doesn't take him down.

"Ouch!" he cries out, and begins to laugh, regaining his loping stride.

"You sick motherfucker!" The portly man again swings, connecting hard against one foot and spinning the tall man into the shadows. He attempts to fall on his side, protecting whatever is cradled to his stomach.

The pursuer is standing over the downed man, flashlight held out in front, bat at high noon. Before Miller can take a step, the man in dirty boxers swings the bat like an ax, striking the thief's legs with a sickening thump.

"Please, sir, I want some more." The tall man's voice is a gleeful, intoxicated.

"Have all you want, asshole." The pale flesh on the attacker's chest and stomach reverberate with each strike, and Miller anticipates agonizing screams that don't come. The blows must be crippling, bits of knee and shin bone splintering every which way. But it's mostly silent when the melee pauses, just Miller's padding feet across the uncut lawn, and the fat man's rasping breath.

"Gimme my fish, you sorry bastard!" The bat is again raised, flashlight picking a target. Miller can see the tall man's olive skin and sharp features. He might be Indian, or Middle-Eastern, his white hair wig-like in the stark light. He looks to be in his sixties, a lot of those years under a heavy sun.

"Hey, stop! He's had enough." Miller is close when he speaks, and the man with the bat yelps, takes a backward step and wheels toward him.

"Who the hell are you?"

"I was walking by, out on the road." Miller maneuvers to put a portion of the pond between him and these lunatics. He displays both hands to show he's unarmed.

"You're with this sorry piece of crap?" The man again brings down the bat much slower, taps the side of the tall man's pant leg that has dark grass stains streaking up to the knee. The flashlight shines on the downed man, is then raised to blind Miller.

"I don't know him." Miller uses a hand to block the beam, tries seeing between his fingers. "I was just walking."

"Jesus, Frank, where you been?" says the tall man from the grass, then laughs again, this time a cackle to unnerve any wildlife hiding outside the ring of light.

"You're some kinda lookout, ain't ya, Frank? Come trespassing on my land to steal my goldfish!" He stalks around the pond, causing Miller to retreat.

Miller holds out both hands, shaking his head. "Listen, I was just walking past, I swear. My name's not Frank, and I don't know this guy."

"Nobody walks this road unless they broke down. I ain't stupid. I know you two is in cahoots." The man's anger renews. His walk becomes a trot, flashlight and bat held like track runner batons.

Miller continues backward, searches for an escape route.

Despite his exhaustion, the hours of walking and lack of food and water, he can surely outrun this man. He is, after all, befitted with top of the line hiking shoes.

"Run, Frank!" the tall man calls out. "Never surrender!"

"I swear to God!" Miller shouts, which unleashes the full rage of his near-naked assailant. Miller catches a glimpse of the guy's penis in the harsh floodlight as it springs loose through the fly hole and bounds crazily toward him, a bulbous mushroom jerking like an injured rodent. Miller is suddenly frozen by an image of Cowboy Boots hovering above his youngest daughter. The man held his penis over her still body until a stream of urine cascaded.

"I'll kill you both!" shouts the man, and Miller is back crumpled on the floor of his bedroom instead of being tackled on some sweat-slick stranger's lawn. The impact takes his air, and he falls over the tall man.

"Hi, Frank," the man says brightly from underneath.

Miller is grabbed by the collar and feels a dull throb of pain he knows should be red hot. The cuts on his neck have torn open, and oily blood seeps from crusty scabs. He smells cigarettes and fried onions in the man's wheezing. Stubby teeth are yellow and crooked in front, but none are missing.

"I'm sorry," Miller says, after managing a breath. "I'm very, very sorry."

"That's a start," says the man pinning him with his great weight. "But it ain't good enough, shithead."

Miller anticipates the blow, closes his eyes, wondering if he'll hear his skull fracture, or if it will be like the flip of a switch. One instant alive, the next you are being fitted for a cushioned coffin pillow.

There's a moment of silence, and then Miller tries making sense of the light right up against his face.

"Hey, I know you. You're that guy who let his family get killed over in Factoryville. Ain't that right?"

Miller nods, eyes still closed.

"So who's this asshole?"

There's the sound of muffled giggling. Miller feels shifting angles, a knee and elbow in uncomfortable places.

"I'm the Ghost of Christmas Past," hoots the trapped man.

"Shut it, fuckwad." The man sprays spittle, his mouth close.

He's addressing the nutjob underneath, but is examining Miller. "Something mighty peculiar 'bout a person who robs fish. He's some sorta retard that don't feel no pain."

"No pain, no gain," says the tall man, and then begins to sing. "Coming for to carry me home!"

"You knocked out his brains," Miller says with no joy, and the weight on his chest lifts away as the fat man grunts and pushes to his knees. The flashlight stays on Miller as if he's some sort of curiosity.

The tall man stops singing, makes the sound of clearing his throat. "Now that we're all friends, anybody got a Band Aid?"

FIVE

The sky behind the two men goes charcoal to lavender. The tall stranger limps in a jarring rhythm, clear plastic bag of dead goldfish clutched to the front of a muddy shirt. A slice of moon is enough to light the road, and Miller hunts for his shadow. No cars have passed in the hours since their escape. Louisville Slugger. Bat man. He smiles and rubs a hand over his own belly that has already shrunk. When had tying his own shoes become a wrestling match? Or cutting his toenails? Jesus.

He lets go of his flab. A few high-flying jets play celestial connect the dots.

"You don't talk much," the stranger says, and Miller only huffs and shrugs. He wants nothing to do with this man who stinks of sweat and swamp, of things decaying. It's a meaty smell that's more than the dirty pond water. Worse, the man is a distraction from the real business of walking. Each step is both pain and a relief. Concentrating, he'd been able to divide the sensations, put all the ache in his left foot, and all the relief in his right. Now you hurt, now you don't. Now you hurt.

"How about a joke?" says the man. "Two guys walk up to a naked redneck armed with a baseball bat. Don't have the punch line worked out. C'mon, a little help and we can brainstorm this. There's gotta be a real good zinger."

"Why take his fish?"

"Ah, my grand savior orates! Have I shown proper gratitude for rescuing this unworthy soul? Name's Christopher." He offers his left hand for an awkward shake of Miller's right. Miller takes it from habit and immediately tries pulling back, but the man's slender fingers are steel pliers.

"I didn't rescue anything." He turns his wrist to slip free, and both men lurch sideways, the stony shoulder making scraping noises underfoot.

"Does my new friend have a name?"

A pause, and a few steps put more road behind them. "Miller."

"You didn't notice the water, Miller?" says Christopher. "No, you couldn't have. It was too dark when you happened upon my unfortunate circumstance. I, on the other hand, had seen it by day. Reconnaissance, you might say."

The man's explanation finishes as though it should make perfect sense.

"I asked why you stole them."

"It was a liberation mission," he says, then swears under his breath when his left foot strikes a pear shaped object. The gray rock tumbles and spins to a stop on the yellow traffic line. Christopher's long narrow toes extend beyond the soles of tooled leather sandals. His dingy toenails are trimmed to points, reminding Miller of a show he'd watched with Mary. It was a tribe who filed their teeth into points, and stood mugging for the camera while brandishing bamboo weapons. Were they cannibals? Miller wanted to think about Mary while the sun came up, not trudge along next to some masochistic goldfish thief.

"You liberated fish by taking them from a pond and putting them in a bag with no water?" He looks at the man, the sky behind finally beginning to design shadows on the road. The man's eyes are set deep, his nose and chin regal. His skin seems fashioned from the same leather as his worn sandals.

"Yes, that's exactly right. The pond was poison, barely a lick of oxygen. It was heartbreaking, let me tell you. Little faces pressed up to the surface, mouths pleading for help. What choice for a sane man?"

"Sane? Really? The guy was about to beat you to death." He wants the man to stop walking, allow him to pull away and be free. He craves silence. There are things to hear when there's no noise, no talking. And how the hell is the guy even walking? He has no business being able to stand. His bones were broken by blows violent enough for Miller to feel through the soft ground. Somewhere in the night, he weighed the possibility that it was a plastic bat, or some bizarre staged confrontation. Or that he'd imagined it all, and the man walking next to him was an aberration the morning sun would dematerialize, and hopefully take his own cruel inner voice with him.

"I needed to give them their peace." The man's tone is solemn, and he seems incarnate in the early morning glow. He holds the plastic bag out for Miller's scrutiny. "They're quiet now. No more suffering."

***

"We're here." It's full daylight when Christopher pivots toward a mailbox with the name L. Onley hand painted on the side in feminine script. The driveway has been reclaimed by weeds and leads to a double-wide trailer with a puffing chimney pipe at one end. "This is a good place for a break. My feet are about to go on strike, and you're hauling a bigger load than me."

"Do you know these people?" Miller absently rubs his round belly, dubious of following the man considering their last encounter.

"The matriarch awaits," says Christopher. "But it's perhaps best that you to hang back a skosh since she's not used to strangers. Takes a little to warm her up, if you know what I mean."

He has no idea what Christopher means as he watches him hobble up two steps onto a small front porch. There's a single planter also full of weeds, and with no car out front, the place feels abandoned save for the billowing smoke. The vinyl siding is dented all over, as though someone has spent hours going at it with a hammer. The gutter is pulled free in two spots, brimming with decayed leaves, about to crash down. The aluminum foil covering the windows stirs the inner voice.

"This is the sort of place where they cook crystal meth."

Miller glances back down the weedy driveway while Christopher raps on the front door. "No, it's too visible from the road."

"Don't be dumb. You read the papers. They aren't hidden in caves. These places are always right under everyone's noses. Let's get our ass moseying down the road, and leave this whack job. Nearly getting us killed once per day is plenty."

"Look, it's just some old woman." He peers around Christopher's lanky frame. She wears a faded blue nightgown and is looking up at the tall man's face. One eye is half closed, lips knit, as if searching a faulty memory. "You think you know everything."

"I know when something is wrong."

The woman nods, listening to Christopher low voice. Before she retreats into the shadowy entryway, Miller sees her bare shins are full of purple and black bruises. It's as though she suffered from the same hammer as the trailer exterior.

Christopher turns and waves for Miller to follow, then steps inside.

"Don't do it, sport," says the inner voice, but it goes silent when he climbs the steps and crosses the threshold into the dreary body of the double-wide. The hanging light above a kitchenette table illuminates the clutter. It reeks of cat urine and mildew, but the smells are muted, as if the cat has been gone or dead for a while. There are no beakers or chemicals for producing illicit drugs, only a covered pot on the stove with escaping steam.

"Take a load off." Christopher points to a sofa stacked with mail and tangled laundry. "I have business with this pretty little lady." He winks over his shoulder as he leads her down the short hallway. Miller watches him slide a hand down her back and onto her buttocks, where his long fingers pinch the gauzy material.

Christopher's bag of dead goldfish sits atop a mound of dishes in the sink. Miller turns to the couch and shovels away some of the old lady clothing and sits. His knees ache from the new position, but a flush of warmth courses up from his feet to deliver a euphoric sensation through his entire body. Is there such as a thing as a walker's high? He leans into the clothing behind and stretches, allows the couch to consume him. He is instantly sleepy, eyelids heavy, and he can't help but yawn so hard he gets a painful neck cramp he can't knead because of the wounds. From down the hall comes flirtatious laughter and conspiratorial murmurs.

Christopher and the woman are sitting on the foot end of an unmade bed, the door wide open. He is still clothed but she is naked, the lump of blue cloth next to a thigh. Miller guesses she's at least eighty, maybe even ninety, with skin so wrinkled and papery that a rough touch might tear it away to reveal what hides underneath. Dust, Miller thinks. There can only be dust inside.

Christopher reaches to cup a pendulous breast, the colorless areola and nipple disappearing into his palm. The other breast lolls above a hairless crotch. The woman's hands are at her side in submission. Her eyes are closed, thin blue lips parted. Her hair is the same white as Christopher's, but a wilder mess, bobby pins and other clips protrude from tangled clumps. When Christopher leans closer, maybe to whisper or just breathe into an ear, her head tilts back and Miller hears her speak for the first time.

"Yes," she says, and her boney knees quiver and inch apart. Creaks, thinks Miller. They creaked apart on rusted hinges. Her mouth again moves. "Yes," she repeats.

Miller is repulsed by the erection trapped against his thigh, and waits for the inner voice to begin mocking. He tries to look away, even just close his eyes, but it's as though he's frozen in a dream in which control has been relinquished to an alien force. Unable to blink, his eyes tear, stomach aching for the pain and relief of more steps on the unyielding blacktop.

Christopher has brought the breast to his face, is dabbing it to one cheek. Miller marvels at the woman's throat, its cascading skin working up and down as if she's chewing and swallowing. The angle of her head makes it appear her neck is broken; she's looking at the pillows behind, if her eyes still see. Her body shudders when Christopher puts the long nipple between his lips to suckle, calf-like, dropping his hand to his lap. For a moment, their only connecting is his teeth and her stretched teat.

Christopher pulls at the top of his pants, works the zipper one-handed, then rolls on top of the woman and pins her to the bed. The air in the bedroom undulates, shimmers as though the pair is underwater, and for the first time Miller notices an aquarium and its bubbling aerator. As if a spell has broken, he's able to blink and look away. He rubs his nose and hot face. On the floor across from the couch is a glass box with algae so robust it encases the bulb and threatens escape. A single black fish bobs against the glass wall, disturbed by the tube carrying forced air. The upside down fish makes teeter totter motions. Miller looks back at the sink and wonders if she'll add Christopher's gift bag, and then notices the human couple on the mattress imitating the motion of the dead fish.

His eyes close to see Mary sitting on the edge of their bed at home. She's naked, too, but alone, her left breast cupped in her own hand. Mary's are small and firm, not a hint of wrinkles or sag. Despite fifteen years of marriage, two kids and a lazy husband, her body differs little from when they first met. He remembers the morning she announced she was getting chubby, and immediately began a jogging regimen. It was her pragmatic way, a life of self-discipline the girls mostly took after. There were never battles over homework or cleaning their shared bedroom space. The girls swapped turns filling the dishwasher and giving Petey a hose bath once every few weeks in the summer. Life was easy because of Mary. It was orderly, and it all made sense. And when she found a thin roll of flab over a tight pair of jeans—hand-me-ups from their oldest—Mary grabbed her car keys and shopped for running shoes and colorful sports bras.

"You're welcome to jog with me," Mary offered while threading virgin laces through shiny eyelets. But he of course stayed put, watching her through the front window with a soda can in his hand. She crossed the road to run toward traffic, which produced the first pangs of worry. He stood behind the wide picture window for thirty minutes, counting cars and speeding trucks. He watched for dented fenders and cracked windshields, telltale signs of a dead jogger left behind in a ditch. He was imagining the awful newspaper headlines when she reappeared alive and safe on the near side of the road. She made the sharp turn onto their walkway and slowed, fists pressed to her hips, chest heaving, the most beautiful thing in the entire world. He saw her flushed cheeks and the triangle of sweat that turned the front of her sports bra from blue to black. Her nylon shorts were knee high and baggy, but he could sense the new muscles flexing beneath the thin material. Across 20 feet and through two panes of glass, he felt the heat radiating from his perfect wife.

"I love you," he mouthed when she looked up at him. He smiled and repeated the words, but she only looked away. She stopped outside the front door to stretch, and he wondered if he'd been hidden by glare, or if perhaps things were changing.

"I love you," Miller says again, and opens his eyes in the filthy trailer. The room seems much darker, the bubbling aquarium louder. The light in the bedroom has been switched off, but the commotion on the bed continues. Or maybe it's started up again, round two or three of Christopher's mummy sexcapades. His legs have gone so stiff that he might have been asleep for hours.

"We're getting closer," the inner voice says, and Miller is too tired to be startled.

"Closer to what?" He coughs, and then swallows hard. His throat is dry, and there's a bad taste. "What are we getting closer to?"

"What happened to Mary and the girls."

He hesitates. "Leave me alone."

"You control me, sport."

"I don't want anything from you."

"We need to know what happened to our family," says the inner voice.

"They're gone. There's nothing else to know."

"You're a regular Agatha Christie. The Sherlock Holmes of Factoryville, Pennsyltucky. Hey, that's a pretty rockin' movie title."

He doesn't respond.

"We both know there's something up with the screwball humping the fossil." The inner voice pauses as if listening to the noisy bed springs. "And it's not just the dead fish. You heard what happened to his legs. Christ, that Louisville Slugger didn't just break his bones, it pulverized them."

He cringes at the memory of the awful sound, was certain the man would never again walk, if he even lived.

"He'll claim to be a drifter, some poor sap down on his luck," says the voice.

"But he's more than that," Miller says, although he can feel the voice has suddenly left him, has slipped back into some shady spot in his brain and pulled a curtain behind it. "I came along and saved him, but it wasn't by accident, was it?"

He listens to the rocking bed, can feel the motion that is carried along the thin subflooring and up through the rickety couch frame. His erection comes back, and he wants to hammer it with his fist, but shuts his eyes instead. He drifts back into a shallow sleep and dreams of walking alone on an endless road.

SIX

The sun floats in a summerlike haze, heat lifting from the pavement to envelope the walkers. A green sign announces the next town is nine miles. Sparse traffic is mostly pickups hurtling down an unpopulated stretch of country highway. The bigger and faster trucks create wind that tugs loose clothing, then releases its grip as if changing its mind. They trudge on the right to keep their faces from being sandblasted, Miller on the outside, wanting to be alone and lost in the rhythm of each step's pain and relief. Someone tosses a brown bottle that misses.

"King of Beers," Christopher says with a smile.

"You're not from around here." Miller has been watching the dense old growth trees that bring deep shadows up to the soggy culverts. At night the woods here would be noisy, full of insects and other things. He's been thirsty for miles, thinking about the crowded sink back at the old woman's house, and how good the water would go down right now. Hell, even the contents of the algae-filled aquarium was wet.

"I've been away for a quite some time. Overseas, not jail." He gives Miller a wink as if it's a good joke. "I tinkered with explosives for an activist group. My folks were from Syria. Beautiful place, really. Nothing like what you see on the news."

Neither had spoken in the hours since leaving the woman's trailer, where Christopher finished his business and stirred Miller. No words as they made their way back out the overgrown drive.

"Interesting hobby," Miller says to humor him. He continues with even strides despite the threat of a muscle cramp in one hip.

"No, it was a job. Full-time. Not great pay, but free room and board. Other perks."

"Tinkered means you made bombs?" Miller again craves solitude, would jog ahead if he was capable.

"I see your wedding ring." Christopher points to Miller's left hand that swings in cadence to his legs. "Let me guess. You're a man working on a change of plans, some family affair, I'm betting. Maybe trouble in paradise? Your gal found a pair of undies tucked under a pillow she didn't recognize? A little of the old grass is greener over someone else's septic tank?"

Miller says nothing, but notices the man's limp has disappeared. His gate is as cocksure as his voice. He's reminded of the smarmy, fast-talking salesman where they bought Mary's car. He had wanted to leave after two minutes of off-color jokes, but Mary's look stopped him cold. She wanted a particular model in a particular color, and she hadn't had a new car since before Lizzy was born. The look meant you aren't going anywhere, buster, so you better deal with this tool bag.

"Well, no need to open up right out of the gate. Don't wanna step on sore toes." Christopher dips a hand into his deep front pocket and withdraws a thin leather strip he puts between his teeth. He gathers his hair with both hands and ties it off in back. "Much better. Hot as blazes out here."

"I planned on being alone. Try and get my head together."

"A long walk can do wonders."

"Maybe, maybe not."

"I'm sure it can, friend," says Christopher. "I do a lot of walking. Good for the heart, better for the soul."

"Now that you're a retired terrorist?"

"Hey now, I said I was an activist. Mighty big difference." His tone makes it obvious he's not offended. "Had to make a career switch after a few years in the field. Chemicals were doing a number on my lungs. Damage is cumulative. Doc said I'd end up with emphysema if I managed to keep from blowing myself to pieces."

"Bullshit," Miller says. But the tall man takes a breath, then barks words in a rapid-fire foreign tongue, brings his long-fingered hands together several times as though striking a tambourine to emphasize certain words. He sounds like a frantic Al Jazeera correspondent delivering a live report from the front line.

Christopher pauses, then switched back to English. "What line of work are you in?"

Miller is dumbfounded, watches in silence as sweat drips from Christopher's forehead, his broomstick-thin body hunched at the shoulders. There's something snake-like about the man, like he might be coiled, ready to strike.

"Now, with a pretty wife at home, you must have a good job? The insurance game? I've thought about selling insurance. Put in a few years of hard work, become your own boss. Nothing beats working for yourself. And you're providing a real service. House catches fire and a check's in the mail. Hurricane blows the roof, you're the go-to guy."

Miller blinks and turns to look forward. The sun plays tricks on the distant road, makes it wobble. "I manage a resort community," he finally says. Of course Christopher hadn't heard Miller's description from the bat-wielding goldfish owner, who stopped his assault to enjoy a good look at the pathetic fucker who allowed his family to be murdered. Christopher had been writhing in pain and laughing hysterically. "We have some year 'round families, but mostly second homes and vacationers."

"Ah, fascinating, so you're more or less a mayor?"

"No, I'm mostly a bookkeeper," he says, thinking how he is probably on the verge of being unemployed. Sure, they'll understand a few days or maybe a week not hearing from him. Given the circumstances, maybe stretch it to two. But it's still a fairly busy time of the year at Whitetail Lakes, and business is business. Tragedy visited one of WL's beloved employees, but life never pauses long for New Yorkers needing stickers for their wave runners and guest badges for cousins coming in from South Jersey. There's a budget meeting this week, and a report due about changing the fishing rules to catch-and-release for all the waters.

"You have kids?"

He pictures Celia and Lizzy tossing a Frisbee in the sand at the main beach. Employees and their families receive the same privileges as residents, a nice benefit to offset the modest pay and lousy medical package. There are two outdoor pools, tennis, and mini golf. "Girls," he says. "Two girls."

"I bet they're pretty little peaches who take after their mother."

"Celia's a dead ringer," he says, then repeats the words silently. Her eyes were closed at the viewing. It wasn't taxidermy, and they weren't creating lifelike poses of the recently passed in their natural habitat. The phrase was laid to rest. Even still, he'd wanted to look into Celia's eyes in particular. She had an adult way of making eye contact, of putting a soft hand on your arm when she had something important to convey. Her arm felt like cold plastic when he reached into the coffin. He touched below the shoulder, then squeezed. They were about to bury a doll, not his daughter. The warm parts and her beautiful blue eyes were somewhere else, lost or stolen. He couldn't decide if it was a good thing.

"I'll bet she's a total sweetheart. How old?"

"Celia's almost thirteen." His voice sounds hollow in his ears. "Lizzy was just seven."

"Thirteen must be the start of the boy-crazy years, not that I'd really know."

"Boy-crazy," he whispers, suddenly struck with the image of the monster in black work boots standing over her, peering down at trapped prey. Miller can't breathe, the chord once again tight around his neck. He reaches for it, rubs at the crusty scabs until they flake and begin to split open.

"Hey, I didn't mean anything," Christopher is saying, and Miller's grimy hand swipes sudden tears.

"It's nothing, forget it."

They walk in silence, Miller at some point guessing he's traveled a hundred miles, but has gotten nowhere. One foot in front of the other. Pain and relief. Left and then right. He recognizes some of the towns on the signs, but the occasional billboards advertise businesses he's never heard of. They are still in his home state, if you can call it that. The plates haven't yet switched to Ohio, but he knows they will.

When the road begins a sweeping left bend, a stabbing pain causes Miller to double over. It's a twisting knife plunged into his stomach, pulling his feet from under as he pitches forward, face slamming to the gravel. He clutches his middle, kneading, trying to brace against the molten lava in his bowels. And then there's something even worse touching him squarely on the back. The hand is flat, but he feels tiny insect-like movements, squirming things crawling over his skin and inside his body. Miller vomits, and then tries catching his breath.

"He's probing you, sport." It is the inner voice, back to enjoy some red meat action. "He's seeing if you're ready to die."

"Leave me alone," he tries saying, meaning both the voice

and the stranger huddled over him, touching.

A horn blares and there are catcalls for the faggots to get a room, as daylight dissolves into blackness. The pain mutes, and his body goes weightless and rises until he is floating. Perhaps this is death. He has slipped out of skin and bones to escape the shackles of his mortal body, and the proposition is glorious and welcome. He begins thanking God, but then recognizes the sound that has become familiar over the miles. It's the steady sliding and crunch of leather sandals over loose stones. And there is gentle singing, a lullaby, in a language he doesn't know, as he is carried forward.

SEVEN

The sheets are slick against bare skin, the bed soft under his weight. He's on his side, knees drawn to his chest. Fetal position. A fetal pig, he thinks, although he's no longer all that pig-like. How long since his big old gut kept his knees from visiting his chin? Mary's gentle persuasion didn't work. Neither did the doctor's stark warnings. Diabetes, stroke, coronary heart disease. Those were bush league, Doc. I found me quite the weight loss elixir. Of course it flays your chest and rips at your heart, but you take the bad with the good. It's an amazing fat remedy that leaves the bearer ample years for lonely pondering. Truth be told, Doc, one day in my shoes and I give odds you'll be praying for any of *your* medical misfortunes in exchange, maybe throw in cancer of the nuts to boot. Tie me to a stake and burn me alive. Just bring them back. Tear me to pieces, but make them whole. I can't sob or scream them back. I see them everywhere, but not the way you imagine. My family snapshots? Here's my baby girl with blue lips. The whites of her eyes have gone red, filled up with blood. And this one? Her cheek is caved in, but that can be adjusted no problem with a cellulose cavity insert. I know because I did my homework.

Stop.

He works to nudge his mind in a new direction. Being indoors is daunting, the walls trapping images, keeping them from drifting away. Outside was better. Moving. One step after another. Pain and relief. Left and then right. What was the word Lizzy chose to replace sunshine? Gave her the giggles. Mom bought fruit to make smoothies.

You are my mango,
my only mango.

It is a motel room with dusty watercolors hung on dark paneling, and a television with rabbit ears that have aluminum foil balled at each tip. He and the girls stayed in similar digs during Catskill ski trips, timeworn properties run by elderly couples, or young hopefuls escaping city life. The vibrating bed mechanism never worked, but the industrial version baseboard heat could turn the room into a sauna on the coldest winter night.

He pushes out from under the covers and lurches into the bathroom. He twists the cold water knob and slurps from the faucet until cramps threaten a curtain call. In the smudged mirror he is ten years older and thirty pounds lighter. He has a ribcage and his penis no longer resides in a shadowy crevasse. Small red and black dots across his forehead are sore to the touch. He vaguely recalls the instant before impact. He rubs whiskers now softening with length. The bristly mix is a queer feeling, and he notices the gray at his chin.

His dripping clothes dangle from the shower rod. They smell of economy hand soap. He pulls down his boxers and flaps a few times before sliding them up his pale legs. The waistband has to be rolled to keep them from dropping to his ankles. He briefly considers his pants when the knocking begins, but it's likely his former bomb-maker companion back from some terrible new mission.

"He slaughtered the owners and stomped their orphaned kittens to enjoy the tiny crunching bones," whispers the inner voice. It then cackles like a B movie mental case.

"Not now." He crosses the room and turns the knob.

"I bring a bounty!" Christopher whisks past with a plastic grocery sack he spills onto the dresser top. There's a half dozen frozen sandwiches in microwaveable packages, a box of candy hearts, fried pork rinds, and a jar of instant coffee.

"I think I lost the room key." Christopher shrugs knobby shoulders, holds them that way in a look of chagrin.

Miller picks up two rock-hard meatball sandwiches and taps them together. "Maybe it's in the microwave."

"What microwave?" Christopher spins to search the room, and then laughs. "Oh, right. Sorry, it's all they had."

Miller drops the frozen packages. "But about this stuff, and whatever this place costs. I have a credit card, but no cash. I need to find an ATM."

"Oh, yeah, your credit card." Christopher chin lowers, white hair falling over his face. He puts one hand on a bag of pork rinds and twirls the snack on the slick surface. "You puked on yourself, so

I took the liberty of washing your clothes."

"God, I'm sorry."

"No, no, it's perfectly fine." Christopher lifts the hand from the bag to gesture. "Your credit card was in a pocket, and I figured you needed food in your belly. Get some fuel back in the tank."

"Okay." Miller hesitates. "No problem."

"But I, uh, seem to have lost the card along with the key."

Miller tries searching the man's partially obscured face for signs of deception. He hadn't thought to bring money when he walked away from his home. He hadn't thought about anything. The loose credit card was in a front pocket by accident. He gassed up the car after the storm—after the murders—and slid it into his pocket instead of his wallet. "We have to go look. It's all I have." He steps toward the door, then looks down at his saggy boxers.

"Wait, no, not actually lost, per say." Christopher turns and drops onto the lone chair that's pressed against the thick, paisley window curtain. "I mean, I must have left them on the store counter. I remember the teen boys behind me, rude as they were. I went back to look, but the clerk was clueless."

"Shit."

"I have a little cash, though, and the room's paid-up for two nights."

"You were a bomb-maker, huh?" Miller let's out a deep breath, works thumbs into pressure points at his temples.

"And you were a mayor." Christopher smiles up at him, reclines, and lifts a foot onto the dresser. "There's a tavern down the street, maybe two blocks. Let's get something cheap but cooked. Wet pants never killed anyone."

***

Two Harley's are angle-parked out front, sandwiched by rusty pickups. The interior is all shiny dark wood reflecting half-lit neon beer signs. The juke plays background country music to drunken guffaws and the clack of billiard balls.

"I love this." Christopher sweeps between empty tables with outstretched arms, Jesus on water that's really just spilled beer. He beelines for the long bar lining the far wall. Miller slinks behind, pulling at his damp crotch, thighs already chafing. He only took time to stick his head under the shower to rinse the road grime, Christopher badgering outside the door. Wet hair and clothes, he feels like the only person in the joint who suffered a rain cloud.

Christopher pulls out two bar stools. "Go check the bathroom for an electric hand drier, maybe fluff your unmentionables. I'll order burgers. Medium rare?"

Miller finds a door with a cowboy silhouette. There's a hand drier that makes a jet engine racket when he palms the metal button. He holds his shirt cuffs under the hot blast for a minute, punches the button again and bends to dry his hair. He goes through two more cycles with his hips forward, pants undone, air billowing down his crotch and thighs.

The smell of frying meat hits when he pushes back out into the bar. The grill has been turned on for them, sizzling meat and onions overpowering the cigarettes and stale booze.

"You look a thousand times better, my friend." Christopher is gobbling handfuls of popcorn from a wood bowl. Kernels litter the space around two beer bottles. "Local brew was cheap."

"Fine." Miller mounts the stool and reaches into the bowl that's already empty. Stray kernels on the bar are wet. "I'm starving."

"I could eat a horse."

Miller takes a long pull from his ice cold bottle, feels woozy before he can set it back on the square napkin. "I'll stick with cow."

Christopher slaps the bar with his big hands as if to deliver a revelation. "There's this hole-in-the-wall Aleppo joint that serves amazing lamb meatballs in spice sauce. Cinnamon sprinkled custard for dessert. It's my shipwrecked on an island food."

Miller glances over his shoulder at the pool players whose noise level has lowered. The bike owners are easy to peg. Harley vests and chained wallets, but clean-shaven faces and flashing gold wristwatches cast doubt on their authenticity. The cowboys on the opposite end of the green felt are plenty farm-fresh. Mud and maybe cow shit splattered Wranglers, oil-stained John Deere caps, both have cigarettes tucked behind their ears.

The barmaid and a man camped at a table under a heavily dented air conditioner are the only other souls in the joint. A mechanic, probably, hands black and clothes a matching dark blue uniform. There's a script filled oval patch on his shirt pocket. He's settled behind a sweating longneck, but seems to be doing more staring at Christopher and Miller than drinking.

"Sweetheart?" Christopher holds the empty bowl sideways. The woman is busy delivering a round to the pool players, and then ignores him when she stalks back into the kitchen to flip the sizzling burgers. Her mostly black hair is piled high, wiry gray strands escaping. She is middle-aged, with broad shoulders and torpedo breasts.

Miller sips more beer, wanting water instead. He feels the mechanic's stare.

"Love a woman with attitude. And this joint is the real deal." Christopher uses one arm like a game show model displaying the goods. "It's what makes being an explorer special. That smell is a potpourri of true Americana. And the music?"

Miller's head swims from the alcohol. He pushes the bottle forward. What he wants more than anything is to be outside, away from the dark walls and Christopher, the road to salvation back under his feet.

"Tammy Wynette was a Mississippi girl, born and raised." Christopher's eyes close, and he sways to the scratchy recording. "Still in diapers when she lost her pappy to a brain tumor. Rough start turned into a brilliant career, a real shooting star. Poor girl checked out of this world before her time."

The onion smell fills Miller's mouth with spit, but it doesn't overcome the invisible force pulling him toward the door, toward the blacktop. The walls edge closer, the ceiling squeezes.

"Tammy had medical issues that turned into addictions," he says. "Fell asleep one night and never woke up."

The mechanic still stares. Miller reaches for his beer, tilting the bottle as if reading the label. "You were a big fan, huh?"

"Just an interested bystander. Three of her daughters lawyered-up against her doctor and manager hubby, claiming all sort of nastiness. They had Tammy exhumed for a second autopsy. Imagine circumstances turning so sour you treat a loved one like that?"

Miller shakes his head, done talking and thinking about death.

Christopher chugs the remainder of his beer and belches. "A final resting place should be just that. Final." He puts the bottle on the bar and pats Miller's arm. Miller grimaces at the touch.

"You came back from the Middle East for country music and

43

dive bars?"

"I'm an explorer," says Christopher. "Been all over the map. Not many of my kind left. Everyone's in such a hurry, busy as bees getting to and from jobs. Family time is a computer message, or pecking at miniature keyboards on portable telephones."

Christopher lifts a hand and wiggles his fingers. They are the legs of a bald spider, and Miller notices the fingernails are also trimmed to points, although less drastic than his toenails. "Imagine me typing on one of those little devices?"

Plates are slid onto the bar before he can respond, and both take equally massive bites out of greasy burgers. They squeeze ketchup globs and shovel fries.

Christopher again belches, then catches the barmaid's attention to order two more burgers, and Miller wonders for a second about the money. She rolls her eyes and drops a pair of mugs back into a sudsy trough. She slings a dishrag over one shoulder, droplets spraying the pockmarked bar.

From behind comes a voice. "I know you."

The mechanic has traded tables, moved right up behind them. His focus is on Christopher, milky eyes narrowing, one clenched fist on the table top. "I said I know you. I know exactly what you are."

Christopher wipes a napkin across his lips, little bits of white paper catching in his whiskers. He turns to the man and makes a face as though searching his memory.

"You're a dirty thief," says the man says, and Miller's mind jumps to the bag of dead goldfish.

"Now we're getting to the gist of this story." Miller's inner voice is so loud he nearly chokes on his last bite. He looks at Christopher and then the man, convinced they heard.

"Go away," Miller tells the voice.

"This ain't your business," the man tells Miller, then points at Christopher. "This is no place for you. You ain't been called and you ain't wanted."

"Just a world weary explorer," says the voice. "An innocent bomb-maker who takes a licking and keeps on ticking."

Miller cups his mouth and tells the voice to shut up.

"You're in the wrong place," says the man.

Christopher has a befuddled expression, looks sideways at Miller and shrugs.

"The mechanic is on to your new best friend," says the inner voice, and Miller tries shutting it off by putting greasy fingers to his ears. He looks beyond the mechanic to where the cowboys and bikers have entered their own hostile stand-off. One of the bikers is using a cue stick to make his point, and the cowboy isn't taking kindly to having it waived in his face.

"You ain't leaving with my Alice," says the mechanic, shifting forward and causing his chair to make a high-pitched scrape.

Christopher's face changes to a mix of recognition and sorrow.

"He's here to do to Alice what he did to the old woman in the double-wide," says the voice. "Or maybe the deed is already done."

"Stop talking," Miller pleads, and Christopher stands to dig crumpled dollar bills from his front pocket.

The mechanic pushes up from his seat. "I ain't letting you have her."

Christopher drops the cash at the same instant the pool cue is snapped over a cowboy's head. The metal feet of the pool table grind on wood when his buddy lunges toward the other biker. Acrylic balls make tick-tock sounds as they spill over.

"Let's vamoose." Christopher grabs Miller's shirt and tugs him into the maze of tables, but the mechanic is on his feet to block their escape. Beyond them, a beer bottle strikes a wall and bounces back unbroken. It ricochets off the pool table and skitters to the floor, spinning.

"We're married forty-one years." The mechanic's voice is more desperation than anger. His eyes are set deep and have come through a lost war.

Christopher brushes the man aside with ease, an unlikely strength that causes the mechanic's shoes to skate over the floorboards.

The pool table altercation ratchets into combat mode, the barmaid shouting into the phone for backup. John Denver has replaced Tammy Wynette to croon about Rocky Mountains and lullabies. Christopher is still jerking Miller's shirt when the mechanic dives past, arms outstretched. He's trying to tackle Christopher at the knees, but deflects off Miller and only managed to attach to one long leg. The mechanic pulls his grip tight, shifting forward, and looks

45

prepared to chomp down on Christopher's calf.

Christopher stumbles and releases Miller. A button breaks free and joins the wobbling billiard balls at their feet.

"We aren't looking for trouble." Christopher catches his balance and stops, bending over to address the man attached above the ankle. "We're pilgrims on a quest to see the world. We have no business with you."

The mechanic lets loose a primitive growl and bites.

"Dammit to hell!" Christopher's howl halts the pool table brawl. The frozen scene is a cowboy with a beer bottle poised to hurl, and a biker with a cue stick ready for a high and tight fastball. The soundtrack is the barmaid giving a breathless damage description, and Denver's song about raining fire.

Christopher swings his leg in an arc, chairs and tables tumbling away from the lower half of the mechanic's firmly attached body. Miller has an image of Petey as a pup latched to a towel, allowing himself to be used as a kitchen floor mop.

"Mother of Allah that hurts!" Christopher slams a fist on a table and sends salt and pepper shakers flying. "Do something, Miller. My rabies shots aren't up to date."

The man snarls, and the bite turns into gnawing. Christopher tries pumping the leg, but the grip is merciless.

"Get away from him."

Miller looks up to see who has spoken before realizing it's his inner voice.

"This might be your best and only chance to ditch this wacko."

Instead, Miller drops to his knees and puts a palm over the mechanic's forehead. He's careful to avoid flashing teeth, reminded of the girls' wind-up chattering sets that were Christmas stocking stuffers.

"He's eating me, Miller!"

The man's face is sweat-slick, and Miller has trouble getting a grip to pry. It's no help that the pool table melee resumes, with furniture converted into weapons. A chair bounds across the room, strikes Miller's shoulder on a bounce, and clatters against an overturned table. He releases the man's face as Christopher begins lunging for the door as though escaping quicksand. Miller grabs at the mechanic's belt as Christopher takes big, drum major steps, causing Miller to slide along before his expensive hiking shoes manage to gain purchase.

"Oh, God!" A patch of Christopher's trousers tears free, along with a fleshy pink chunk of calf muscle. The painful liberation allows him to limp toward the exit. Miller recoils from the detached mechanic, but the man makes no move to continue the assault.

"Forty-one years," the man repeats, the fight gone out of him.

Miller shakes his head. "I can't help you."

"Come on," Christopher calls back, propped crookedly against the front door.

Miller gets to his feet and steps over the now docile man wearing a bloody frown, but has to wait for the pool table scrum to shift tide. The outside air is cool and fresh, but instead of savoring the freedom from chaos, Christopher has found another battle. Already halfway down the block, he's swatting at the head of what first appears to be a cowering nun. Her dress is black, hair concealed by a dark scarf. She has a bright red oversized purse at the elbow, arms raised to fend off her hobbled attacker.

"Shoo! Get away!" Christopher makes lunging motions, and she finally turns and begins a retreat. Christopher's arms flail, torn pants flapping with each step. Blood splashes from the wound as this new confrontation becomes a graceless chase.

Miller sucks a deep breath, and begins a half-hearted jog. It's been too many miles in a shorter stride, his muscles threatening to unravel like the steel belts of a worn tire. He knows he should take his inner voice's advice and turn from this chaos, but guilt draws him to protect the woman. He calls to Christopher, but the tall man settles into a giraffe-style lope at the heels of the scurrying woman, a monster threatening to consume her. They cross two side streets and come to the town's main shopping area, but Miller is cut off by a car making a slow right turn. The duo goes out of sight, veering off somewhere ahead. He runs to a closed insurance agency storefront, THE COMPANY YOU KEEP in big letters. His inner voice guffaws at the irony, but he doesn't have time.

He listens for footsteps or screams, but it's only his own breathing and another car rolling between the two and three-story buildings surrounding the nearly deserted main drag.

I spy something red.

He searches, locates the blood flecks on the concrete walk, and begins tracking. The trail turns at a drugstore, then crosses a side street and makes a left into a residential area. He backtracks once, follows along at a fast walk for at least 100 more yards until the trail is no more.

"Christopher?" It isn't until a mower's low drone cuts out that he hears the woman's hysterical pleading. He follows the voice, at first not realizing he's left the narrow road and entered a cemetery's gravel driveway.

"How appropriate." The inner voice is back. "I guess this is where our little odyssey turns into that B movie. Will it be zombies or vampires? The mummy thing's already been done, am I right?"

The woman's crying is close, and Miller goes into stealth mode, hunched at the middle, knees bent. He stops when he hears Christopher's cajoling voice, dropping to his butt with his shoulders against one of the markers. Leaning across a vase of dead flowers gives a partial view of the woman also propped against a headstone. Hers is shiny black, a winged cherub with hands in prayer posed on top. There are flashes of Christopher's white hair.

"I'm not going with you." Her voice is shaky but defiant, and it takes Miller a moment to see the knitting needles she is brandishing.

"I only want to help," says Christopher, which elicits a miserable laugh from the woman.

"You're not the police."

"Of course not."

"You're something much worse, aren't you?"

Christopher goes silent, and Miller leans forward, lowering to his stomach to relieve stress from his back. Late afternoon clouds threatened rain. The highway isn't far, its black tar still warm and inviting as fresh baked bread. Other road smells offer the odd comfort he craves. The diesel exhaust hugging the ground, stirred by smaller traffic. The tang of flattened squirrels. Worms chased from flooded holes now desiccating on painted yellow lines. Get up and walk away. Left and then right. Walking is the only thing. Stay here and the ground will open. Hands will reach and pull you under.

"Well," Christopher begins in a calm tone, part salesman and part priest. "I guess that depends who you ask. But we have time to talk, right? We're in no hurry. It's a beautiful day. The birds are singing."

The woman looks away, and gravity takes its toll on the knitting needles.

"And you're not frightened of me, or you'd be pointing the gun instead of those," Christopher says.

She turns toward the bag that has partially spilled. There are balls of colored yarn, and what might be the start of a grandchild's sweater.

"I never once touched Marvin's gun before today." She uses a needle to poke at a lump still in the bag.

"But you're Quick Draw McGraw when it comes to knitting needles," Christopher says in a lighter voice, and Miller can see a half-smile alter the woman's face. It last a few seconds.

"He took up with another woman. Denied it for all his worth, but she came calling to confess their sins. Know what she told me there on my front porch?"

"Tell me."

"Said she felt better, that the guilt was too much to bear. Confessing to me let the weight of the world drop off her shoulders."

"And it fell onto yours," Christopher gently adds. "You went to the tavern to shoot him, and then turn the gun on yourself."

"You know about killing," she says, her voice a higher pitch. "It's why you came for me."

"That's nonsense." Christopher is indignant. "I couldn't kill a fly."

The goldfish, thinks Miller, and the ancient woman in the trailer. Had Christopher killed them? What about the bombs? Were they lies? He'd talked about suffering and bringing peace.

"I have grandbabies," the woman blurts, covering her face. Her body hitches, the sobs returning. "I don't wanna die, but I can't live this way."

"Honey, we all die. I bet dying was the last thing most of these people wanted." Christopher's left arm unfurls, his creepy long fingers indicating the graves. "Worse than dying is what you might have done with that gun."

The woman calms a bit, then pulls the scarf from her head. She folds it once and blows her nose long and hard into the shiny material. She holds it out to Christopher. "He gave this to me."

"Pretty."

"I watched a program about murder-suicide," she says.

"It's become popular."

"They said it saves families from the embarrassment of a trial."

"Noble," says Christopher. "But guns aren't best for first-timers. I can't begin to tell you how many knitting club ladies botch the suicide part. They get the first half right, especially if he's a cheater and the gun is fully loaded. But then those girls usually only manage to shoot a very painful hole in their cheeks. Poor things end up in handcuffs."

"Oh, that's awful."

"Tall buildings are good," says Christopher. "It's like flying, right until the end. Are you afraid of heights?"

"Isn't everyone? I'm a nervous wreck climbing a chair to dust the China cabinet."

"Too bad," says Christopher. "Well, let me think. Drifting off with your car idling in the garage is another favorite."

"Marvin's truck would be perfect. It has a leaky something or other and makes a cloud of smoke. But it has to be parked in a garage?"

"You don't have a garage?"

"Marvin built a carport to tinker out of the weather, but it fell over when he backed into it. Was coming home from the bar."

Christopher draws a noisy breath. "I don't suppose you have a charcoal grill? The kind with wheels?"

"We sure do. It was next to his tools and all, but I don't think it was ruined."

"Bingo!" Christopher claps his hands. "It's called Death by Hibachi, or at least in the magazine I've read. Wheel the old girl into your bedroom and fill it with charcoal. Drop a match and climb into a snuggly bed. You'll take the hand of Jesus into the Promised Land in no time. And it has a pleasant smell."

"Is the quick start kind all right?"

"Sweetheart, is there any other?"

"Marvin will have a fit if he finds out I touched his grill."

"Honey, you need to focus."

"Oh," the woman says after a moment, and then lets out a sound like a giggle. A child's giggle. "I shoot him first."

"I know you'll do fine."

The pair sit quietly, content with this new plan. Miller rises from to ground and slumps against the grave marker, his back to Christopher and the woman. Fat rain drops splash on nearby headstones, drip down the names of the dead.

"We're not afraid of heights," whispers the inner voice.

EIGHT

They forfeit clean beds for a road cast in a partial moon's ashen glow. It was an unspoken agreement to leave. They again washed up, took turns on the crapper. No conversation. Miller was the first out the door. Christopher followed.

Occasional horns in the first miles, more beer bottle and trash assaults, but the hurlers are drunk or lousy aim. Christopher's gate is uneven, bitching under his breath as he struggles along. But Miller knows the damage is healing, imagines the pain is akin to fresh scabs over bad burns. The bomb-maker turned explorer could be smashed, torn and broken, but the mending that begins immediately is superhuman.

"You meant to say inhuman." The inner voice is matter of fact. "Listen, sport, there's one of two things going on with Mister Limpy. Door number one says he's a crazed hypnotist making you part his traveling sideshow. But what's behind door number two ain't so adorable."

"I'm losing my mind," Miller whispers over the sound of scraping shoes.

The voice chuckles. "Step in front of the next truck. Wouldn't it be a hoot to jump in front of a speeding taxi for a ride into the afterlife?"

"Yeah, that's the funniest thing ever."

"Aw, come on, sad sack," chides the voice. "Maybe it'll be peaceful end."

"Or the start of a nightmare that lasts forever, with you giving running commentary."

"We used to be friends," says the voice with mock indignation.

"Friends," Miller repeats.

"Of course we are," says Christopher, who is walking very

close, arms swinging to their slow rhythm.

The walking is relief and the air is neither cold nor hot. The road is dead flat for as far as he can see. Christopher is perhaps bolstered by the mention of friendship and begins a song in his foreign language. It helps drown out Miller's inner voice, and the rest of his suicidal thoughts.

***

It's after midnight when the road tilts into a long uphill stretch that disappears into the sky. Miller thinks of the gigantic conveyor belts quarries use for piling crushed stone. Maybe he'll crest the hill and plunge into a squirming mass of other pathetic souls who've walked away from tragedy. Chin on chest he's been been dozing, in and out of a dream in which Celia is filled with anxiety. Kindergarten has started, full school days instead of morning pre-K, and Mommy is about to give birth to a baby sister who is already stealing attention. Celia wants to play a game she claimed to have outgrown, the box pulled from the high shelf with books stacked on a chair in a danger-filled sortie. He thought it was a step back, and Mary explained the comfort from small reversions, said it will help her transition into independence, according to the book she's reading. Spend more time with her. Lots of hugs, and really give her an ear. And for heaven's sake, play whatever silly game.

On the rising pitch that steals his breath, he is overcome with sadness that he had resisted Mary's suggestion. And he should have protected Celia from the kids who might have teased her into again abandoning her game. You should never be made to forsake simple things that bring such joy.

It was an autumn Sunday, the Eagles game in the second quarter, not that he was much of a fan. Celia had set up the Candy Land board, shuffled the cards, and put their favorite yellow and blue pieces in place. She wore a Disney princess tiara, and a pink dress with satin sleeves and puffy shoulders. She shaped him a crown from rolled construction paper, jewels drawn with green and red crayons.

"Your Majesty." Celia's small fingers tucked his ears under the brim, her warm breath on his cheek as she made adjustments. She had a slight cold, and her sound is a cat's purr. He knows in a week he'll be stuffy and sneezing, but no matter.

"How's school so far?"

"I like Miss Hollister. She has a jar of pretzels on her desk for sharing. Pick a card, Daddy, it's your turn."

He chose from the stack, moved Mr. Blue to the first green space. "Miss Hollister was really nice when we met her."

"Did you meet Johnny Munson?"

"I don't think so."

"He eats his own you-know-what." She pointed up her nose, faced scrunched. Her other hand turned over an orange card, and she took the Rainbow Trail shortcut. "Guess where he sits?"

"Close to you?"

"Have you ever seen someone eat boogers?"

"Pretty awful, huh?"

"Remember when Petey ate his poop and you yelled at him?"

He'd scoured the internet for advice, learning about a lack of nutrients and low-quality foods. "We bought him different food and he stopped."

"Johnny Munson's mommy should buy different food. It's your turn."

"You think that might be it?" He advanced two spaces.

Celia reaches for the pile of upside down cards. "Angela Rodriguez says Mommy might die from having the baby."

"That can't happen. Mommy is perfectly healthy, Sweetheart. And she has the smartest doctor in the whole world."

"What if her doctor is on vacation when it's time for the baby to come out? And Mommy keeps saying she's tired and fat. She says she has elephant feet. I thought it was funny when she said it, but not anymore. Not after what Angela said."

He moved his piece to the pink space at the Peppermint Forest, a smirking Mr. Mint swinging a candy cane ax. He wasn't a fan of Mr. Licorice's bats, but the ax-wielding character with a cherry nose and red sneakers was far more sinister.

"The doctor promised he'd be with her, so there's no reason to worry. Mommy said the same thing about her feet when she was pregnant with you, and look how great you turned out."

Celia considered his words, forgetting the game, looking around the bedroom she'd soon be sharing with a stranger. They could have converted a storage room into a nursery, but Mary wanted the girls together from the start. He worried the crying and commotion would make Celia resentful, that a six-year-old needed her own space.

"Do you promise Mommy won't die? Cross your heart?"

"I crossed my heart and I hoped to die," he tells Christopher, who seems startled out of his own deep thoughts.

The sky is lightening, the moon gone. They've put the long hill behind them. Miller's head pounds and his throat is so parched he can barely swallow. It's been miles of dense forest, probably state lands. Wooden signs mark access to trailheads on both sides of the highway. Christopher grunts and turns onto a path where a swampy pond has come to greet the road. They follow an animal trail in the gloom, kneel side by side at water's edge. Both scoop handfuls of murky liquid that smells of decay, dunk their heads, and then sit back. Miller guesses from all the dead trees sprouting from shallow water that it's a beaver pond, low ground flooded by woven dams. The trees have shed their bark, stand naked and full of angles, haunting configurations picking up the early morning light.

"It's spooky," Miller says, their breathing the only noise. It's the very brief period when neither night nor day creatures hold ownership.

"It's peaceful." Christopher sprawls on his back, stretches, then rolls onto his side to look at Miller. "I spent years in cities. The noise and stink of traffic. People always on top of you, cursing each other. Planes overhead, and trains rattling the windows. Cities put you in a cage. Knowing these places exist kept me sane."

Miller doesn't mention all the car and truck noise they've had here on their lonely highway. "Did you really make bombs, or was it just bullshit?" The man had rattled off some language that sounded Arabic, but what did Miller know?

Christopher props on his right arm, rubs pale whiskers. "The work was in Lebanon, but my mother and father were Syrian. They came to Northern Virginia when my mother was pregnant. My father took a job as a State Department translator. I was raised Shia, but without radical teaching. I was educated in public schools, and probably sat next to Jews in a dozen classes. Had no idea I was supposed to hate them."

"How did you end up in Lebanon?"

"I was a grad student studying family counseling at the University of Maryland, but had very little direction. What does a young man in a classroom know? Then I was assigned an internship, and experienced what humans were capable of doing to their young. It was the spark that turned me idealistic, and I needed to make a difference. I saw a chance to help children overcome the limitations brought by household chaos, from parents who beat and humiliated them. Or who drank or smoked crack and failed to protect them. So many ways to fail as a parent."

Christopher's voice is gentle in the still air. Miller yawns, fights the urge to close his eyes. The exhaustion is good. The open space. Being near the highway.

"Children are brimming with potential," Christopher says. "I wanted to remove what stifled their capabilities, not stand in judgment. I wrote papers that were passed along to a Lebanese national who convinced me to follow him to ash-Sham, the City of Jasmine. He was one of many campus recruiters who'd come to this country after the Israeli invasion. The Lebanese are the brothers and sisters of Syrians."

"This was all that PLO, Yasser Arafat stuff, right? The early 1980s?"

"We were the infant child of Hezbollah, the Party of Allah. Arafat was a pig, but we shared a common enemy."

"And you built bombs in the name of god."

"I was a young, starry-eyed romantic. The Israelis brought misery, and our best weapons were our own bodies."

Miller lifts to his own elbow to look at the man, as the morning creatures begin their music. "Suicide bombs."

"We used C-4 when we could get it. Chinese-made fishing vests mostly, pockets loaded with ball bearings and screws. Anything for shrapnel. In a pinch we used the marbles children flick across circles drawn in the dirt. But we were pushed to use cheaper explosives that were available in bulk. Acetone peroxide was common. You've seen news footage of bomb factories accidentally blowing neighborhoods to smithereens. It was highly unstable, and came to be known as Mother of Satan." Christopher pauses, stretches. "I need more water."

Miller watches him struggle to his feet, then hobble to low bushes and work his fly. He rinses his hands before scooping to drink.

"I wired the initial wave of female bombers during the first months of *al-ijtiyah.*" Christopher drops back down to sit cross-legged. "Blessedly, a fatwa granted Paradise to the successful women. But the Israelis got wise after we'd struck several checkpoints. Our last heroine wore a belt to make her appear pregnant. Funny that she actually was expecting, only not far enough along to be convincing. An Israelis soldier condemned her with a bullet to the head. No attempt to disarm, even though she was stopped in a wide open space. Not that it matters. War is war. You adapt."

Christopher's voice trails off as a thumping helicopter flies in low over the treetops, banks around the pond's far edge before heading north. They watch the sky as the noise recedes.

"We turned to our eager little beavers."

Miller is at first confused, looks out over the beaver pond, then realizes Christopher means the children. Barely audible over the morning creatures is the howl of distant sirens.

"It was like offering a visit to Santa's lap," says Christopher. "Who wants to be a hero, to live forever? They clamored for selection. Little hands waved, begged to be chosen, and the international press ate it up. We were on the cutting edge of a new type of warfare, and it didn't matter that the explosive packs were more modest. It was an exciting time, but also quite somber in the larger picture. Imagine the mixture of pride and loss for the families of those brave youngsters. It was all bittersweet."

"You were helping children reach their potential," Miller says. "Did you choose them yourself?"

But Christopher is back on his feet before answering. Dogs bark somewhere deep in the woods. Their racket shifts, as if tracking a scent.

"Maybe it's your lunatic travel companion they're hunting," says the inner voice.

Christopher's loping gate takes him back out toward the highway, and Miller knows the tall man is running toward the commotion, not away. He gets to his feet with an old man's grunt, and begins to chase the sound of sandals slapping pavement.

NINE

Christopher's ragged clothes flap from skinny appendages, a cartoon scarecrow with a pressing engagement. Miller is running more carefully in the gravel, shouting Christopher's name. Three pickups and an old Chevy roar past, and Christopher is twice nearly clipped as he weaves on and off the shoulder, sometimes crossing into oncoming traffic. Each vehicle has a twirling blue strobe light, volunteer firemen or EMTs.

"Christopher!" Miller's lungs burn, a stitch bores into his side. The low flying chopper and clamor of hounds are connected to whatever is pulling Christopher down this stretch of road. But Miller isn't interested in the emergency. He's suddenly desperate not to be abandoned. Christopher will be gone forever once out of sight, and Miller's not ready. Not yet. It has to be on his terms. He can't spend tonight alone next to a swamp full of dead trees. Or huddled alone anywhere. His mind flashes to Mary, to the way they were drawn together when she was sick. She was the tough one between them, the rock. That she went to the first doctor was typical of her, but coming home and making an appointment for a second opinion freaked him out as much as anything. She knew she had cancer before any lab results were in. He held her hand the way he needs to hold Christopher's.

"He grows on you like a tumor," huffs his inner voice, also out of breath. Miller is struggling too hard to respond.

Christopher maintains the pace for more than a mile of small green markers, always about 50 yards ahead. He runs faster than Miller, but his zigzag course causes him to cover more ground. Christopher slows in the middle of a bridge that's pockmarked by missing concrete. Exposed rebar twists from several gaps like human tendons. Miller dances around water-filled potholes that have claimed hubcaps that now rest upright against the inner retaining wall.

58

Christopher sidles up onto the ledge and peers down the 30-foot drop, studying the fast-moving muddy current.

It takes Miller a full minute to catch his breath enough to speak. "What is it? What do you see?"

Christopher waves a hand, keeps searching.

Miller leans over the edge for a better look, both hands gripping the rough surface. Steep hillsides rise from the river's edge to form a narrow gorge. There's been heavy rain upriver, and the debris-filled water rages against one bank, threatening to undercut rows of trees.

Christopher surveys the surface, hands shading his brow. He tracks the path of several bobbing objects until they pass under the bridge, then raises his head to again scan upstream.

The helicopter sweeps in from behind, following the river's course. The rotors are evil laughter from a matinee horror, the machine's hulking shadow momentarily stealing all color, but Christopher's concentration doesn't waiver. Miller can't imagine what he's looking for, is anguished over the man's precarious perch. He wants to grab hold, be an anchor, but fears he'll send them both over the edge.

Christopher is silent, eyes locking onto something Miller can't see. He teeters in his worn sandals, pointed toenails curled down. And then he jumps.

"Jesus Christ!" Miller watches him enter feet-first and disappear in a white splash, the roiling water immediately consuming all evidence. Frantic, heart pounding, Miller turns and sprints across both lanes to search the far side. Nothing. He runs to the end of the bridge and hurdles the steel barrier, then drops down to the incline and scrambles between trees like a ski racer in a slalom course. He twice nearly cartwheels head-first before reaching the bottom.

He maneuvers downstream at nowhere near the speed of the current. His hiking shoes slosh through mud, small limbs slapping his face. He cups his hands to call Christopher's name, then trips and nearly joins the murky torrent. Another 50 yards and a rocky outcrop creates a dead end. The hillside above is far too steep, and he only briefly considers attempting to wade around the giant rock. He grabs his knees, exhausted, looking out over the raging surface for any sign of the man. Broken tree limbs appear and disappear, long boney arms reaching for help and then giving up.

He once more calls Christopher's name, then collapses backward in the leafy slop. How long has it been? Two minutes, or maybe four?

"I count five," says the inner voice. "Humans don't survive five minutes in that water. Some fisherman will find the body a mile downstream, tangled with other trash at the first tight bend."

"Christopher," he says, but his energy is gone, and he's suddenly alone again.

"That's it, sport. Time to kick back for a spell and asses our not-so-sparkly situation. Not to be a Negative Nelly, but it appears we've come to a bona fide dead end." The inner voice has softened into a cajoling tone. He looks up at the boulder blocking the way, then back at the muddy slope. The road is impossibly far away. The voice is right. Dead ends are everywhere. "No money or food. Dirty and cold, with no way forward. Home is not an option. C'mon, just you and me, sport. Those fancy hiking shoes are wearing thin in spots. Let's go for a swim."

He defiantly shakes his head, but struggles upright, wiping muddy hands on already filthy pants. He takes a tentative step, trying to convince himself it's only to feel how cold the river is, nothing but a little test. Both feet disappear to the ankles in brown water. The ground underneath tips at a slight angle, but probably falls quickly away. The water is numbing, tugs at his laces and leaches up his pant legs as he stands staring forward, hypnotized by the constant motion, the immense power.

"It's all right, sport. Feel how much it wants us. It's chilly now, but it'll be toasty warm once we're inside. It'll hold us, and carry us from this shitstorm. No more walking, and no more nights waking up believing we're in bed with Mary. Imagine not suffering any more of those disappointments. We'll have peace."

A small step brings the water to his knees. Another and it's massaging his thighs. The pull is almost a riptide, and he digs his heels, not quite ready to let go. He is a teeter-totter that's balanced perfectly level, poised for the tiniest disturbance to tip one way or the other.

"You tried your best," says the voice, but it's void of sympathy. The words are an accusation that yank him from the hypnotic state.

"There were two. They came from the storm. I had no way of

knowing."

"Congratulations for being unprepared."

"It was supposed to be safe. I checked the locks. I always checked them. I turned the knob, and sometimes went back and turned again. It was supposed to be enough."

"You for sure did the minimum."

"Mary called it our nest. And she called the girls our chicks. We were raising two little chicks in our happy nest."

"Monsters are everywhere."

"Monsters were other places. These came out of the storm. They came, and I couldn't save them."

"You *didn't* save them, sport."

"I didn't save them," he concedes, and is completely deflated, chin drooping to his chest. The perfect balance is lost, and he tilts forward into the rushing water. Miller closes his eyes and doesn't take a breath as he slips under.

TEN

Miller recoils from an object bumping his hip. The peaceful state shatters when he realizes the thing is alive and seems to be reaching for him, or trying to climb through him. His stomach and chest are probed as it blindly comes at him in the inky tempest. His crotch is assaulted by a fist or an elbow, and a gasp fills his lungs with water. The creature pushes into him, rotating his body in the cold, and he's forced backward, struggling to dig his heels against the current. The underwater beast bullies past and then his hair is snatched in an iron grip, head yanked. His body is turned face down as he's pulled like a rag doll, knees bumping across the rocky bottom.

"C'mon, sport, at least put up a fight."

But he's a helpless fish at the end of a line, lugged into an alien world and deposited in a place with air he cannot breathe. The fisherman pounds his back and then rolls him over. A finger jams into his mouth, exploring, finds his tongue. Miller tries his eyes, but there's more of the grit that clouded the water, makes the sky and tree tops a mottled blur that is eclipsed by a familiar shape. His captor's face comes close, the leathery skin, white hair, and chapped lips. There's a glimpse of teeth also once sharpened to points, but ground smooth by gnawed bones of innocents. The fisherman kisses wide and hard, replaces the warmth the river had promised. The kisses come and go, and he accepts each without resistance.

"Open wide for some tongue, faggot."

Another face flashes in and out of his vision. Each time the fisherman comes for another kiss, a female child's motionless body is exposed. Her eyes are yellow wax, hair in shadowy tangles. Her shoulders are pallid knobs. Dead leaves hang from her gaping mouth.

Miller vomits river water, and a fit of violent coughing bring stars and lightning. Christopher releases his grip and allows his retching body to slide away. He hacks phlegm and blood, then pushes to his knees, forehead in a patch of moss, hands to his stomach to keep his guts from bursting.

"Come back." Christopher's voice is low but demanding. Now in dry heave spasms, Miller manages to roll his head sideways to peer at his companion now cradling the girl. Christopher rocks, one hand buried in matted hair. A child slightly older than Lizzy, naked to the waist, skin bereft of contrast except for two nipples that are black freckles. Pajama bottoms are torn wide at the crotch, some kind of cartoon pattern that elicits a plaintive moan from deep inside Miller. Her feet are bare, and dimpled as if dragged over coarse ground. "Come back, come back," Christopher pleads.

Miller's raspy breathing evens, and his attention goes to the drone of an outboard engine echoing from the gorge walls. Aboard are four men in bright orange life vests, the one in the bow standing tall, gesturing and excited. Miller witnesses the approach upside down, fearing any movement might bring another round of retching. A holster is unsnapped and a gun freed in the seconds before the hull beaches. The engine is killed when fiberglass scrapes over exposed roots. The armed man wears a blue baseball cap with a gold star, and is the first to jump down in heavy boots, the sound of shit hitting toilet water.

Miller senses movement on the outskirts of his vision. With a slight shift he sees the girl's left hand close into a fist. Tendons in her thin wrist flex and contract, the muscles working, trying to be alive again. He has a sideways view of her wan face, and the frail neck twisted too far. One stuffed cheek is puffed like a greedy chipmunk full of seed.

"Come back," Christopher repeats, and Miller beholds the change. Her head sways, assailed by unfair gravity, her throat pulsing as if trying to unclog. One pupil begins to lower, an upside down brown sunrise over dirty snow. Miller roots for the eye's return to life. It vibrates into a thick crescent, then pulls back to a tiny sliver. Below, the hand clenches and unclenches as if she's inflating herself back into this world, this life.

"Let her go, motherfucker!" The cop's black weapon is held out in front, leveled at Christopher. The hopeful eye goes lifeless.

"She's dead." It's a simple statement from Christopher. He loosens his grip on the limp child as if proving his veracity. "She won't come back."

The other men clamber from the boat, one tying off on the nearest tree. Miller watches the girl's hand, but it remains frozen.

"I said let her go!" The cop steps forward and kicks Christopher squarely in the face. The impact tumbles Christopher backward, the girl rolling from his arms. Slithered. Her body slithered from his arms. The cop takes another step, raising a black boot and stomps with a heel, snapping ribs and causing air to whoosh out like a child's fart toy. Christopher lifts both hands in defense, elbows pulled in close. He's making breathless sounds, trying to say something, but is unable. The cop bends, uses the gun to flick away one of Christopher's hands.

"What is it, asshole? You got something to tell me?" The cop's crimson face looms, the gun barrel pressed to Christopher's temple. "What the fuck are you saying?"

It takes Miller a moment to realize Christopher isn't trying to speak. The strangled noise is laughter.

Two men come from behind to pull back the cop, but he shakes them off. Relenting has to be on his terms. He taps the barrel to Christopher's forehead. It makes a knocking sound. "Cuff these motherfuckers," he says, and then slowly straightens. "Before I save our taxpayers a whole lot of money and trouble."

ELEVEN

The police station's main work area has the look of a town library sans the books. Two side-by-side cells are in the very back, separated by floor to ceiling bars. Miller and Christopher each have their own cell, and bunk beds with stiff rubber mats. Both have chosen the top, and lie staring at the cement ceiling.

"Some days are so excellent you can't believe you forgot your camera," Christopher says, shivering in damp clothes, teeth chattering loud enough for Miller to hear. An emaciated gray dog sits directly outside Christopher's cell, head cocked, high-pitch whine escaping every few minutes. Nothing is weird anymore. Miller isn't sure about breeds, but it has some kind of German name. Christopher, whose face is red and puffy on one side, lips with a vertical cut, doesn't acknowledge the dog.

"It'll get worse if they decide not to believe us." Miller rubs the heels of his hands to knead thigh muscles. His legs are tired enough to keep the desire to walk at bay, but he'll go crazy once they've rested.

"Are there police in the community where you work?"

"Not exactly," says Miller. "Full-time security keeps an eye on empty homes, directs ambulances, stuff like."

"No guns?"

"We had one guy get certified for a Taser," Miller says, the dog again makes the sound of air escaping a squeezed off balloon. "But that didn't turn out well."

"Went Taser happy?"

"On a Russian grandmother who forgot her pool badge and wasn't about to be turned away." Miller was in charge of gathering statements and dealing with the insurance company. The worst part was calming the lawyers. "She hit the deck hard. I had to fire the imbecile. He had no clue he'd done something wrong."

"Will you get over what happened?"

The dog turns and trots to the front window before Miller asks if he means the *babushka* or the murder of his family. The dog barks, tail thwacking the side of a metal desk. The lone cop guarding them hasn't stirred from a magazine since they were delivered. The sheriff had unlocked the cuffs and shoved them into the cells, then slammed the doors and headed off in his car. The room is a collection of messy work spaces. There's a table with portable radios and charging stations, but all the gear looks disassembled. Wastebaskets are surrounded by missed shots of balled paper. A padlock hangs from the latch of an empty steel cabinet along one wall.

"Stop your fuss and go lie down." The cop tosses the magazine on a stack of papers, removes his shoes from the desk. The dog is on its hind feet pawing at the window. When the sheriff throws open the door, the dog scrambles to him and is abruptly kicked with the same boot used on Christopher. The dog is driven to the floor hard, and then recovers to cower off to a blanket folded in a corner, tail tucked, piss trail left behind.

Miller looks across at Christopher, whose eyes have gone narrow, mouth pursed. Christopher is seething, and Miller is somehow certain the sheriff would fall dead to the floor if he were at that moment to wander anywhere near the cells.

The sheriff ignores the prisoners, goes about sticking a coffee cup in the microwave, then sits at a desk and reaches for the phone. Twenty minutes pass before another car pulls in front. The dog stays put.

"Woody," the sheriff says when the door swings open. The man wears a dress shirt and tie, is a foot shorter than the sheriff, who's built like a former high school linebacker turned heavy beer drinker.

Woody drops a manila folder next to the sheriff's cup. "Not adding up," he says in a low voice, glancing beyond the sheriff at the cells. "Timeline's all wrong. And before you ask, I tripled checked. There's no possibility."

"You gotta be wrong." The sheriff picks up the folder and then slaps it back down without looking inside. "My gut says these are the bastards. We got 'em cold."

"Grab me the keys, and I'll have a little powwow with these

boys," says Woody, retrieving his folder. "Take your mutt over to the school field and air him out. He stinks something awful, in case you haven't noticed. And don't hurry back."

"This sure as hell ain't the way we used to get things done." The sheriff lifts the ball cap to rub his forehead with a meaty palm, and then gets to his feet with a loud groan. He removes a set of old fashion skeleton keys from a hook above the other cop's desk and tosses them underhand. He marches toward the cowering dog. It rolls over in submission, long tail still tucked, the very tip trembling against its belly. "Get the fuck up." He uses a boot to shove the dog hard enough to spin the entire blanket. "Maggoty piece of shit."

The dog scrambles to its feet, trapped in the corner. The sheriff works a boot around behind and propels it back across the pee trail. He stomps to the door, grabs the knob and pulls. Once again he boots the dog's ass, and they are gone.

"Stay put," Woody tells the remaining cop, who reaches for his magazine, and then sinks back in the chair with a shrug.

Miller and Christopher are sitting up on their bunks, legs dangling, while Woody rearranges furniture. He clears a table and moves two heavy chairs to face the sheriff's desk, then comes to unlock the cell doors. "Please join me, gentlemen."

Miller looks across. Christopher's chin is pinned to his chest. He is sucking air through his teeth, eyes fixated on the window and beyond. Not the ideal frame of mind for convincing authorities you aren't responsible for the half-naked dead girl they found in your arms. Miller drops down and slips into Christopher's cell, where the temperature is a few degrees warmer. He taps Christopher's ankle to get his attention, to break the spell. Feverish heat radiates from the man. Miller steps back and hisses his name.

Christopher slides from the bunk, clothes still wet, sandals making a squishing sound on the concrete. "How can someone do that?"

Miller tugs him out of the cell by his shirt. "Forget it. Just forget it."

"Please sit." Woody motions with his chin, opens the folder and pulls out several faxes and Miller's stolen credit card. "I'm sorry for your loss," he says without looking up. "A horrible tragedy."

Miller is confused at first, but of course the cops would know. He says nothing.

"He's killing the dog," says Christopher, who continues looking out the window, paying no attention to Woody.

"I'm Daniel Woodman. Woody's just fine." The man sits back in his chair, stretches his arms behind his head. "I handle things pretty much like a district attorney in this county."

Christopher points at the window. "It's the sheriff you should lock up."

"One of the volunteers said he assaulted you at the scene."

"He means for kicking the dog," says Miller. "My friend is an animal lover."

"I need to tie up a few loose ends," Woody says, not interested. "You were on the bridge when you saw the body. You jumped in to attempt a rescue, which was either heroic or crazy, or plenty of both, if you ask me. You didn't know the girl or her family, and had nothing to do with her disappearance. I get anything wrong?"

Miller looks at Christopher, then back at the man who is now leaning forward and frowning over one of the papers. "That's exactly what happened. We saw the helicopter and heard the dogs. We were camped down the road, next to a pond. I swear there's nothing more."

Woody slides the credit card in front of Miller. "State liquor store manager next town over took it off some boys trying to buy a case of beer. Care to explain how that came to pass? You have two strikes when it comes to the kids in these parts."

The credit card pulls Christopher's attention back from the sheriff and abused dog. He blinks and clears his throat, looking as if he is waking up in a strange place. "That was my fault."

"I was sick when it was stolen," Miller says, and Christopher nods fast. Like an idiot, thinks Miller. Jesus, it's as if he wants us put away. "We were staying at a motel. He went for food and left it on the store counter."

"They got the key, too," Christopher adds.

"The card wasn't reported stolen," Woody says. "Most people I know would at least cancel it. You didn't."

Miller takes the card, flips it over. His signature is elegant, almost prissy. Was it the card he'd used to buy the bed in which his wife had been murdered? He thinks so. The small piece of rectangular plastic is hot against his fingertips. It feels tainted, somehow responsible. He wants to put it back on the desk and leave it behind.

"The girl went missing when you were miles away. A witness puts you in some sort of bar altercation, and described this one right down to his sandals. Quite a brouhaha, but out of my jurisdiction, so not my business." Woody puts the fax sheets back in the folder. "It's a shame, because this case would have wrapped up nicely."

"What's his name?" Christopher asks.

"You're asking about the sheriff?"

The chair makes an awful screech against the hardwood floor when Miller stands. "I'm pretty sure we're free to go."

"The dog," says Christopher. "What's the dog's name?"

The man looks at Christopher as if he's crazy. He *is* crazy, Miller thinks. More crazy than you could ever imagine.

"The hell if I know. Calls him Maggot or Shithead, most of the time. Might not have a name."

"We can be on our way? We're done here?" Miller has the credit card in one hand, a grip on Christopher's shirt with the other. He begins pulling him to his feet.

"Hang on. Lemme find your property bag." Woody turns without getting up. He opens several file drawers before locating a plastic bag containing a clump of soggy cash. He turns it upside down, shakes out the floppy bills. Miller scoops them. "This is still the good old United States of America, and I have no legal reason to keep you locked up. I would, however, suggest getting a move on before your less than hospitable host returns. Unless, maybe, you'd like to stick around and press charges for what he did to your face?"

Christopher glares over his shoulder at the door, and Miller's skin spreads in gooseflesh over the low snarl coming from the tall man's throat. The inner voice has been absent, but Miller knows it also sees murder Christopher's eyes.

***

Miller is again jogging to keep up with Christopher's strides. He's following the man toward more trouble, and this might be of the catastrophic variety. He looks with longing to the west, the direction his entire being yearns to travel.

"I know what you're planning," he says to Christopher's

swishing tangles.

"Then you'll help me. What do you figure he does to that dog when nobody's watching?"

The police station is on the town's main drag, gas station and grocery to the right, a school and compact houses with neat lawns to the left. There's a bike lane in one direction and sidewalks on both sides of the road. Christopher continues away from the late afternoon sun that calls Miller.

"You know this is big trouble," Miller says, but it's useless. "The guy's an armed redneck with a badge. You can't mess with a cop."

Christopher stops and whirls, fists on hips. Miller nearly bowls him over in front of the single-story elementary school. "Then walk the hell away. Turn around and disappear into the sunset for all I care. It's what you do best. I sure wouldn't want you to grow a set of balls that might weigh you down."

Miller stands silent, mouth agape. They are nearly chest to chest, Christopher hunched to speak directly into his face. So much heat radiates from Christopher's body that he expects steam to rise from his wet clothing.

"There's fire inside," says his inner voice. "Your fingers will burn if you reach out and touch him."

"It's not sane," Miller says to both the inner voice and Christopher.

"Maybe you don't know what sanity is," says Christopher, whose hands reach up and gently settle on Miller's shoulders. Hot, yes, but there's also something else Miller's mind races to understand. It's what he imagines it's like being trapped between two powerful magnets pulling at one another. "You need to understand the importance of equilibrium. There is chaos when things lose proper balance. That's an easy enough concept, isn't it?"

Miller can only nod, wants the hands off his body but can't move.

"One fucked up person with power creates havoc." White specs have gathered in each corners of Christopher's mouth. Miller's shoulders smolder, but he's locked in place by the slight touch. "And we can't have that. Those situations are bad for everyone. The sheriff is a poison that spreads. Imagine the ripples from a stone dropped into a pond."

"Please let go," Miller manages.

"Oh, sorry." Christopher lowers his hands and backs away. The heat is gone, but Miller's skin itches and feels branded. "You had a taste of what it's like to be that dog when your monsters came in from the storm. You got the condensed version on a dark and rainy night, but it definitely made an impression. And right now you wouldn't know balance if it walked up and kicked you in the ass."

Christopher turns and charges through a manicured hedgerow, sandals annihilating blooms of newly planted flowers. The school parking lot is empty, and Miller sees the target Christopher is zeroing in on like a guided missile. Visible from the rear, the hulk of a man is seated on a bench maybe 50 feet away, the blue sheriff's cap tipped up. Cigarette smoke wafts in the still air. Beyond him is a yellow and blue playground set, the same shades Miller and Celia always chose for their Candy Land games. The gray dog squats on his haunches trying to crap in the wood chips at the base of a tube slide, but is having trouble. The dog tenses, muscles straining, tail straight out and shaking.

Christopher tramps across the painted parking spaces. The slap of leather on pavement catches the dog's attention, but the sheriff remains oblivious, his only motion is to take a drag and blow a single smoke ring. As Christopher steps onto the grass directly behind the bench, the dog finally releases a huge bowel movement.

"Now we become cop killers." The inner voice sounds resigned. "Whatever headlines were printed about Mary and the girls will be added to this story and run all over front pages. Enjoy your last hours of being yesterday's news, sport. This is the big time."

Miller steps through the hedges and angles to the right. He has no intention of interceding, but feels a need to bear witness. Christopher looms over the sheriff, pausing for a few long seconds, and then reaches with his right hand as if to caress the man's cheek. Christopher leans forward and puts his lips to his left ear, and the two stay like that as the moments pass. Miller scans the fields and then the windows and doors of the school, but they are alone. The dog kicks wood chips to conceal his pile and trots around to sit next to Christopher, head turned up, hopeful. He looks about to bark, but doesn't. His tail thumps grass.

The cigarette dangles from the sheriff's lips, smoke rising around the ball cap. Christopher separates himself, standing tall and casting a shadow over the seated man. There is a distant horn, and a single gust of wind ruffles the tall man's white hair as he turns back toward the parking lot. Christopher's face is pale and without expression, his movements almost slow motion. Or perhaps time has slowed inside Miller's head while experiencing a cold-blooded murder.

"Did you hear that?" The inner voice is a whisper. "Know what the click was?"

"What?"

"They were switching on the electric chair, sport, testing it out. Getting it good and ready. It's what they do to cop killers."

"I heard his ribs break when the sheriff stomped his chest," he tells the inner voice, watching Christopher's approach. "He had a black eye and bruised face. Now he doesn't."

"I get the feeling you'll fry alone for this."

The dog is walking with Christopher, bumping into his thigh while greedily licking at his right hand, the one that touched his master's cheek. Christopher smiles, the crow's feet at each eye grow deeper. Everything speeds back to normal, and there's a new bounce in Christopher's step by the time they are face-to-face.

"Look at this handsome guy. Isn't he something?" Christopher drops to his knees, allows the dog to cover his face in sloppy kisses. "Yes you are, yes you are!"

"Christopher … "

He rubs at the dog's sides with long boney fingers as they nuzzle each other's necks. Both make happy whining noises, the dog's tail whipping in a gray blur.

"You have that credit card back, right?" Christopher laughs and has to turn his face to avoid getting a dog tongue in his mouth. "Let's find a store and buy him a sweater."

Miller's voice is a croak. "It's got to be 80 degrees."

"Okay, then a shirt. A doggie t-shirt!" Christopher grabs the animal by the jowls and ears, rubbing deeply, adding to the dog's ecstasy. "One with a cat on it! Wouldn't that be some funny shit? We need to find someplace that sells dog food. The good stuff."

"We better go." Miller eyes the desolate school grounds, and the bench with its slumped figure.

"Excellent idea." Christopher uses both hands on the dog's sides, loose skin jiggling. The dog leaps and tries for another lick when Christopher stands. "C'mon, Maggot! Let's go, boy!"

Miller moves to keep up with the happy duo. "Maggot?"

"That Woody guy said it was either Maggot or Shithead." Christopher is hunched to continue rubbing the dog's ear. "Look how he moves all wiggly like a maggot when he's happy. Don't ya, Maggot? Who's a good boy? Are you my good boy?"

They find their way to the highway and head toward the falling sun.

TWELVE

They walk into the night, dog toenails ticking on the warm pavement, the men not talking. A convenience store bag filled with energy bars and cans of dog food bumps against Christopher's leg. Lights from another town glow on cloud underbellies. Lightning flickers, but the air is dry and smells of honeysuckle long past bloom. There are signs for New York and Ohio, and small towns Miller has never heard of.

It's an hour since the last car rocketed by, fragments of a country music song left swirling. Christopher is first to speak.

"You think I killed him."

Miller has been listening to the symphony of the woods and trying to decipher firefly language. Lizzy had explained they were looking for boyfriends and girlfriends by writing messages with their lights.

Miller coughs, clears his dry throat. His left knee is sore, the sensation of trapped air bubbles under the cap. "I don't know what you did."

"It's a complicated thing." Christopher pauses as if gathering his thoughts. "I mean, it's both complex and simple. Guy like that has time bomb for a heart. Overweight, a heavy drinker, and a cigarette always jammed in the corner of his mouth. Not to mention the evil inside."

"It's complicated, huh? The balance was all out of whack."

"He was alive and now he's dead. And there are a dozen good reasons for his ticket getting punched, all of which were his own doing."

Miller watches a firefly make the letter J with a downward swoop. He waits for the next letter to begin, but it doesn't come by the time it's behind them. He holds no more sympathy for the sheriff than he does the men who murdered his family. What happened at

74

the school playground could have been a scene flashing across the TV, a show he might have watched for a minute or two before clicking onto something else. He decides his anger is solely for the selfish reason that Christopher jeopardized what he's come to think of as his disappearing act.

"My youngest daughter told me fireflies use their lights to communicate. There's a picture on our fridge, with little yellow dots trailing out behind."

"It spells love," Christopher says in a gentle voice, and Miller stumbles and nearly falls. Christopher looks at him, his face a half smile in the dark. "What else would a little girl draw?"

Miller concentrates on the insect noise. There's an entire universe, and although the sound isn't loud, it comes from everywhere. Vibrating bodies fill the surrounding vegetation, the sound giving texture to the air that tingles on his bare skin. It's a mile before he can speak. "There are so many surprises when you have kids. It's not that you see things in a new way, but more that you see things in a way you've forgotten."

"A lovely thought. I've heard similar sentiments."

"The layers of cynicism strip away, and you find yourself looking forward to the smallest things. I'd sit with a cup of coffee in front of the Saturday morning news, and Lizzy would come bounding down the stairs in her pajamas. She'd jump in my lap, grab the remote and make lightsaber sounds as the channels changed to Bugs Bunny, or whatever."

"A father with his loving daughter."

"Thing was … " Miller stops, his throat closing and his eyes filling with tears. They walk for a while before he resumes. "She knew those were the cartoons from when I was a kid. She found them specifically to watch with me. Mary told me that she'd asked what cartoons Daddy liked as a boy. So while I'm seeing things through her eyes, there's this little kid doing the same thing. We'd watch Elmer Fudd shoot Daffy in the head over and over, and the wisecracking duck has to keep rearranging his beak. And she giggled like crazy because she could see how her Daddy would have loved it as a little boy."

"Breaks your heart," says Christopher. "I can only imagine the pain."

"There is no pain." Miller shakes his head, then rubs at his face and eyes, sees white sparks. "There aren't any feelings left. You're a zombie when it's taken away. I'm an empty shell putting one foot in front of the other, too chickenshit to step in front of truck."

"Perhaps you'll see them again."

Miller snorts, has to wipe his nose. "There is no Heaven, no God."

"Belief would keep a man motivated."

"Like strapping on a suicide vest to earn 72 virgins? Do you really buy that glass slipper and gingerbread house shit? It's another shitty fairy tale to make us less afraid of what's coming."

"What if you could again hold one of your children? Take her in your arms."

"Shut up." Miller walks faster, needs to get away. Favoring one knee makes the other hurt.

"Scoop her up and embrace the warmth," Christopher calls from behind, his voice rising, preaching. "Smell her hair, and look into her smiling face."

"They're cold and dead, you fucker. They're gone forever."

"I could help if you stopped thinking like a zombie. You know I can."

"Fuck you."

"Which one would you choose? Is there a favorite? I imagine parents don't like to think that way, but it would seem natural to have a preference."

Miller is panting, snot and tears streaming. He swings his arms to compensate for the rubbery weakness in his legs. A hand will touch his back any second. It will be burning hot, and squirming things will flood out of it and into his body. He'll collapse here on the side of this road listening to the rants of a madman wanting him to make a deal with the Devil. Instead of 72 virgins, he'll get one little girl. It's suddenly clear. A daughter for his soul. He almost laughs because he knows Christopher is insane in the worst of ways. A cold-blooded killer and savior of abused dogs. A man who entices children to raise their hands and beg to die. Pick me, pick me.

"Which one?"

"Leave me alone."

"The oldest? The one you had more time to love? Or the more vulnerable one? She must be frightened wherever she is. It has to be terrifying for such a young thing." Christopher's voice is so close he feels breath inside his ear, the words loud despite being delivered in a moist whisper.

"Stop."

"The young one looked so much like Mary, didn't she? Same crooked smile, same frown when she concentrated."

"Please don't."

"You can pretend it doesn't hurt, but we both know better. And there's a reason you haven't stepped in front of a truck."

Miller's unsustainable pace tapers, and he feels the inner voice searching for words that don't come. There's a rumble miles up ahead, a trucker finding another gear, bearing down, but he knows he'll keep walking.

***

Christopher leads them to a break in the woods, several miles after the last truck thundered past. He once again stops as Miller's legs are on the verge of giving out, as though they've developed a rhythm for their limits. They tramp down a game trail that is swallowed by black foliage. It dead-ends at a shallow brook that's lined with light-colored stones set aglow from distant stars. They find a flat spot to sweep clear with their feet, then sit propped against fat stumps that smell of decay. Joints pop, and both groan as their limbs are forced into new positions. Miller thinks of the noises his car made after a long trip, the drips and ticking, and the sound of something deflating.

Christopher pries open a can for Maggot, then unwraps and rips in half a store made hoagie, handing one side to Miller.

"I may have gotten carried away." Christopher's voice is apologetic.

Miller's sandwich sits on the crotch of his pants. The miles have muted his anger and revulsion the same way it mutes the pain. What remains is not whole, only a cracked voice and emotional fragments. "People talk about acceptance and healing, but those words mean shit. Everything is gone, and nothing can change it. It would be better if I could have a few memories. Just one for each would be okay. But it's not safe to remember. I hear screams, and see what I can't erase."

"I know it feels hopeless." Christopher speaks while he chews, and Maggot makes wet sounds with the can. "But it's also the balance I tried to explain. The world is in disorder when it's missing. Isn't that how it feels? Like you're falling?"

Miller yawns instead of responding, sleep about to overrun his consciousness. The pulpy wood against his back is comforting. It's the only part of his body not numb or throbbing. If he sat long enough he'd melt into the stump, rot into the ground. Another yawn seems to go on forever. He hopes there are no dreams.

"My guess is that you aren't walking toward or away from anything." Christopher's raised voice jerks him back. In the dim light, Miller watches him pull his remaining sandwich meat to offer the dog. Maggot gulps it down without tasting, licks Christopher's fingers with gusto. "Your tilted world causes you to walk. Simple as that. You move without choice. And you will keep walking and falling until you find balance."

Or until I fall off the edge of the world. Miller watches a firefly begin a new message over the grasses beyond the water. Christopher coos at the dog, rubs his floppy ears. Miller falls asleep with half a sandwich in his lap.

THIRTEEN

There's a familiar weight on Miller's neck. It's the warmth of a nuzzling dog being passive-aggressive, wanting to be fed while maintaining a patient front. Petey would sometimes forget his stomach, falling back to sleep with jowls drooped across Miller's throat, the dog's deep breathing becoming a snore.

Petey was a Christmas present for the girls, although Celia had led the begging because Lizzy was holding out for a pony. Mary put the puppy in a box with holes, a red ribbon stuck on top. For company was a small stuffed panda, which he gutted in the few brief moments spent hidden under the tree. For sure it was a harbinger. Petey was born from the box, loved by the girls, and destined to chew everything to pieces, including a pricey goose down comforter that first January. He was an opportunity for the girls to learn responsibility, feeding and walking him before the bus, making sure he had water. A job relegated to Miller by mid-winter, but he hadn't minded. And the name was part of it. Celia had conspired with her mother, picking a name her dad would have to love, since he'd watched Little Rascals repeats as a kid. Miller's first dog was also named Petey, and he'd gotten in trouble for drawing a circle with permanent marker around the dog's left eye for authenticity.

Miller reaches to stroke Petey, tells him he needs five more minutes, but the head is too big, the brow too boxy. No, this is the new dog and he isn't in a comfortable bed with his wife, but lying in a forest, head on a pine needle cushion. It's still night, and the sounds of life have come dizzyingly close. Warm drool traces a zigzag line down Miller's neck, puddles at his collarbone.

"Five more minutes," he whispers again, drifting back to sleep.

***

The minutes become hours, and he wakes to laughter and splashing water. Christopher sits naked in the shallow stream, hair and chest lathered with soap, Maggot playfully bowed in front of him, remaining just out of reach.

"Mmm, soap smells good and makes you less noxious." Christopher is crooning, the green bar held under his nose. "Come boy, I'll give you a scratch."

The dog creeps forward on bent legs. He allows Christopher to rub his ears, but bounds away, barking and snapping at the water as soon as the soap comes near. A frustrated Christopher splashes his own armpits and head.

"You'll go through life stinking and infested with fleas." Christopher shifts to his knees, works new lather in his palms. "I promise it won't hurt."

The standoff continues as Miller goes to the edge of the woods for a piss, comes back to scrub his hands in the cold water.

"He thinks you're playing," he calls to Christopher, who makes one more reach for the dog before giving up.

"He's not the most cooperative animal."

"Maybe he's trained as a bomb sniffer, and you have him confused."

"Is that possible?"

"The water is freezing," says Miller.

"The water's fine. He thinks the stink of whatever he rolled in gives him character."

"He told you that?"

Christopher shrugs, finishes rinsing his hair, then leans forward and shakes the water from his fine white locks. "The lights we saw were probably a town. I could handle a little civilization, some hot coffee and a soft diner seat."

"I could use a plate of eggs, and maybe a fresh shirt."

Christopher dunks his face and comes up laughing when Maggot barrels into him from behind, soap bar sent flying. The dog circles, barking and playfully lunging.

***

The trees are filled with chattering birds in the bright

morning, the road an easy downhill grade. The forest gives way to farms, then residential homes yield to gas stations and storefronts. The town is more a small city.

"We need a leash," Miller says when they pass a woman walking a fuzzy little mutt that yaps at Maggot. "We can't have any trouble."

Christopher doesn't answer, and Miller is struck by a sense of déjà vu when he finds himself out of breath keeping up with the tall man's accelerating strides. They are single file on the sidewalk, mostly low brick buildings on either side of the street, then an entire block consumed by a car dealership with flapping pennants. A bank clock flashes that it's 70 degrees and just past 8 o'clock.

"Hey, slow down," Miller says, but Christopher angles off the sidewalk, jaywalking through traffic. A driver honks, causing Maggot to yelp, but the dog stays on Christopher's heels, head down, looking like he's on a scent. They both look to be on a scent. Miller crosses at the next light, then jogs to catch up as man and dog disappear into a convenience store. Well, isn't this great? Perfect way to keep from drawing attention to a dead cop's stolen dog.

When Miller pulls open the store's heavy glass door, the scene is confusing. His first thought is that it must already be Halloween. There's a man in blue jeans, a dark windbreaker zipped to the neck, and a cheap plastic clown mask. At the end of his outstretched arm is a gun pointing across the counter. A flustered middle-aged woman is punching keys, trying to work the register. Christopher is standing a few feet behind the robber, hands up in surrender. Maggot crouches at his side, a low growl rumbling through bared teeth.

"Open it!" His voice is muffled by the fake mouth and big red lips matching the color of its nose. The cashier continues her fumbling efforts, and the man lowers the gun to the growling dog. "You better shut him up."

Christopher doesn't move, keeps his hands comically high, pointy nails nearly scraping the ceiling. Maggot's lips draw back to display rows of dangerous teeth. The sight of such raw power leaves Miller dumbfounded as to why the dog tolerated the sheriff's abuse. Maggot's transformation into something capable of serious damage is disturbing. Teeth that were an inch from Miller's throat a few hours earlier drip glistening saliva.

"I swear to Christ I'll shut him up for good!" The robber brandishes the gun, which causes Maggot to erupt into a menacing bark, strands of drool lacing out across the robber's dirty sneakers. But then the dog is distracted and loses his threatening pose. Fleas on his haunches have come to life. He sits back to wildly scratch, his banshee image further deteriorating when a loud fart releases against the scored linoleum. The smell will surely penetrate the clown mask and be the dog's death sentence.

The robber turns back to the woman. "Open the fucking register!" He slaps the counter with his unarmed hand, and sweeps two glass display jars onto the floor. Neither break, but the contents of the one stuffed with beef jerky fans out around the clown's feet. Maggot forgets his fleas and lunges for the treats. The robber shrieks and pulls the trigger.

Miller recovers after ducking away, expects to see the dog either dead or attached to the man's leg. But Maggot is spinning circles on top of the jerky strips, nipping at his tail that has apparently been grazed.

"Grab your dog or he's dead meat!"

Christopher stands frozen, with the same pursed-lip look as when the sheriff kicked Maggot inside the police station. The robber's gun draws imaginary circles in the air following Maggot.

"Don't." Miller's voice is a resigned croak, and the robber turns toward him as if seeing this new person for the first time.

The clown mask shakes back and forth at Miller. "Who the fuck are you?"

Maggot's rear end clips a display carousel and sends cheap sunglasses flying. It causes the robber to open fire without aim. Two, three, then four shots strike the floor, one ricocheting down the aisle and slamming into the refrigerated display case. The cashier howls, and a two-liter bottle sends soda jetting through the damaged glass panel. Maggot forgets his injured tail to chase after this new commotion, charging down the aisle and sliding to a stop amid cream-color foam. The robber raises the barrel to where Maggot attacks the fizzing liquid. The man is oblivious to Christopher having squeezed between him and the counter. The cashier watches with her head cocked, as Christopher reaches to touch the man from behind. A half-foot taller, Christopher leans forward and whispers into the man's exposed ear. The robber's knees buckle, extended arm wavering, as the gun slips from his grasp and bounces on the littered floor.

"Good," is the single word Christopher says into the man's ear, barely audible over Maggot's exuberant slurping. The robber teeters like a drunk trying to maintain balance, finally collapsing face first. The cashier gasps and makes the sign of the cross, puts her fingers to her lips. Maggot goes on lapping soda, bloody tail wagging.

FOURTEEN

The store swarms with police, and the cashier is kin to at least two red-faced young deputies who call her Aunt Deb and mull with hands jammed in pockets, watching their shoes and stealing glances at the corpse as if on a dare. An older cop wears pajamas under a grimy windbreaker, hair still shaped from a pillow. Another is out front directing traffic, maneuvering the looky-loos around abandoned squad cars, while jealously eyeing the real goings-on.

"You set those boys free right now, Ernie." Aunt Deb is lecturing a stout cop fully dressed in a tan uniform, notepad and stubby pencil at work. "You put them in handcuffs for saving my hide? I know for a fact it's not what Big Ernie would have done. Nothing Christian about it."

Officer Ernie is frowning, looks from his pad to where the strangers lean against the chip rack. Next to them is a young guy in jeans and a police uniform shirt holding a pepper spray vial in one hand, a monster truck magazine in the other.

"Something is fishy," says Officer Ernie, who stands over the body. Maggot sits attentively at the cop's side, tail missing hair and skin at the very tip. It leaves little red dots where it taps the floor. "Pretty convenient for a couple of vagrants to wander in right behind an armed psychopath."

"They're heroes, not vagrants." She comes around the counter to collect lollipops and jerky from the floor, stuffing them back in jars. Some of the meat strips have to be pulled from under the robber. "You're too darn suspicious. I suppose you forgot your Sunday school lessons about Jesus wandering the earth? I don't imagine you'd call our Lord a vagrant, now would you?"

"These two aren't healing the blind, Aunt Deb."

She nods her chin at the body. "This devil clown turned my store into a shooting gallery. Could have been a flock of precious children right down that aisle. Thank the Good Lord your little princess wasn't helping Mommy pick out an ice cream dessert, like she has a hundred times."

"I'm sorry, but I have a crime scene to get right. This is police business, not Sunday school."

She squats to give Maggot a jerky strip, strokes his head. He devours the treat without tasting. "I've heard you say how to best judge a man by his dog. You can't tell me this animal belongs to someone with malice in his heart."

Miller sneaks a glance at Christopher, who seems bored for someone who just committed murder.

Officer Ernie glares at the pair, then down at the dead clown. "It's my sworn duty, Aunt Deb. An officer of the law is required to be suspicious. It's how crimes get solved."

"Fine, then be suspicious about this one all you want." Aunt Deb pokes a jerky stick at the dead robber. Maggot's nose follows every movement, tail tapping away. He lets loose an anguished whine. "But I wouldn't be standing here if it weren't for those brave souls."

Someone has covered the robber's head with a dish towel patterned with pink bunnies and bright orange carrots. It still has a price tag. Officer Ernie nudges the dead man's leg and breathes an overly dramatic sigh. "These men not knowing one another is hard to swallow. It doesn't add up. When was the last time the store was robbed?"

Aunt Deb rubs her chin. She pulls balled tissue from a front dress pocket and blows, her eyes searching the dirty white ceiling panels. "Sixty-eight, I think it was. I remember Pops saying it was hippies. But we've got our share of shoplifters," she adds, looking across at Miller and Christopher, offering them a kind smile. "You had a talk with Johnny Sheppard not two weeks back. Boy's folks will have a handful once that child gets his driving permit."

The glass door is shouldered open by a harried, middle-aged man holding a camera and flash, ID badges flapping from a string around his neck. The half-dozen cops making their way up and down aisles hunting evidence in doughnuts boxes and cookie sleeves go for their holsters, and then relax.

"Jesus, Bradley, for crying out loud!" Officer Ernie flips his notepad pages and reaches to stroke Maggot's head. Miller's eyes catch the dangling tags when the dog leans into the cop's leg. From across the store he can make out the word Sheriff and the official-looking police department stamp. The tags flash and jangle each time the cop rubs the loose skin over Maggot's skull. Miller elbows Christopher and nods down, but the tall man is watching his dog and the cop with the expression of a scorned lover.

"Whatcha got here, Ernie? Looks gang related." The photographer steps past Officer Ernie and the body, finds a good angle and kneels to compose a shot. He's a thin fellow, with a white dress shirt and a narrow tie that tangles in the press pass string.

"Goodness, my hair." Aunt Deb licks her palms and presses them at the sides of her head. She runs the tissue under her eyes, then pulls a purse from beneath the counter and digs out lipstick.

"Christ sake, let me finish my job before you take photographs," says Officer Ernie, straightening his own tie and smoothing his collar. "And for God's sake, no more writing about imaginary gangs. You had every Nervous Nelly in the township ring my phone off its hook."

"What's with the pooch?" Bradley fires off the flash, and then twists camera buttons. Maggot stays glued to Officer Ernie, ignoring Miller and his master. "The robber had a four-legged accomplice? Boy, wouldn't that make a headline. Doggy and Clyde! Scooch down a little, I wanna frame you up with the deceased."

Officer Ernie bends at the waist and tilts his head to provide the lens a stern look. He straightens up after a few more photos, rubbing at the small of his back. "Nope, it's their mutt," he says, thumbing toward the cuffed duo. He reaches down and strokes Maggot's soft coat. "Deb says they came in after this dumbass, and saved the day. Guy was shooting up a storm when the tall one used some sort of Kung Fu move. Sonofabitch musta fell and cracked his skull. Clown was deader than a doornail by the time I got here."

"No, shit?" The photographer takes out his own tiny pad, finds an empty page and turns on Miller and Christopher. "Names and where you're from, please. Dog's name, too."

Miller glances at Christopher and then answers for both. "He's been staying with me after being out of the country. The dog is a stray that started following us quite a ways back, was hungry and needed a bath. We've been caring for him," Miller adds, looking over at Aunt Deb.

"Wait, you mean you're traveling on foot?"

Miller shrugs, nodding. The newsman points his pencil at Christopher. "Some sort of missionary, am I right? You look like one of those Peace Corps nuts. That where you learned Karate?"

"Yes, the Peace Corps," says Miller. "He just got home from a really difficult assignment. Saw terrible things, and doesn't open up to people. I'm sure you've seen a lot of the same in your line of work."

"That I have, that I have. What did you say his name was?" The photographer points at Maggot, just as Officer Ernie takes notice of the dog tags and begins shifting the nylon collar.

"Maggot!" Miller calls, and the dog slips from the cop's grasp and trots with his tail doing happy loop de loops. Maggot sits, waiting to be pet. Miller gives an embarrassed eye roll. "Yeah, I know, but it's French. A Peace Corps thing," he adds, as vaguely as possible.

The photographer knowingly nods his head, then unpockets a cell phone. He tells the person on the other end it'll be a half-hour, while also maneuvering camera buttons. He checks the image on the back screen. "This isn't working, Ernie. I need to get your ugly mug closer."

Officer Ernie grunts to his knees, then gathers the body's upper torso across his lap. Miller thinks it's probably the same pose he strikes each deer season.

"Get him a little higher," says the photographer, but the jerking motion causes the bunny dish towel to slide off and expose the clown mask. "Holy ravioli, what's with the getup?"

"The boy's disguise," says Officer Ernie. "And it ain't nothing to do with any gangs, you hear?"

"Looks like one of those Batman villains. Gonna scare the bejeebers outta my loyal subscribers."

"Then put the damn towel back on. C'mon, he's heavier than he looks."

The newsman ponders the scene, then puts the camera to his eye. "Nah, this is too gosh dang good. Cheese!"

"Speaking of cheese, Ernie, your boys have helped themselves to about thirty dollars worth of my goods." Aunt Deb is back behind the register, leaning over the counter.

"It's a crime scene," he says.

"What in Heaven's name does that have to do with them scarfing down Butterfingers? It's these two heroes who deserve a reward," she says, gesturing with a tissue. "Not your useless bunch of Keystone Cops."

"I'll take it out of their pay next Friday. Are we done here Bradley? The meat wagon's gonna be along any minute."

The group turns toward the window, and Christopher lets out a strange hiccupping noise. Dozens of faces have crammed up close, are clamoring for a view. Miller recognizes the centermost face as the cop who'd been directing traffic. Judging by the number of onlookers, the street is likely impassable anyway.

"Send one of your boys over to the Army Navy for two sturdy knapsacks, would you, Ernie?" Aunt Deb lifts a hand cart from a rack behind the counter and shuffles to the canned goods aisle. "You boys like beef stew? I have whole and creamed corn to make a nice hot meal."

"I have a credit card," says Miller, unsure if it's been cancelled after the district attorney phoned his bank.

"No, sweetie, your next meals are on me." Aunt Deb plucks items from shelves, then stops with the half-full basket and glares at Officer Ernie. "It's about time you find your keys and unlock our new friends. And I don't want to be waiting all day for those knapsacks. I have a business to run, and you have a body to clear on out. And don't leave any chalk outlines, thank you very much. Not a sight people want to associate with their olive loaf."

Officer Ernie rifles through his keychain, ordering one of his men with a powdered sugar mustache to get a move on those Army Navy bags. He works the locks on both sets of cuffs, then takes a cautious step back. "If no warrants come back on you fellas, you'll be free to ease on down the road. And none too soon, in my book."

FIFTEEN

Miller sprawls in the tall grass that conceals them from a busy stretch of highway. The wind gives energy to waves that sweep across timothy. Clouds move in the same direction, lagging slightly. The sun is best with eyes closed and chin tilted. It's warm and enveloping, and Miller could sleep all day. Officer Ernie drove them 30 miles, offered a ride all the way to the Ohio border, but Christopher had seen this 100-acre field and begged him to pull over. He'd more than begged, in fact. It was fortunate the rear doors of the cruiser only opened from the outside, or Christopher would have launched into the field at 70 mph.

Maggot begins barking, and Christopher adds his lunatic laughter. Miller opens his eyes to watch the puffy clouds, searching his memory for their scientific names. He once also knew the constellations, but is even unsure of the easy ones, like which Dipper was big. More things he has lost.

"Get off!" Christopher shouts, and Miller lifts up to peer through the oscillating seed heads. Maggot has tackled Christopher and is enthusiastically humping away. The tall man is on his side, shielding his head, laughing too hard to defend himself.

"You two seem to have made up."

"Help! His thing is touching me!"

Miller doesn't budge. He instead arranges one of the new backpacks behind his head. Aunt Deb stuffed both with canned goods, peanut butter jars, and dog food for a week.

"Miller!"

"That's getting pretty nasty." Miller is smiling. "I read you're supposed to let a dog finish, something about rejection causing heartworm."

"That can't be true."

"I wouldn't risk it."

89

Christopher manages to untangle, scurries to his feet. "Knock it off and maybe we'll find you a girlfriend."

Maggot begins to circle, dropping to the ground and barking each half-revolution.

"I'm done playing until you stop that shit," Christopher scolds, but then lunges at the dog, continuing the game. "Hey, Miller, how 'bout some SpaghettiOs?"

Miller rolls over to dig through his pack for an opener. There's also a box of plastic spoons. He finishes peeling open the second can when Christopher sits in the grass next to him, Maggot panting at his side and scratching behind one ear.

"He needs a flea collar," Miller says, handing over one of the cans. Christopher spills out half for the dog. With his free hand, Christopher strokes Maggot's sleek gray coat from behind his head to the base of his tail. Miller watches Christopher's face change from smiling to something slack-jawed, pupils dilating and shifting up as if he's trying to look at his own forehead. Miller is about to make a snide comment, but stops. Christopher lifts his hand and blows away small black dots after each stroke. Miller realizes that what looks like pepper flakes are dead fleas. The dog is in ecstasy, whether from being touched or from relief.

"I'm okay with resting here a few hours," Miller says, and Christopher blinks fast and seems to return from a daydream.

"It's nice, isn't it?" He takes a spoon and digs the rest of the can out onto the flattened grass. Maggot licks the ground clean, then circles the spot and lies down nose to tail.

Miller again stretches out with the backpack for a pillow. "I think I know who you really are."

"You do, do you?" Christopher maneuvers the second pack to lie parallel. "Hell, even I don't know who I am. I sorta envision myself as one of those seventies-kids trying to find his mojo."

Miller and his wife weren't religious. She described attending a Methodist church as a little girl for Grandma's sake, remembered bake sales and bright dresses, but not much more. When the matriarch passed, her family did other things on Sundays. Miller had fielded most of the girls' questions about religion, a job simplified by their copy of Disney's The Lion King. The hamster was buried in the flower garden to become part of the soil that grew the plants eaten by the animals, and so on. Even the little orange fish sent down the toilet made it back to the ocean, reborn as nourishment for something new. It was the circle of life.

Miller knows it's ridiculous before speaking. "You're some kind of Grim Reaper, only without the black robe and scythe."

Christopher laughs so hard it throws him into a coughing fit that causes Maggot get up and anxiously sniff at him. Christopher pushes at his muzzle, catches his breath. "Sorry, it's the way you said it. All serious and stuff."

"But you are."

"I told you it was complicated. Better to let it go, or you'll give yourself nightmares."

"I already have nightmares."

Christopher turns to look him in the eye. "What I do is nothing special."

"You killed a cop." Miller shifts to lean on his right elbow. "I know he was a bastard, but still. And you made me an accessory."

"You're worried about prison?" Christopher crosses his legs and folds his arms behind his head. Maggot settles in next to him. "You told me your life, and everything it was worth, was gone. Mister Sad Sack with nothing to live for."

"My family ... "

"I know what you lost. I wish I could do something, but what's done is done."

"So what are you?"

Christopher makes a grunting noise and pulls an arm free. He points up at the sky and the streaming clouds. "What do you see?"

"The clouds?" It was a game he'd played with the girls dozens of times. It was how most kite flying days ended. Exhausted from running, they'd collapse on their backs and one girl would point skyward and ask the same question. *What do you see?*

"Yes, the clouds. Tell me."

Miller decides to humor him. "A cotton ball."

"Really, Miller, a cotton ball? A billion things to imagine and that's what you come up? What's wrong with you?"

Miller points to the far eastern sky, where a large cloud has piled up and might have rain building within. It has layers of bright white and deep shadows. "All right, so that one is a cow," says Miller. "A black and white Holstein, like the ones down the road from my house."

Mary sometimes walked the girls over with a bag of wormy green apples from one of the trees now shading Petey's grave. The cows loved it, would coming mooing over to the barbed wire, meaty tongues flopping out and probing like greedy hands. The girls considered it the most gross and fun thing in the world.

"Fine, a cow will do," says Christopher. "Concentrate on its legs. Imagine they are moving. Form a picture in your head of the cow walking."

As Miller concentrates, nubby protrusions at the base of the cloud become four discernable legs.

"Harder," says Christopher. "Put them in motion. See each movement as you would draw them. Make them walk."

Miller imagines they bend at the knees and reach forward two at a time, and the cloud does exactly as he pictures. The rest of the cloud also becomes more cow-like, including the markings across its fat body. By the time it drifts overhead, it seems as though a cow has been painted over an enormous azure canvas.

Christopher moves his long index finger toward a much smaller cloud trailing Miller's cow. The white puff elongates, grows tube-like, then sprouts a snake head and a rattle on the tip of its tail. The cloud doesn't drift but rather slithers toward the cow, which breaks into a trot on its own accord. Miller tilts his head back to watch the formations disappear into the western sky, then turns to look at Christopher, who is staring back.

"Boo!" says the tall man, his face etched in deep lines from a wide smile.

"It's a trick. Some kind of hypnotism," says Miller, knowing better. He hides his shaking hands, tucking them under his thighs. "You're a street magician happy as hell to find some gullible idiot like me."

"I love magic shows."

Miller shudders over how helpless he is in this man's company. "It was summer vacation with Mary and the girls. Orlando, I guess. Guy dressed like a mime was working one of the main drags. Opens his mouth to pinch one end of a little string, starts pulling. He pulls and pulls, and then razor blades start popping out every few inches, as though he had a stomach full. Celia starts screaming bloody murder. Didn't faze my youngest, but Celia freaked-out like I'd never seen."

"Oh, my."

"I turned her away from him and hugged her. It's only a trick. I promise it's only a trick."

Christopher nods and shrugs. "It's all tricks, same as the clouds. There's always a simple explanation."

Minutes pass as they ponder the sky. Maggot snores, then makes noises like he's on the chase, legs jerking. He stops and growls, maybe has it cornered.

"Lizzy loved it," Miller says. "She wanted a magic set for Christmas. But then she wouldn't do any of the tricks. She read the instruction booklet and lost interest."

"I bet she wanted real magic."

Miller watches Christopher's big hand stroke the dog, more fleas dropping away. "Parents are supposed to teach kids magic is only pretend," Miller says. "It's okay to pretend, but understand what isn't real."

"Is that right? You mean like the Easter Bunny and Tooth Fairy? Not to mention Santa Claus and God Almighty?"

"It's not the same," Miller says.

"You mean it's complicated? There's no one simple answer?" Christopher reaches toward the sky with his right hand and points an index finger, turning it into a play gun. He closes one eye to sight down the barrel, searching for a target. Miller sees for the first time the variety of birds he hadn't noticed while making clouds change shapes. Six vultures circle in a distant formation. Crows bicker in treetops near the busy road behind. Small birds flit overhead at high speed. Christopher scans them with his make believe gun, thumb cocked and ready to fire.

Minutes pass, Christopher's pretend gun going from bird to bird, tracking each potential target for a few seconds, then moving on to another. Maggot is awake, head on his front paws, eyes also following the hand. He begins a high-pitched whine.

"Bang!" says Christopher. Miller and Maggot flinch.

Christopher's finger still points, but is dropping toward the horizon. Miller searches the sky and finds its mark, a small bird, yellow he thinks, tumbling through the air in free fall.

"You bastard!" Miller rolls and jumps to his feet, trying not to take his eyes from the bird, muscles punished for the move by sharp jabs, grass poking through a hole in the sole of one shoe. He pushes into the higher timothy as the bird disappears dozens of yards away. There are no landmarks and the waving grass erases any solid picture he tries to keep for estimating where it has crash landed. The grass swallows the tiny creature, but he continues forward, keeping his head level, eyes steady. Closer, he slows, afraid of stepping on what he hopes is only a stunned animal. He sweeps aside great armfuls of grass, scanning the bleached dead stalks covering the soil at the base of the live plants.

He spots the bird, one wing extended, one folded beneath. It is belly down, unmoving, as he bends to scoop it. He cradles the bird that's not yellow at all. It is a plain brown starling or barn swallow, or whatever, but it's not one of the bright yellow canaries set free from his daughters' bedroom window. He glances at the sky knowing there isn't a companion that's suddenly alone. He loosely holds the bird against his stomach in cupped hands and feels the head loll on its pencil-thin neck. The bird is lifeless as he stands with his hair blowing across an unshaven face.

He turns to curse at Christopher, the anger and rage welling as he holds the tiny murdered being that innocently wandered too near a monster. But Christopher had followed, is suddenly in his face, and before Miller can say a word, Christopher grabs his hands, incredibly powerful fingers clamping down. The dead bird is trapped.

It is somehow electric, an intense vibration that moves inside muscle tissue, or maybe through blood vessels. It begins at Miller's wrists, travels along his forearms and continues to his shoulders. It tickles the tip of his nose and makes his earlobes itch. He knows that if the vibration reaches his chest there is no way his heart will handle it. He will keel over dead as the bird, as dead as the robber and the asshole sheriff on the schoolyard bench. He'll be as dead as Petey and his newly buried family. He is inches from oblivion, can feel the muscles at the end of his collarbones cramping. A dull thump at the base of his neck makes him swallow hard, but he isn't frightened. He listens for the inner voice, expects a last few cynical words about his wasted final days running from a ruined life. Make that walking, he corrects. But the voice doesn't come, remains dead silent.

Miller's eyes are open, but he only sees shadows and vague movement. He feels Christopher's breath on his neck, the warmth from his body, smells his sour odor, but has lost the ability to focus. He waits for his legs to give out, for the plunging elevator sensation before hitting the ground. Instead, there is a sharp pain in the fleshy part of his hand between thumb and index finger. He tries pulling free, to open his hands and wave away the searing heat. But his hands are in a vise.

"Stop struggling." The words arrive on moist breath in his left ear, and he shivers, knowing it's the last voice Christopher's victims hear. "Relax, my friend. Allow it to happen."

He stops fighting and closes his useless eyes, bracing against the pain in his hand. The knife-like stabbing moves to his palms, then the sensitive spots along his fingers. He realizes the movement in his cupped hands is the bird, once again alive and searching for freedom.

"Its stomach is full of parasites." Christopher's voice is no longer a whisper, and although he's backed away a little, his grip over Miller's hands doesn't let up. "It hasn't eaten for days and cannot drink. Its suffering was over, but is now back like you wanted. You see how it only seems complicated? The answer to suffering is simpler than anyone cares to admit."

"Let me go," Miller huffs.

"We aren't done." Christopher's spittle lands on his face, and Miller can't wipe it away. The bones in his wrist are near collapsing. "Do you feel it? Has it reached you? It's balance being compromised, being fucked with. Are you getting the idea?"

Miller's stomach churns, bowels hot and heavy. It feels like he's swallowed a molten bowling ball, his newly loose pants bursting at the leather hair tie Christopher had given as a cinch. The pecking at his hands becomes frantic, but the pain is overwhelmed by what's happening inside his guts.

"Please." His knees buckle, his weight almost entirely supported by Christopher's iron grip. "My stomach. Please stop."

"You want the suffering to end?" Christopher laughs with contempt, but Miller comprehends little beyond his stomach's turmoil. He's been invaded, worm-like things squirm in a swelling mass, consuming his intestines and searching for a way out or more to eat.

"Help." The writhing works into his chest, is at the bottom of his throat. They'll be on my tongue, in my mouth. I'll know how they taste.

Pressure fills his ears, as though he sank head first to the bottom of a deep swimming pool. Or maybe he stumbled into

Molasses Swamp and is being pulled down by the ever-smiling Gloppy.

"Molasses Swamp is a sad place," Celia explained years ago, when the Candy Land game was still new. "You're almost at Candy Castle when Gloppy gets you. It looks like chocolate, but it's not."

"Right," he told her. "It's sweet and comes from sugar cane, but it's different from chocolate."

"I think it's quicksand," she said. "The coyote that chases Road Runner got stuck in quicksand and started to sink. Know what Road Runner said when coyote disappeared?"

Miller had smiled at his daughter. "What did Road Runner say?"

"Meep meep!" his daughter shouted, laughing.

The stomach pain begins to recede, the heat diminishing. He opens his eyes to Christopher's shadowy face, and yearns for the road to lead him away. He tries taking a step forward, through the man or around him, it doesn't matter. He wants nothing more than to be back out on the edge of the endless highway, the steady sound of scraping gravel beneath his worn shoes. Instead, he is being pulled close again, four hands trapped between their bodies, the wriggling bird still attempting to peck free. He is enveloped by Christopher's appalling energy and ripeness, as the tall man hunches to put his mouth back to Miller's ear.

"Meep meep," Christopher whispers, and the trapped bird stops moving.

SIXTEEN

It's sometime after midnight when they zip their packs and march single file to the black road. The breeze that usually dies after sunset persists, has even grown stronger. Kite weather, Miller thinks. It's a cooling headwind, and an earlier shower tamped down the worst of the dust. That the wind makes talking difficult seems fine with both men, as they work their way in and out of small towns with single traffic lights blinking yellow or red.

Maggot is energized, hunting new smells and chasing tumbling trash. He's a gray ghost shadowing the humans, trotting through culverts and along rocky hedgerows. His nose works the ground, his misshapen tail pointing skyward. Christopher has given up chastising him for sampling roadkill.

The walking is good, and the rhythm of moving body parts through night air brings relief. Miller fantasizes this new world is a blown-up snapshot that's black from edge to edge, top to bottom. Each step adds a single color pixel, another miniscule piece to an enormous puzzle he will always be too insignificant to properly see and therefore understand. But it doesn't matter. Putting scale to the universe is out his brain's league. Filling in the vast empty space is his workman-like job, an obsession that delivers comfort. Slaughter a man's family, but at least give him a task on which to focus. Left and then right. One foot in front of the other until there is no more ground to cover. And so be it if the path turns out to be infinite. There's no rush here. I have all day, all year. I have until my two bloody stumps cannot support their burden.

"I asked about your stomach. How's it doing?"

Miller looks from the road. The wind pins Christopher's clothes to his stick-figure frame. They are tattered flags over sharp angles. Miller shrugs, craves only the satisfaction of coloring more blanks.

"You also have a question." The inner voice nearly makes him trip over his own feet. "It's about that little birdie back in the field. Or maybe you're too chickenshit for the answer?"

"Leave me alone."

The voice chuckles. "Come on, sport, you know I'm not going anywhere. I'm here for the long haul."

"It's too late." Miller's real voice is consumed by the wind, so he's not even sure he's spoken. He walks stride for stride with Christopher, matching his pace. With such different lengths of gate, they've come to an unspoken agreement as to speed.

"Mary would go to the ends of the Earth to save your life, not to mention the lives of the girls," says the inner voice.

He is silent, doesn't want to be drawn into thoughts about the funeral home and the things he forced himself learn. But he senses what's coming.

"She'd have thrown a shovel in the car and had your sorry ass dug up the instant that bird ... " the inner voice trails off, perhaps searching for the perfect words.

"Was resurrected," Miller says thickly, wind filling his mouth, drying his tongue.

"There you go! That's what I'm sayin'. If a dead bird can be zapped back by Mr. Creepshow, what's to say it won't work on people?"

The funeral home had a special room where chemicals were pumped into the dearly-deceased, compounds used to forestall decomposition and keep loved ones good as new for decades. He learned the details online, typed the word embalmer into a search engine the night his family experienced the process firsthand. Some part of him demanded knowledge, forced him through page after page at a clinical website. Mary's mouth was being sutured into what the site referred to as a natural expression. He read about eye caps, and the difference between arterial and cavity embalming. He learned about the incision made above the navel to puncture hollow organs and aspirate contents. He looked up the word aspirate to be sure. He read how the close-up photos he provided were used by the embalmer to restore faces that were lopsided from settled fluids. Mary and the girls would be kneaded into peaceful presentations.

"They would be made acceptable," he whispers, wanting to stop remembering, but it's too late. "Painted with makeup to hide damage." He fills in another pixel with his feet, forges through another powerful gust. Left and then right.

The air in their tidy farmhouse had turned toxic. The poison choked him, but he'd been assigned tasks. He tore the framed family portrait from the main staircase wall, turning away to gulp air that burned his lungs.

In the disorder of the master bedroom he pulled the closet door from its track, then piled Mary's clothes on the stripped bed. Petey's blood formed two large egg-shaped stains, one on the mattress and one next to the door frame where he'd slid from his arms. He chose a green dress for the embalmer to fit over his naked wife. Panties were easy, but deciding on a bra nearly drove him insane, lacy straps with hooks and material too sexual for this ceremony. Would Mary want something with a lift, or one with racy animal stripes? He found a sports bra tucked among satiny running shorts.

He did much the same in the girls' room, tears saturating his filthy t-shirt as he picked through their delicate clothing. He smelled each piece, breathing in memories, the sweet little-girl perfumes, the hint of nail polish and strawberry shampoo. Every smell was a fading bit of their lives, and he held the soft material pressed to his face, tried to pretend.

"They can't come back," Christopher says over the noise of wind gusting through trees, tossing their hair.

Miller's hands are still covering his nose and mouth, the very last scent of his oldest child a memory he's trying not to lose.

"There's nothing to balance it with," says Christopher. "I'm sorry, friend."

Miller lowers his empty hands, appalled by their weakness. His weakness. He wonders if Christopher is lying, if there isn't some way. "I didn't know how to ask," he says.

They are the last words for the next few miles, and Miller fills in more specks of the boundless canvas. The wind dies before dawn. Howling one minute, quiet the next. The only sound is shoes sliding through loose gravel, and sometimes slapping the black road. And there is the occasional excited bark from a ghost dog finding vague scents of long gone animals.

SEVENTEEN

Christopher leads the way along a curvy stretch. The busy morning traffic has returned for the afternoon. Commuters with invisible problems are in comfortable seats, coffee cups or phones in one hand. Miller appreciates the need for routine. Breakfast with his girls. The debate over sugary cereal, and the morning Lizzy sounded so grown up declaring Mommy's *jihad* on things that tasted good. Celia sprayed milk from her nose. He was in his car at quarter to eight, and sitting in his cubical twenty minutes later. Staring back is a family photo from Disney World, and a Mickey Mouse letter opener that had never opened a letter. Mornings were for troubleshooting, neighbors complaining about neighbors, and assistant bank managers bitching about missing deposit slips and bounced checks. There were phone messages left by irate weekenders from the city. Nobody was doing anything about the wandering deer herd threatening to maul children and dent BMW fenders. A woman referred to the herd as a gang. Afternoons were for dealing with clubhouse and restaurant vendors, and other in-box paperwork. Then back in his car at quarter past five, and home twenty minutes later. The routine was gratifying, but never the work.

The sky has no entertaining clouds for passing the time. He concentrates on tire track puddles in the softer earth. He imagines an ocean wave sweeping across the surface, points a finger to condense his mental energy as they trudge by. Maybe a breeze he doesn't feel moves a ripple. He stirs more puddles in the next mile. Beyond a house with a yard full of rusted junkers is a field of tall grass. He images a tsunami that begins along one tree line and powers over a sea of green. He uses his left hand to move the wave, watches the grass bend and flatten as if a helicopter was hovering close. And then the energy sweeps westward, birds escaping ahead of the shifting grasses, where the wave dissipates in a distant feathery shrug.

Christopher doesn't notice, and the dog is busy with a dead squirrel. Miller considers showing off the new trick, but decides to keep it secret. When they reach the next cluster of trees, he selects a brown leaf dangling from an overhanging branch. He targets with his index finger, causing the leaf to flutter and its stem to break free. The leaf falls halfway to the ground before it's back in his sights. He concentrates on the empty space just below it and imagines another wave, this one smaller, nothing more than what a pebble might cause in a deep pond.

The leaf stops falling, defies gravity. The trio is abreast of the tree when he points again, this time with more force, compressing the energy behind the thought. The leaf is practically annihilated when it explodes in scattered flecks that spin to their feet. He cocks an elbow to blow on the tip of his finger as though it's a smoking gun, then eyes the back of Christopher's skull and wonders how much energy it would take to separate the head from Satan's shoulders. The magic is proof he has gone insane, the tricks and taunting inner voice born from the same illness.

There is a cloying sweetness at the edge of the next field. Milkweed and picked-over blueberry bushes alive with insects line the road for 100 yards. Mary had a small Monarch butterfly tattoo, the same orange and black as the dozen or so flitting stem to stem. It was in a hidden spot below her bikini line, and the tip of Miller's finger covered both wings. She teased that it was a remnant from an old boyfriend, but he knew it was from an old Mary, the one who had composed poems and wrote long stories, maybe even the beginnings to novels, before they were married. The remnants of Old Mary occasionally painted in secret at the kitchen table, sending her work off to her mother in New Mexico, the turpentine odor left in the air to mingle with the good smell of toasted bagel. And while he wondered about her subjects—he suspected they were things with wings—he was careful to never ask. He was happy to guard her secret, appreciating the mother and daughter bond from the artwork on their own refrigerator.

It had been Celia's idea to buy her mother live butterflies for her birthday. He timed the overnight delivery for a Friday, so they could release them together on Saturday morning. They arrived from a sanctuary in a sturdy box with pinprick holes, accompanied by a pamphlet and a note encouraging you to make a wish when setting them free. He hid the paperwork, and the box was placed on the dining room table with a red bow for her to guess the contents. The girls giggled, and scolded her when she threatened to shake it. It's too small and too quiet for another puppy. Your father's in mighty big trouble if it has scales or fangs. Not a bird. Could it be an egg? The box was left on the dining room table, and Miller went back outside to water the three strikingly fragrant butterfly bushes he'd planted weeks before.

He was brushing his teeth when Mary called to him the next morning. The box was gone. The girls were still groggy in bed, claimed to know nothing. They were upset, and eager to search. The doors had been locked, and Petey still hadn't been let out. Miller and Mary jokingly accused each other of sleepwalking mischief, and lamented over what another year had done to their memories. Only Petey was left to blame after combing the house. There was no other explanation. The dog must have pulled down the box and massacred its contents. Miller hoped the butterflies had died quickly. Petey buried the box in some perfect hiding spot to be uncovered when searching for Christmas decorations or storing winter blankets.

Two days later, Mary took Lizzy's temperature when she wouldn't get out of bed. She was four, he thinks, but isn't really sure. Mary was worried all morning, realizing Lizzy had skipped dinner and maybe even lunch. Lizzy rolled away and pulled the covers over her eyes, shook her head at a list of what hurt. Mary went downstairs to call for a doctor's appointment, leaving him to watch over their anguished child. Lizzy lowered the covers to her chin when he eased onto the edge of her bed. Her eyes gave her away.

He leaned across his daughter and touched a flushed forehead. "What happened to the butterflies?"

Lizzy confessed in her small voice. "They were the wrong color when I peeked inside. So I made them orange like the picture on Mommy's tummy."

Lizzy began crying, her body shaking as she clutched her stuffed bear to her face. "I tried to make them pretty," she said, wiping her eyes and nose on the bear's fur. "I was careful not to hold them too tight when they tried to get away. But they all died."

He imagined her panic when the butterflies stopped waving their painted wings and went still. The shame of her first real lie was enough to induce a fever, but there was more.

"I didn't put them in the ground like I should have. I flushed them down the potty and killed them forever."

The three explorers pass the last of the milkweed along a country highway somewhere close to Ohio. Miller resumes work filling in more tiny pieces of the giant black picture, imagining them the same orange as Lizzy's butterflies. "Like I flushed your blood," he whispers.

EIGHTEEN

Nothing changes when they walk into Ohio. It's the same grinding truck engines and rusted-out tailpipes. The same blacktop bubbles ooze from the surface in polished onyx orbs. The dust on Miller's tongue is the same grit. He chews his spit, and wipes it on a sleeve. Bottles still whiz past, bounding and spinning, and dogs bark behind fences made from the same chain links.

There was a novel in college that chronicled a hitchhiker's travels. Not a great read, but it sparked a yearning. The milk-toast stories with hints of danger fueled Miller's plans to backpack across Europe with a frat buddy. They'd step it up a few notches, find what the book missed. They jotted scrap paper wish lists of exotic girls and forbidden drugs, but they never went. It was always a new girlfriend or some family emergency in the way.

Miller wonders if bumming around Europe would have altered what had been his hopeful view of the world. He's skeptical that travelers along those highways are treated differently. We're all human beings, after all, and the temptation to fling garbage at someone surely has no borders. Most trash is hurled from behind, before the culprits have seen the face of the devil, or the man who did nothing while his family was murdered.

If he'd discovered the real world as a 20-year-old, would he have still fallen in love with Mary? With anyone? Multiple piss-filled jars have shattered at their feet. He crouched beneath a tree at the edge of an abandoned corn field and used leaves to scrape baby shit from pitched diapers off his pant leg. Would he have seen something different when he first looked into Mary's eyes?

"What is wrong with humanity?" Christopher asked, his bare toes soiled by brown goo.

He wonders if Christopher keeps tabs for future reference, a version of Santa's naughty or nice list. Will the mother who threw the diaper suffer one day longer from cancer?

For Maggot life as a target is pure joy. Hit me all you want with half-eaten burritos. I've eaten week-old frog pancakes, so take your best shot! The game is awesome, each volley chock-full of delicious possibilities.

When the sun drops over the flat horizon, a glow in the western sky lingers. They find a good spot with soft grass to rest.

Miller knows the route number and state, is otherwise lost. "A city?"

"I guess we'll see." Christopher shares spoonfuls of beef stew with Maggot. Both chins drip brown gravy. "Try this," he says to Miller, offering the spoon. "It would be better warm. We should invest in a pot."

"It's all yours." Miller watches a light move across the clouds in figure eight patterns. His legs need to move again. He tells Christopher to finish.

They shoulder their bags and make the careful climb back over a rock wall. Barbed wire strips snake from crevasses. Miller's shoes are almost done, parts of the thin soles flap behind. He'll buy a new pair instead of a pot.

Closer, the lights are wrong for a city or town. And traffic is almost entirely one direction, drawn to what produces the glow. Christopher raises an arm and points at the searchlight's dance. Over the noise of passing vehicles are screams and the metallic clack of a roller coaster, country music, bells and buzzing alarms. Traffic forces them single file, and Christopher glances back with an idiotic grin. He's speed walking again, but Miller at least knows his destination.

It's another timothy field that's been rolled and stomped flat by hundreds of cars, dilapidated circus trucks, and families who must have come from miles for there to be so many. Christopher tugs the pack from Miller's shoulder, and stashes both in the last stand of trees before the wide parking area.

Maggot leads them past ticket booths and toward the midway, but seems anxious now, almost miserable. His head is low to the ground, hackles up, not on a scent he's eager to follow. Maybe he knows some of the smells belong to dangerous things.

Miller's feet suffer from peanut shells, and globs of cotton candy mixed with the hay used to manage mud. One sole has worn entirely away in the last half-mile, although the top of the shoe is laced and appears normal. His left shoe is experiencing a similar fate. And so am I, he thinks.

Christopher is practically euphoric, an unruly toddler touching and prodding everything they pass. He strokes the numbered countertops of the game booths, the fence that keeps people from being trampled by a giant green metal inchworm. He runs a hand along a funhouse mirror's curved plastic facade, tapping knuckles on his elongated face. When he begins touching people, Miller grabs his shirt and jerks hard. Stop, Miller warns. Christopher shrugs with a chagrined look, resumes touching objects and settles for only sniffing people.

A barker with a red megaphone picks Christopher out of the flowing crowd, invites the silver-haired gent to experience otherworldly prestidigitation he's not soon to forget. A mere two dollars for a thrill that will make his pants dance. Pennies really, half the bill for a cup of coffee. Christopher smiles and waves back, then skips across the busy lanes of people to slide one hand along an antique popcorn wagon's arched glass.

Miller catches up. "Your folks didn't take you to the circus?"

"Oh, man, what's the word I'm thinking of?" Christopher leans against the wagon and closes his eyes, hugs himself, still grinning. "Take a whiff of that air. You can literally taste it. Transcendental! That's the word. This place is transcendental."

"I smell fried onions." Miller is grateful nobody is noticing them. It's a fine place for two weirdos to blend in. The crowd marches on, color balloons bumping heads. A nearby game buzzer announces a winner amid cheers and catcalls. Christopher plunges back into the crowd, touching again, and sniffing in a way that makes Miller think he's searching for something deeper than smells.

He expects Christopher to angle toward the main tent, prepares for a confrontation over the dog, but he continues walking, peeling from the flow. Maggot cowers along at Christopher's knee, whining as they make their way beneath strings of bare bulbs, away from the screams and loudest music. The midway branches off to where tents are fronted by canvas paintings of nature's freaks and abominations. A two-headed man, Crab Girl, and a boy who is half-fish are overseen by barkers making change from belts.

Christopher stops, turns wide-eyed to Miller, head nodding spastically. "We have to see this." He claps, rocking on tiptoes. "Two heads, Miller. Half-fish. Oh my God, where's my camera?"

Christopher digs for crumpled dollars, but isn't waved through until buying another ticket for Maggot. The music inside is Middle Eastern, and there are 30 mostly empty folding chairs crammed up to a low platform stage. A belly dancer finishes her jingling act, and is replaced by a man with a handful of narrow swords. Two beefy young men in filthy clothes stand sentry at either end of the stage, smoking and flicking ashes with grease-stained fingers. Bouncers, Miller thinks, in case one of the five onlookers gets out of hand and decides to try a little sword swallowing on their own.

Beyond the stink of cigarettes is caramel apple sweetness, woody incense, and the tang of hay bales lining the perimeter. One of the bales has been split open in a corner to cover some mystery remnant.

Christopher tugs his sleeve. "This way."

To the right of the stage is an open flap that connects another tent, and there are more compartments beyond. Lizzy's hamster cage started out basic, and was extended by a maze of passageways, square boxes with exercise wheels, dead-ends, and ball-shaped chambers for naps.

He follows Christopher through the domain of the fat lady and the world's strongest man. The hulking masses loom over cards dealt on an upended wire spool, and the travelers go unacknowledged as the muscle-bound giant slides coins with a stubby finger. Maybe it's their act, or maybe they're on break.

"C'mon, boy!" Christopher calls to Maggot, who hesitates at the next opening. From over Christopher's shoulder, Miller sees a human figure seated on another spool. Two stage lights balance on stands for the only illumination inside the otherwise barren tent.

The performer sits cross-legged, bent at the waist, head lowered to his shins. The visitors shuffle to a respectful distance in the middle of the room, the freak of something or other perhaps in meditation, or maybe asleep. Maggot squeezes between the men, no longer whining, possibly relieved to be more isolated from the danger smells out on the midway.

The lighted subject slowly unfolds, hands sprouting from his lap and bracing at his sides. He unbends at the waist, head lifting to unveil he is a young man, long sleeve shirt unbuttoned, a scaly skin disorder having ravaged every visible inch of flesh. The malady creates an alligator roughness and renders him a deep shade of green. Miller's first impression is that it's too fake not to be real.

"Hello," Christopher chimes, causing Miller and the dog to flinch.

The young man smiles, his teeth are wide and bright against dark lips. "Welcome to my tent."

Maggot scoots backward with a low growl, peers around Christopher's leg.

"Come on, boy, that's not how you make friends." Christopher puts a hand over the dog's snout, then refocuses his attention. "Guess it doesn't get busy down this end."

"It will later, when the hoochie girls take over." The young man's voice is muffled, as if the skin condition is also inside his body, although his eyes are as bright as his teeth. "My name is David."

"So you're some kind of freak?" Christopher says, and Miller moves to jab him with an elbow. "I mean, you don't perform, right?"

David chuckles, and with what seems like exaggerated effort, begins removing his shirt one arm at a time. He painstakingly folds and places it next to him. "Nah, nothing like that. I'm the Martian Man. I used to be the Martian Boy, but none of the hoochies would fool around with a Martian Boy, so I changed it. Now I have to fight them off." He winks, and sticks out a long tongue that has a scarred surface.

Miller begins a question, but David holds up a hand. The palm is smooth, normal except for a hint of pale green.

"I'm not really from Mars." David begins, then falls into a rapid, rehearsed speech. "My dear, unstable mother left a wailing babe on a church step, from where I was shipped to an orphanage until my legs grew long enough to run away."

In a Groucho Marx imitation, complete with an imaginary cigar in one hand, he adds, "And allow me to share one odd little nugget I solemnly swear is the truth. Father, Son, and Holy Ghost, on the Pope's payroll resides a cavalry of eager sodomites hungry for a pint-size green pickle. Even a monster-child such as myself was not safe." He trails off, shaking his head, then resumes in a normal voice. "I take coins of all sizes, but green money is even better. Get the joke? The sideshow rescued me, and now I see the country and can live happily ever after. The cherry on top is that my ass is again a one way street, thank you very much."

Miller looks at his ruined shoes, wants back on the road and away from these people. He'll gladly walk barefoot into the night, is anxious to get back to work on his giant black canvas, filling in more spaces. Left and then right.

"Come touch me."

Miller can't help but look at the young man, whose eyes glimmer from the harsh lights. He holds out both green-tinted arms, inviting. "Everyone is scared at first, but they want to know what it feels like. You can't catch what I have. You have to be born like this. Please come."

Miller's voice is anemic. "No," he says, but does want to put fingers to the rough skin, know if it's warm or cold. He wants to confirm it's real, and see if it flakes away or leaves something oily. It's pathetic, shows what a sorry human being he's become. He should be sympathetic, not full of grotesque curiosity. His eyes close to picture the seductive macadam that appears abrasive but is sleek underfoot. That's what he really yearns to touch. The good road keeps dreams at bay, and will lead him far away.

"Oh, hell, I sure do!" Christopher lunges forward, leaving Maggot exposed. The dog whimpers, shuffles to crowd behind Miller.

David lowers his hands and tilts back his chin, as the tall man's shadow envelops his small frame. Christopher's palms cup Martian Man's bumpy shoulders as if giving absolution. A minute passes and Christopher begins to shake, or maybe it's the young man causing the motion.

"What are you doing to me?" David's voice is low, accusing.

Miller hears Christopher whisper for the young man to be still and not speak.

David begins crying, quietly at first, but his sobbing intensifies. The sound of distress halts the bickering card players next door, and the music switches off in the tents beyond.

"No, Christopher, absolutely not!" Miller calls out.

"Shush! It's not what you think," he says over his shoulder.

The Martian Man begins convulsing, his grief turning into a hacking cough, and there are heavy footsteps in the soft earth.

"Let's get out of here," Miller says, and Maggot begins to bark, backing away from the tent opening, perhaps worried whatever exudes those dangerous smells is coming to rescue the distraught human.

The world's strongest man stalks into the tent and goes straight for Christopher's neck with both hands, confident the skinny assailant will peel away. But Christopher doesn't budge, simply goes on holding the lurching young man now producing hungry infant caterwauls. The giant sports a sleeveless t-shirt and elastic tights, fanny pack riding beneath an oversize belly. He digs in his feet for another heave, neck veins bulging, great sweaty arm muscles flexing.

"It's okay," Miller says idiotically, and makes the mistake of approaching the connected trio. As if to say okay I'll try this one, the strongman turns, grabs Miller in a bear hug and squeezes out his breath. He then tosses Miller to the ground and kicks him squarely in the gut. Miller wheezes for air, puts out a hand to wave surrender. He watches through teary eyes as the strongman resumes his initial attack, looping both arms around Christopher from behind and attempting to jerk him off his feet.

Despite a variety of leverages and weight lifting maneuvers, Christopher does not yield until he is ready. His hands slip from the young man's shoulders like a lover saying goodbye, as the giant delivers three sharp elbow strikes to the side of Christopher's skull. Miller knows each blow would mortally wound any normal human.

The strongman abandons the assault, stands dripping sweat, chest heaving and mouth agape, peering down at where Martian Man lies curled on the table. David's skin is no longer that of a scaly alien. It is an irritated pink shade, as though he'd spent too much time in the sun. His head is bald and his face pockmarked from acne, but any sign of his birth defect has vanished. Miller catches his breath and rises to an elbow, watches as the Martian Man opens his eyes and brings a hand near his face. He turns it over, then rubs the palm against a cheek.

"What have you done?" Both hands prod his entire body. "What is this? What's wrong with me?"

Blood seeps from Christopher's right ear, and he takes two stumbling backward steps, face pallid and dazed. Christopher doesn't seem to notice the people crowding into the tent, only looks down and makes half-hearted finger snaps to Maggot.

"You stay," orders the strongman, who pulls a cell phone from his fanny pack and pokes at the keyboard. "I want the boss to see this."

The tent fills with roustabouts and performers coming to the aid of one of their own. News travels word of mouth as Miller struggles to his feet, hearing snippets passed from those closest to David. A bucket brigade of voices transfers through the tents and out into the night.

"Who?"

"Where is he?"

"A miracle."

"A curse."

Eyes search and find Miller, linger for a moment and move on. Christopher has backed against the canvas at the rear of the tent, obscured by shadows, but the shock of white hair is an easy target. Silver, the barker had called. It's the silver-haired man who did something to David.

The strongman has reinforcements block exits, while other large bodies try pushing the hoard back out. Miller is jostled, and someone steps on Maggot's paw.

"Get a mirror!" And the words are repeated a dozen times, a magic echo that changes voices, even sexes. Also like magic, a mirror appears in an instant. Round and with a handle, it is passed above heads, crowd surfing to a woman who delivers it to David's hand, or so Miller assumes. The dozens of people circling Martian Man are pressing inward, the jostled light stands causing the beams to sway. Miller thinks of the spotlight that led them here, and how much he regrets ever seeing it.

It is surely David who screams so fierce and long that Maggot can take no more. He bolts for the exit, eluding the startled sentry, damaged tail straight out behind. Miller watches the gap close, and is jealous of the dog's freedom. They are sealed in, and at the mercy of whatever these people decide is proper justice. Christopher stands bleeding, the canvas behind him alive, prodded from the other side. Miller slowly makes his way to him. No sudden moves, just a meander to his queer accomplice while the strongman watches, one finger stuck in his ear, mouth working into the phone.

A boy with an unfortunate cleft palate slips from the crowd and comes to Christopher, face lifted in a portrait of everything gone wrong. Teeth are turned outward like the mouth of some yet to be discovered deep sea creature. The boy, about Lizzy's age, reaches a filthy hand and pulls at Christopher's shirt.

"Fix me, too, mister," the boy pleads, or at least it's what Miller thinks he says. The words are wet and sloppy, full of spit. He points a dirty finger at his disfigured mouth and chants. "Fix me, fix me."

Christopher is in a zombie trance, the entire right side of his shirt has gone scarlet. Blood drips from his middle three fingers.

"Fix me!" shouts the boy, who begins pummeling Christopher's stomach until a woman tears from the sentry's blockade and rushes to scoop him away.

"The devil."

"God."

"A true miracle."

Miller recognizes fragments of prayers.

More words echo out into the world, and the response is an angry swarm. The remaining country music is devoured, as is the clanking metal from the rides and all the cheery midway noise. The road is gone, thinks Miller. It too laid to waste, broken to pieces by bedlam and swallowed. Gone, he thinks, as another of Christopher's bloody drips is cut in half by an extended blade of hay and disappears into the shadows at their feet. Something will grow, Miller thinks. Something that should be mowed and then stomped to dust.

"Out of my fucking way!" An old man's voice shaped by cigarettes and booze cuts through the buzzing and deadens some of the murmur. Dull thuds and cries of pain come closer, and the sentries part the way at one tent flap. The old man emerges, brandishing a walking stick at anyone blocking his path, or looking as though they might consider doing so. He wears navy blue uniform pants, maybe from a marching band, bedroom slippers and a ratty pajama top that is buttoned askew. Trailing are two men probably recruited from the trapeze act. They have enormous upper bodies, with skinny legs encased in sheer tights.

"Where?" booms the old man, and it seems as though everyone in the tent turns at once to point toward Miller and Christopher.

"There boss," says the strongman. "They did it."

"Lemme see the goddamn boy." The old man pushes to the circle, whacking people who have no space to move.

Minutes pass, and Miller realizes Christopher has taken his hand. His long face has gone purple on one side, a strand of drool hanging to his navel. Christopher's eyes are still down, unfocused, but he attempts mouthing a word. Miller thinks it might be Maggot's name, and that he's asking where the dog is.

"Get Sasha!" shouts the old man. "Get her now! Be careful, or I'll rip your balls off."

The men in tights push through the mob and are swallowed by the swarm. Miller can't imagine anyone surviving whatever is out there, let alone make their way back.

"All you people outta here now," the old man orders. "Any of you fuckers still standing here in ten seconds is fired."

The sentries pass the order back through the tents, and the tide of humanity begins a slow-motion retreat.

"You, you, and you stay." The boss man jabs his stick at the strongman and two mountainous roustabouts. Miller glimpses David's balled figure, rocking while being stroked by the woman who'd grabbed the mirror. "You stay with the boy," the boss tells her, and turns toward Miller and Christopher.

The old man plants the stick and leans hard, gnarled fists cupping the handle. His eyes shift back and forth at the two men who've caused the ruckus, until shouts to clear the way come from the outer tents. One trapeze artist drives a wedge for another cradling a milk crate.

"Bring my baby," says the old man with a less caustic tone, and the box is gently presented by meaty hands. With equal care, the old man lowers to his knees to reach inside. He looks up at Miller. "Come," he pleads.

Miller pulls Christopher along, worried at first he'll stumble forward and crush whatever is in the box. But Christopher's legs work, and they move hand in hand to peer into the crate.

"My Sasha." The old man strokes an ancient dog, a bald and tumor-covered Chihuahua nestled among colored silk scarves. "Closer," the old man whispers, and Miller squats and forces Christopher to his knees.

The dog's bulbous eyes are cloudy and ooze a viscous liquid that cakes underneath. A rapid pant is the only movement for which it seems capable. The old man reaches into his pants for wadded tissue. He wipes bits of feces from under the dog's tail, brushes around its eyes, then stuffs the tissue back into the same pocket.

"She was my wife's, but she's dead now," says the man, and

Miller wonders if he means that his wife or the dog is dead. "She's all I have left in this shithole. You make her better, same as you did the green boy."

Miller looks at Christopher, whose eyes focus on nothing in particular. His drooling has stopped, which is good, but his entire shirt is blood-soaked.

"You do this for me, yes?" The boss man's voice is saccharin, hopeful. "She is worse all the time, but you can heal. You make her right."

Miller puts a hand on Christopher's shoulder. "Christopher?"

The tall man looks at Miller, and it's a full minute before there's a sense of recognition. The corners of Christopher's mouth turn up slightly. "Miller," he says.

"The dog, Christopher, he wants you to make it better."

"Maggot?" Christopher's head tilts, eyes squinting. He looks left then right. Blood drips from the tip of his long nose.

"No, he wants this dog fixed. His dog is sick." Miller puts a hand on the edge of the milk crate, the other on Christopher's damp back, as they go to their knees. The skin is ice cold through the shirt.

Christopher peers into the crate, regarding the animal for the first time. His brow furrows, and he wipes his nose across a bloody sleeve. "What the fuck is that?"

The old man gasps, maybe insulted or maybe from dread.

"My Sasha is sick," he explains, and Miller sees the fear in his eyes. More than fear. They are the eyes of a man who believes he's on the narrow ledge of a bottomless pit. It's a place Miller has come to know, forced there by two strangers on a dark and stormy night. Miller's ledge isn't on the side of a mountain or some steel and concrete skyscraper. If it still exists, his ledge is a road headed west, sometimes named but usually marked by a single black number on a white metal sign.

"This man needs your help," Miller says, and the jealous pangs return. This old bastard gets a reprieve, a do-over, while my family lies in their coffins, loaded up with chemicals to delay decomposition.

"I can't." Christopher looks up at the man, puts both hands on the crate to push away. But the old man lunges forward and grabs Christopher's bloody wrists. Miller sees the strongman take a step forward and then stop.

"I beg you." He is face-to-face with Christopher, yellow eyes wide, imploring. But then he slowly lowers his head and releases his grip, hands suspended over the languishing animal, fingers hung into arthritic claws.

Christopher bends and roughly scoops the dog and several of the thin scarves in one hand, then shoves the box with so much force it tumbles and splinters near the trapeze artists' satin-sheathed feet. The strongmen are frozen in place by this sudden energy, and Christopher also grabs the old man and pulls him against his bloody body, the bald Chihuahua emitting a plaintive squeak when it's pinned between them. There are guttural human moans, and Miller is unsure who makes them until seeing the old man's leathery tongue extend beyond thin lips pressed into a tight circle.

Christopher rocks on his knees, the old man entombed in his mighty grip, and there are sounds that might be cracking joints or snapping ribs. The old man's moaning transitions into something euphoric. His neck muscles go slack, head lolling and twisting to frightening angles, as if it might tear off. Miller reaches to put a hand back on Christopher's shoulder. The rocking slows, winding down like an old key operated toy.

The tent is silent. Not a cough or scuffed shoe. No sound comes from beyond, no words or menacing buzz. Christopher releases the old man, his pajama top and few gray chest hairs now mottled red. Miller thinks the old man is dead, balanced on his knees, only a feather's touch from collapsing onto his face or back. But the old circus owner manages a half-turn toward the strongman, whose own mouth is a gaping hole under a bushy mustache, and utters a few very clear words. "I see my wife," says the old man, who is then brushed by an invisible breeze and tips forward. His last breath escapes in a single puff against the dirty hay.

Christopher rises, the scarves and tiny dog gathered to his gory shirt. He leads Miller past the sentries, through the mass of spellbound people, and out into the night.

NINETEEN

Miller pulls his pack from its hiding spot, then helps with Christopher's. There's enough light to see the man's head injuries are already healing. Blood stopped flowing before they'd left the midway, the red marks next to his eye and cheek fading. Christopher emerges from his fog with some of the earlier jubilance.

"I love the circus," he says. "So many characters."

"This wouldn't be a bad place to bury that dog."

Christopher holds the Chihuahua away from his stomach and folds back a powder blue scarf. "Nah, she'd dig her way out."

Miller shakes his head. "How is that creature still alive?"

The dog makes a chirping sound as if to confirm its status, probably a sneeze.

"Takes a licking." Christopher smiles, wags his eyebrows, then starts them in the direction of the highway.

Miller looks back. The noise of the circus has changed. Generators have kicked off, taking out many of the lights, and rides no longer rumble and clank. Operators abandoned their post to check out the hoopla near the hoochie tents, cigarettes smoldering in the beaten grass beneath emergency stop buttons. There is a growing crowd demanding refunds, strips of blue tickets brandished like clubs. A man in overalls and John Deere cap is rocking one of the booths, getting it near the tipping point, while his wife tries talking sense into him with swipes of her big shiny purse.

Vehicles jam the exit in a sea of red tail lights, and for once it's Miller and Christopher hurrying past, oblivious to the lives left behind. It's two men on foot with a pressing engagement, leaving cars full of families trapped in isolation.

"I think she's too old to walk," Christopher says, their feet splashing through muddy grass. "We'll find her a good home in the next town. She'll make a great pet for someone. I don't think she bites."

"She doesn't have teeth."

"Right," Christopher says. "And no shedding."

"Because she's bald." Miller laughs. "Aside from looks, age, and god-awful stink, you have the perfect dog."

Christopher stops suddenly, and Miller walks right into him. Christopher turns and pushes the ghastly animal into Miller's hands. It's coated in sticky blood that has begun coagulating. Miller grimaces. It's like a newborn *something*.

Christopher paces back and forth in the slop, pulls at his hair with balled fists. "Shit! Shit!"

"What?" Miller bundles the creature in the scarves so he doesn't have to touch its skin.

"I have to find Maggot."

"I'll come."

"No," says Christopher. "Get her away from here, as far down the road as you can. If one of these roustabouts decides we hurt the old man, they'll come after us. Take her, and we'll catch up."

Christopher is consumed in the glare of headlights and the orange winks of puffed cigarettes.

"This would be a good time for one of those classic country western tunes," says Miller's inner voice. "Tex Ritter singing a ballad for a dead man and a dog that's gone missing."

"Shut up."

"And Lawdy in Heaven above, I got me a hole in each shoe!"

Miller turns and walks to the exit, a clogged artery with nobody directing traffic. There's a fender-bender among the mayhem, voices looking for a fight. He pauses on the pavement to kick off his battered shoes, then takes an involuntary step toward them, would have bent to scoop them up if not for his miserable cargo. He stares down, expects tears. If I'd been in better shape, stronger, able to put up a fight. If I'd had a gun in the nightstand like so many talk about. How did everybody else know? Guns don't kill people; violent, home-invading rapists kill people. Miller looks at the still-tied laces, the high-tech, space-age material that has reverted to useless garbage. Mary's gift is nothing more than two lumps of roadkill. The expensive hiking shoes were an expression of love he didn't deserve. She wanted him to live longer, and he let her die. Nothing complicated about that.

He leaves the scraps, walks barefoot under what's become a clear night sky. The dog continues to radiate heat, vibrating with each exhale. It's a mystery how the sack of loose skin and brittle bones is able to generate so much moist energy.

"Hey, sport, I know a secret about your self-healing travel buddy."

"Fuck off," Miller tells the voice.

"Oh, real nice. We finally get some alone time, and you cop an attitude."

"Fine," says Miller. "What is it? What's the secret?"

"Not so fast," says the voice. "We got miles to go and places to see."

"I'm not interested anyway." Miller's feet slap the pavement and he takes care not to stub a toe in the dark.

"The old reverse psychology, eh? Bet a shrink would have a field day with you and me. Wait, I'm thinking of a number between one and ten million."

The inner voice makes him feel tired. "Two," says Miller.

"Ding, ding, ding! How'd you do that?"

"By going insane," he whispers.

"Jeez, that's heavy, sport. Nothing like a buzzkill when the party's just getting started."

"I'd be happy with some peace and quiet."

"A little quality time with this balled up rat-dog?"

"Look who's talking."

"Oh, zing!" says the inner voice. "All righty, I can tell you aren't in the mood. I'll take a pause for the cause, but you know where to find me."

He sucks in a deep breath and suffers a painful twinge. His ribs will be all sorts of purple come daylight. But the road is smooth and cool under naked feet, and if there are sharp stones or broken glass, he doesn't feel them. For good or bad, he knows Christopher will find him, will appear while he rests in some field still on the horizon, his stick figure body casting a scarecrow shadow from the sun or the moon.

For now the walking is fine, and he sets about filling in a good bit of his grand picture, maybe with a million steps before dawn. Left and then right. One foot in front of the other. The nightmares are a world away as he marches into the inviting gloom to the faint sound of a snoring Chihuahua.

TWENTY

Miller hobbles into a quiet town after sunrise on a section of road that's become Main Street. He tries to be invisible while hunting a place to lie down and rest, conscious of his appearance, and what he's become, to the man driving a truckload of bundled newspapers, to diner patrons looking up from their steaming coffee. He keeps his eyes forward, his pace steady, pretending his feet aren't throbbing and his clothes don't reek, and that his burden is something less depressing than a bug-eyed canine encrusted in a tacky sheen of human blood. Invisibility is difficult to maintain now that some of the scarves have unfurled and trail him in a short, multi-colored kite tail.

"You look like a Gypsy who just got his ass kicked behind a bowling alley," says the inner voice. "You're gonna be quite a hit here in Mayberry."

"I need sleep."

"What you need is a bar of soap and to stop talking to yourself."

The town has exactly 4000 residents according to a Rotary Club sign. But even the inviting green lawn of the town square, bookended by a white church and brick courthouse, is desolate at this hour. Are they oaks? Maples? Another subject that confirms his inadequacy in the world. Mary would have known by the bark or leaf shape.

He steps from the sidewalk to sink his toes in dewy grass, gloriously cool on open blisters. He weeps from relief until his aching knees propel him toward the equally inviting park benches, their smooth slats free of twigs and shifting stones, and are suspended out of the reach of creeping insects. Each side of the square has two benches, eight heavenly slices when Goldilocks had only a choice of three.

He strolls to the farthest, which sits in the shadow of the church steeple and the oldest trees. With his pack for a pillow, he arranges the shivering dog on his bruised stomach. His last waking image is a bird's nest in the overhead branches. He wonders if there are eggs, and then he is asleep.

He isn't painting with footsteps. He instead holds a wide horsehair brush in his right hand. The head-high canvas is 10 feet long, locked in place by an invisible easel as he works with sweeping strokes. His choice of colors is limited to pink, green, and blue, the same as the dog's silk wrappings. He makes due, switching from one color to the next as he outlines square after square, creating a meandering stepping stone path.

Miller composes a benign version of Candy Land, with no ax swinging Mr. Minty, no Lord Licorice with pointed shoes and swarming bats, and no Gloppy overseeing a treacherous Molasses Swamp that may or may not taste like chocolate. The path doesn't end at the striped feet of King Kandy. Instead of the ice cream topped turrets of Candy Castle, he paints rudimentary people, the brushes being too large for proper detail. It doesn't matter, though, because he recognizes his wife and daughters. With three meticulous wrist flicks each get a smile, which brings a similar expression to his own bristly face.

He is being gently shaken, a hand on one shoulder, and his eyes blink open.

"Hello, my friend. Hello, hello."

The man is in silhouette, too wide for Christopher. Miller first mistakes the dangling red tie for a very long tongue.

The dog barks or maybe convulses, and Miller puts a hand on her curled body. Sasha, he remembers the old man had said. My Sasha is sick.

"You could use a good meal," the man says. "And your skinny companion, as well."

Miller swings his legs from the bench and sits up, lower back screaming from the miles and the hard bed. Stretching, a yawn, and then elbows on knees, he's ashamed of his awful feet. He clears his throat, wants to be human. "Thank you, but we have food."

"Then I'm sure we can rustle up a decent pair of shoes."

A man in his 60s with sympathetic eyes behind wire rim glasses. Miller envies his clean-shaven face, the lack of dirt in any creases. He is a doctor or maybe a preacher, or some other vocation that makes use of a compelling aura. He is the anti-Christopher, thinks Miller, and lets out a laugh that sounds more like a sob.

"I'm sorry," Miller says. He experienced a similar emotion when looking up at a cop's face last summer. It was a DUI checkpoint after two beers and finishing one of Mary's fruity vodka drinks. That night he was trying to keep his driver's license. Here he is trying to keep his humanity.

Miller looks beyond the man's shoulder, where the church steps are crowded with people in their Sunday best. Nearest on the sidewalk is an older woman in a blue dress, arms crossed and eyeing the park bench. The offer of shoes is tempting. He needs a good fit and doesn't know if he'll be welcome to try a pair with no socks. He'd probably be run out of a store for his smell. And the dog?

The man follows Miller's gaze. "My sister is a worry wart, but slow to anger and plenteous in mercy. That's a Psalm from today's service. I never recall the numbers, only some of the more comforting thoughts."

"I don't want to be any trouble," Miller says. "We're passing through and I needed to rest."

"I don't intend to make you uncomfortable." The man displays the kindest smile Miller has ever seen. "We're here to care for our brothers. You'd do the same in better circumstances. My name is Henry."

"Miller," he answers. "This is Sasha. She could use a hose and a bar of soap even more than me. Or maybe the same."

Henry chuckles. "We have a basin under the kitchen sink that would do her just fine. Come along. Home is a short walk if you can manage."

Miller pauses before rising, the dog quaking in his lap. "I'm not homeless," he says, stroking the animal's bony ribcage. The kindness is jarring after so many bottles, makes him lost for coherent words. Being the target of garbage was easier to accept. "I still have a job."

"That's fine," says Henry.

"It's not how it looks." Miller is suddenly depressed, needs to explain, but can't even begin. "I started walking and couldn't stop."

"I wasn't asking," says Henry. "Every man is on his own journey, has his own demons to slay. Believe me, my current demon is one for the books."

Miller groans as he gets to his feet, his chest and sides a mix of aches. Henry grabs the backpack before Miller can shoulder the straps. It's more disconcerting kindness, although Miller can't help notice Henry's grimace, and the way he holds the nylon bag away from his clean suit.

The pair walk side by side toward the church, where Henry is greeted by his sister's icy look. "Janice, this is Mr. Miller. He's coming back to my house for a meal and a change of clothes. Maybe you'll keep an eye on Toby for a few hours?"

"Mr. Miller." The woman of course doesn't offer a hand, and Miller is grateful for the dog wrapped in his arms, an excuse not to show his filth. "Does he know?"

Miller scans the surrounding faces. The people on the steps, both the men and the women, use handkerchiefs to wipe tears and blow noses. Miller recognizes the grief.

"No, but I'll fill him in. I'm sure Mr. Miller has plenty on his own plate, but it'll give us something to chat about. You take Toby with the ladies and have a nice lunch." Henry smiles and waves to a boy sitting alone on the far edge of the top step. He's five or six, with a cherubic face to match Henry's. "My handsome grandboy."

Janice adjusts Toby's dress shirt and hikes his pants. "We'll go for a grilled cheese."

Toby nods. His eyes are bloodshot, and his nose raw. He points to Miller's feet. "You forgot your shoes."

"That's right. Mr. Miller and I have to go find them." Henry bends to kiss the boy's forehead, ruffles his hair, then turns and leads Miller away.

They cross the square and walk into a neighborhood of tight fitting two-story homes. Henry lives one block in, a neat house painted bright yellow and trimmed with gingerbread woodwork. The front door is unlocked, and Henry leads them straight to the kitchen. He goes about finding the basin, fitting it into the sink to fill with warm water and a few squirts of dish soap.

"The grandkids used to take their baths in this." Henry stirs the water with one hand. "It should do fine for that critter of yours. No offense intended, but it hardly resembles a dog. I'm sure God had a reason, but not a particularly clear one."

Miller lowers the trembling animal into the water and gently rubs her back, regretting he hadn't first washed his hands. Each fingernail is a crescent moon of black dirt amid white bubbles. The dog quakes, tries swimming even when Miller turns her on her back. Clotted chunks break free from her skin and turn bright red as they dissolve. He has no idea how to explain what is washing from the dog, but his new friend doesn't ask.

Henry locates an old towel, and offers it after the water goes cool.

"There's an unused cat bed on the rear porch. It's clean enough, and the deck is screened."

"Perfect, thank you," says Miller, relieved at the prospect of no longer having to hold the animal. He realizes it might be blind, that the film over its eyes is far too thick. He sympathetically touches her chin, but she tries nipping his fingers.

"I'll make coffee while you get cleaned up. Shower's at the top of the stairs, fresh towels on the rack. We'll have a talk when you're done." Henry empties the basin while Miller finishes drying the dog, only mildly surprised it no longer shows signs of tumors. Heck, dip it in enough of Christopher's blood and it'll probably start fetching tennis balls. "We have piles of clothing in the garage, enough to outfit an army. I oversee church donations, mostly because I don't have a car anymore. Seemed like a good use of the space out there."

Miller deposits the dog on a pet bed in a sunny spot on the porch. She curls into a ball and begins snoring.

Under a hot spray the grime washes from his body in oily streams. He soaps from head to toe, then lets the water fall over him until it goes ice cold. A folded stack of clothes sits on the closed toilet lid. On the floor are three pairs of almost new sneakers, each a different size.

The coffee is strong and sweet, served in a kitchen decorated in 50s motif. Miller listens to the man's soft voice. Henry's son had taken his two children camping for the long Labor Day weekend. Toby has just turned five, about to start school. Big sister Olivia, now almost eight, is headed to the third grade. Their dad had slept late on Sunday morning, knowing good and well his girl is as responsible as they come. Goodness, Toby could be trusted to do the right thing if he ever got lost, or a stranger tried anything funny. Toby is a Cub Scout and sharp as a tack. They'd lost their mother going on two years to the same cancer that took their grandmother, and were now extra careful to mind after one another. It was all the more reason they wouldn't find trouble.

Henry's son had stayed tucked in his zipped sleeping bag, dozing in and out. He listened to the sound of his kids discussing the wild animals they were going to find, and what kind of berries might still be ripe. They needed this sort of time, healing together in bits and pieces. He drifted back to sleep, looking for another twenty before starting the day gathering wood, then maybe taking their poles down to the stream.

"But then came two words that reopened the gates to more heartache." Henry removes his glasses, rubs his face hard. His shoulders lurch, and it's a minute before he finishes. "She disappeared," he tells Miller, who has a fair idea of the pain behind the man's lost, raw look. "That's what Toby told his father. She disappeared. Like it was something from a magic act."

Miller reaches across the table and settles a hand on one of Henry's. They sit listening to the ticking clock.

TWENTY-ONE

The sound of a slamming car door is followed by hurried footsteps.

"Grandpa?"

Miller's heart races at the possibility of the girl's miraculous return. But it's Toby who trots through the house and stands in the doorway.

"Where's Grandpa?"

Miller is settled into a cushioned wicker chair on the back porch, legs spread in front, the cat bed tucked between his ankles. Alone with the dog, he became obsessed with checking its breathing, sitting close enough to hear the rhythmic wheezing. In the good light it now appears less close to death. Thin skin stretches over absurd eyeballs that move in its dreams. Henry had accepted a ride out to the rescue staging area to begin the eighth day of searching for his granddaughter. Miller had napped in a downstairs bedroom, but was uncomfortable lurking inside the empty house. His job is to take phone messages, and be there in case a little girl walks through the door. Watching the dog stay alive is all he's done.

"He went with friends to see the police."

Toby stands on his toes to see across the porch into the cat bed. "I like your dog."

Miller glances down and can't help smiling. "You must really like dogs."

The boy wears jeans and a Cleveland Browns jersey. His roundness destines him for the offensive line if he plays the sport.

"You found your shoes."

Miller flexes his ankles. The leather Nikes are soft and comfortable, but a poor substitute for Mary's gift. They won't last nearly as many miles. "Your grandpa gave me these."

"He gives me coins," Toby says, then scrounges in his front

pockets. He turns them inside out to show they are empty. "I had one before. I can't use them because they're too old, but Daddy says I shouldn't ask for new coins to buy stuff. I like the machines at Save-Mart because they have super balls."

"Some people think coin collecting is lots of fun."

"I don't think old coins are fun, but I don't tell Grandpa because it would hurt his feelings," Toby says. "I collect super balls. If Grandpa gave me new coins I'd have more. The Save-Mart machines are next to the doors that open by themselves. They aren't magic, or anything. They open because they're electric. What do you collect?"

"I mostly had baseball cards, I guess."

"Can I see them?" Toby looks around the porch.

"It was when I was a kid. They got lost a long, long time ago."

Toby tucks his pockets back into his jeans. "My sister got lost."

"Yes, I know. I'm very sorry, Toby."

"I was supposed to start Kindergarten, but I think they stopped having school because of Olivia." The boy comes onto the porch and sits on the floor next to Sasha. Pudgy fingers stroke her thin skin. "I was happy about school. I was going to be brave and not cry. I got Mrs. Applegate. Do you like her?"

"I don't know Mrs. Applegate."

"Mrs. Applegate is old, but Grandpa says she's not as old as him. Your dog doesn't have hair."

Miller pulls his feet back and leans forward. "Yeah, she's pretty old, too. And she sleeps all the time."

"Do you think Olivia is dead like my mom?"

Miller takes a breath. "They'll find Olivia. Your grandpa says they have hundreds of people looking, even helicopters and dogs. Kids sometimes get lost, but they're always found."

Sasha makes cat-like purring noises. "Your dog wouldn't be so good at looking for kids."

"She's not really my dog," he says. "I'm trying to find her a good home."

"Is that why you were in the park yesterday?"

"Kind of. I'd walked really far. I sat down and fell asleep."

The boy nods. "Grandpa doesn't have a car either. He kept

crashing into other people, so they took it away and gave him tickets. Your dog can live here if Grandpa says it's okay. I'll feed her every day, unless they start having Kindergarten."

"Maybe we'll ask when he gets home."

"We were looking for a four-leaf clover to give Daddy," Toby says. "We were following a long path. Olivia said we wouldn't get lost, even though we went too far. I started knowing we were getting lost. When you get lost in the woods you're supposed to sit down and not be upset. I know what to do because I'm a Cub Scout. Olivia isn't a Cub Scout because she's a girl."

The boy's eyes are filled with tears when he looks up. They are the same desperate eyes as when Lizzy or Celia had a pet that went missing, or wouldn't wake up.

"The fields had blue flowers and then there were trees." Toby wipes his nose, leaves a wet line on the jersey sleeve. "I said we should go back, and that Daddy would be mad we were gone so long. But Olivia made us keep going. She kept saying the next field would have four-leaf clovers. She called me a baby for crying, but I couldn't stop."

Miller wants to comfort the boy. "I bet it was scary."

"It was really scary when she wasn't there anymore. I thought she was playing a trick. I thought she was hiding. But then I knew she wasn't. I called her name until my throat hurt. I told Daddy she fell down in quicksand, but he said there isn't any in Ohio. Can I pick her up?"

Miller nods, but is thinking about Molasses Swamp.

TWENTY-TWO

"She fell down," Miller tells Henry when he walks into the kitchen. Miller has torn open all the unread newspapers accumulated inside the front door. Lost girl stories fill headlines, and there are maps and drawings of the camping area and her last known whereabouts. There's a picture of Olivia, probably her second grade school photo, with a wide smile and blue eyes. Miller had touched the ink that was her face and hair.

"Who fell down?" Henry's khaki pants are mud-stained, his lumberjack shirt dotted with briars. He looks dead tired.

"Toby was here most of the afternoon," he says. "Your sister didn't know you were getting a ride."

"The search has gone deep into the woods." Henry drops into a chair, limp hands spilling onto the table. He pushes the newspapers aside. "So much farther than Olivia could have wandered. They go on motorized vehicles and horseback. I stumble around with the other old men from the church. We look in the same places that have been checked a dozen times. Eight days is an eternity for a lost child. Never in my life have I wanted time to stop more than now."

Henry pauses, looks up from his hands and squints. "Who fell down?"

Miller pulls out a chair. "Toby is sure his sister fell down." He rearranges the newspapers, puts the one in which Toby gave his account to a reporter on top. The boy said the same thing then. "She fell down and disappeared. One second she was there, the next she wasn't. And they were tired. He said they'd been hunting four-leaf clover, following a trail until he was worn out and scared they'd be in trouble."

Henry pulls off his glasses and rubs his face until it turns red. "Animal trails criss-cross everywhere. A confusing maze. Even the

129

trained dogs have lost her scent. Famous trackers from a television show came, but still nothing. They allowed a psychic to come talk a bunch of mumbo-jumbo. I fear our Olivia is in God's hands. There's talk of changing what the search is called. They speak in whispers to protect the family. Like we could be hurt worse? They want to call it a recovery instead of a rescue. Our precious Olivia is a body to be recovered, instead of a lost child."

The resemblance between Henry and his grandson is greater than ever when he wipes tears on a wool sleeve.

"I'm sorry, Henry. Believe me that I understand your loss. But there's something about what your grandson said that I can't get out of my head. Do they search at night? Were they in the woods when you left?"

Henry nods. "Not as many, but yes. Some brought tents. Wonderful people who have pledged to remain until she's brought home, despite warnings from police and game wardens. Black bears and coyotes, and there are plenty of bobcats. I've prayed for the Lord to watch over Olivia and all those kind souls. My God, how it must be for a lost child, especially at night."

Both men look to the window above the sink, to the darkness beyond.

"Animals hunt her in my dreams," Henry says.

Miller envisions her terror. The magnetic draw pulling him toward the road, to put one white sneaker in front of the other until all the bad things are far behind, is now muted by the image forming in his mind. A girl almost eight—Lizzy's age—caught in quicksand or tumbling down an abandoned mine. Was Toby's father right about there being no quicksand in Ohio? Another subject Miller doesn't know.

"I need to feed Sasha while you call someone to take us up there," Miller says, standing up from the table.

"I'll come, but I can't manage going into the woods."

"That's fine, Henry. Make the call."

***

There is a moment of panic when the enormous tent comes into view, fear the circus has relocated, packed up after the old boss's demise to land in this remote forest clearing. Harsh lights create moving ghosts in low hanging mist amid the drum of generators. Henry's friend behind the wheel wears a suit jacket over flannel pajamas, threadbare and as worn as their owner, but Henry says he's the sort of person who never turns away a friend in need. The man apologizes as the car bumps through ruts, Miller's head brushing the roof. Henry is repeating a prayer in the front passenger seat.

"I hope you don't mind if I catch some shuteye in the car," Henry's friend says.

"I'll join you after introducing Mr. Miller to a few important people," says Henry, who then strains to turn and look at Miller. "Is that all right?"

"Yes, of course." Miller hops out to open Henry's door, extending a hand. The field is in shadow, and he holds the back of Henry's arm to guide them toward the brightly lit open tent.

What they find is disheartening. He feels Henry waiver and nearly collapse, hears the air go out of him. The inside space is occupied only by folding chairs and a table. There's a scattering of trash, flattened coffee cups and dirty paper plates spilling from a black garbage bag. There are no people.

Miller turns and calls a greeting into the darkness, but there's no answer over the generator noise.

"There's been fewer and fewer each time." Henry is defeated, goes to a chair to lean. "Who can blame them? Eight days is a long time. Earth was created, and God had rested."

"They wouldn't leave the generators running," Miller says, rummaging through a cardboard box on the table. There's a stack of graph paper and stubby pencils, bottles of insect repellant, and a cache of flashlights.

"Maybe they forgot," says Henry, who seems in shock. "Everyone is so tired."

"Damn batteries are dead." Miller tosses a last flashlight back into the box, then mellows his tone. "They wouldn't forget."

Henry pulls a matching yellow flashlight from his coat pocket and switches it on. He offers it to Miller, and then unfolds a sheet of paper from a different pocket. It's a copy of the map used by the newspaper. "We're standing on what was their campsite," Henry says, then points out the tent to an opening in the trees where a thousand boots have trampled the weeds. "That's where my grandchildren went in, and where Toby came out. Everything else is a guess."

"Can you make it back to the car on your own?" Miller is anxious to get moving, but Henry comes to him, grabs him in his arms and hugs fiercely.

"God delivered you to us for a reason." Henry's voice is tired but his grip is still strong. "Bless your hope and efforts, my friend."

Henry drops his arms with a heavy sigh, turns and shuffles toward the car. Miller clicks on the flashlight and walks into the woods.

TWENTY-THREE

The moon lights the way across vast meadows of bent grasses and wildflowers. The worn path is a black stripe, a narrow road, and Miller's stomach stirs, part of him wanting to be out on the highway, attending to his own demons. He conserves batteries for the wooded sections that are sometimes no more than 20 paces, and sometimes the better part of a football field. He tries gauging how long before a five-year-old boy would tire, exhausted to tears in front of a big sister. He stops to scan the paper grid, and the landscape seems to match. Each rectangular meadow, perhaps once tilled farmland, is bordered by wooded areas that grow increasingly dense away from the campsite.

"Are you ready to stumble over a decomposing child?"

The voice is no surprise, and he vows not to respond. He listens instead to the sound of his feet moving along the path, the briars catching the cuffs of his new pants. The generators are long out of earshot, replaced by the familiar insects he's come to know from the road.

"Not just bugs out here. There's something else you need to be concerned with. Maybe the same thing that visited you, Mary, and the girls on a stormy night."

He concentrates on the effortless walk over soft earth in his springy new sneakers. He can walk like this forever.

"I'm trying to look out for you, sport. I've got a vested interest in keeping your hide intact."

His night vision has adjusted enough to discern color under the moon's blue cast. The path climbs to a rocky high point and robs his breath, and then becomes a long stretch running adjacent to a shallow brook. He should have grilled the boy for landmarks. Surely a bright little Cub Scout would have remembered the hill with two big boulders and the water.

"She's dead," says the voice. "It's been eight long days. She fell down, all right, and she was hurt so bad she didn't get up."

"Shut up."

"Well, hello! Started to feel like I was talking to myself. Look, I'm trying to lay it all on the table. Your track record is pretty pathetic when it comes to decision making. You don't see a problem by walking off into the woods with nothing but a flashlight and a credit card?"

"She's alive," he says in a petulant voice.

"Then what's he doing here?"

The words freeze Miller in place, chest heaving, skin sweat-coated despite the chill. The only sounds are the insects and water running over the rocks in tiny rapids. There are black woods to his left, the stream and then maybe 20 yards of meadow to his right. He switches on the flashlight and searches the shadows, turning a slow circle, until catching a flash of white in the thicket to his left. He aims the beam toward a heavy tangle of brush where the meadow meets the deeper woods. He takes measured steps, light dancing over multi-textured bark and the glistening wide leaves that have begun collecting the first dew. He can't force himself to believe any plant would have reflected that glimmer of white.

"Christopher? Are you here?"

He is answered with a dog's plaintive whine and a single sharp bark.

A moment passes with only trickling water and the hum of crickets. But then comes a sound both human and inhuman, a feral cry that sends sleeping birds into rabid flight. The sound is from Miller's childhood nightmares; and from a thunder and lightning filled night of his recent adulthood. There's a crashing noise to his left, a body charging through the brush, spinning and bounding off trees, thrashing out of control. It is accompanied by strangled laughter, and a word that is repeated.

"Coming," Miller thinks it says, and he too begins running along the path, trying to keep pace. He can hear the slapping skin and crunching bones as it strikes tree trunks—head-first, maybe—then lurches and continues its mindless stampede. It's a doll made of flesh and topped with a full head of white hair, moving as if mercilessly tugged at the end of a lunatic child's invisible rope. At its heels is a slash of gray that easily avoids the trees and brush, a lithe shadow slipping past obstacles.

"Coming," it repeats, and Miller chases after his light beam, parallel to the creature's spastic, twisting advance.

"You bastard!" Miller's one arm pumps, the other tries steadying the light. The path veers from the stream and plunges into the woods where surely he'll be run over by the charging beast. But the trail disappears in a grove of old pines, and the monster is suddenly gone or hidden. He slows to search the disturbed needles, startled nightcrawlers snaking back into their escape holes as if to clear his way.

"Come out, come out, wherever you are," the inner voice chants, but Miller is too winded to respond, to tell it to shut up. The last thing in the world he wants is for the creature to come out. He hopes it crawled down with the worms, or fell into Ohio's deepest pit of quicksand.

Back into the moonlight he stops to listen. The trail seems gone forever. He aims the flashlight, sweeps it across yellow and red wildflowers at the edge of another meadow. With his next step he trips over a solid object, falling to his knees. His light examines a stone that's been purposely set, one piece of a continuous row. He stands and follows to a right angle what appears to be and an old building foundation. From behind comes a human sound, a kind of throaty snort that might also be a sneeze. He shines the light, searches the cover of flowers. There's another sound that's either laughter or weeping. He steps over the foundation and the noise begins to change. As he creeps closer to the source, his beam sweeping in an arc, the sound becomes softer, and more feminine. And although he knows he's closer, it seems further away. It's a low sobbing, the hollow echo of a vintage movie ghost.

He moves forward, crushing tiny pedals under white sneakers, when his light shines across what can only be a pile of shattered bones. It makes no sense until realizing the bones are made of wood, and are the broken cover of what had once been the cap to a well that is now holding the body of a living child.

TWENTY-FOUR

The morning sky breaks purple beyond flowered window drapes. Miller sits alone with his thoughts in Henry's house. The girl was within reach of his dying light, semi-conscious in shallow muddy water that had broken her fall and kept her from dehydration. One bare leg was twisted and whiter than the rest of her. Her shorts had been pink. She hadn't responded to his words, and he had no way of reaching her. The beam turned amber while he was carefully pulling away teetering boards that rained rotted fibers into the hole. The vertical wall was exposed root and jagged rock, and she'd plunged through spider webs that had gone unrepaired. It was the throat of a monster that might finish swallowing her any second.

When the batteries quit he sat listening to the tortured respiration that was sometimes a whimper. The moon lowered, the shadows creating a third dimension all around, and he considered the chances of finding the path and keeping it through the thicker woods. But going for help would be a blind walk, leaving the unguarded girl to whatever lurked. The creature was still out there, circling easily because it was used to seeing in the dark. Branches snapped, and even the tallest trees rustled as if something powerful had brushed against them. Maybe it was climbing and swinging to pass time.

"I'll give you credit, sport. I pictured you stumbling into the well and breaking your skinny neck as you fell on top of the kid."

The words startled him as he leaned one elbow in the dirt. Your own voice always sounded strange on a recording. You were never quite convinced when pressing the playback button. The inner voice was like that.

"No mood to chat? Content to sit here listening to the boogie man's footsteps?"

"It's only a few hours until dawn." He looked at the moon and tried recalling from which direction it had risen, knowing it was where the sky would first lighten.

"She doesn't have a few hours," said the voice. "Her breathing is worse. She's right on the edge. If you walk out now, you'll still have enough moonlight before it sets. Nights like this really are darkest before the dawn."

He thought about the pitch black sections and shook his head. "I can't. I want to, but I can't."

"It'll be all right. He's not here for you. He doesn't want you dead now, just like he didn't want you dead back on that stormy night."

"What do you mean?"

The voice laughs. "I'll go out on a limb to say he likes having you around. He gets his jollies by having a witness, especially one without the guts to interfere."

"Bullshit."

"You sure about that? Scoop a handful of dirt and drop it over the edge. Go ahead, make like something has gone screwy in your head and you've decided to see if you can fill in that great big hole one handful at a time."

"You're insane," he said, but noticed his hand had burrowed into the soft earth. The dirt in his palm was cool and moist, and black as tar under the moon.

"Jesus Christ, it's not like you're holding a bucket full, just sprinkle a little like you did over Mary's coffin. Give us a little ashes to ashes, dust to dust."

Miller extended his hand out over the hole, saw how badly he was shaking, as dirt trickled between fingers and disappeared into the blackness. Distant thunder rumbled, followed by the sound of approaching wind. It was a gathering summer storm, or a giant train without tracks. He recoiled the empty hand and looked up, expecting perilously bent treetops, leaves being snatched in bunches. But the air all around was still, and not a hint of clouds caused a twinkle among the million stars. He jerked from a nearby thunder clap that was accompanied by invisible rain. He reached to turn his collar against the noise of drops pummeling a shingled roof, whipped sideways against glass windows. Their tidy farmhouse windows that balked as you slid them up or down in high humidity. The wood expands, Mary had explained. He knew about gutters full of dead leaves. He needs to drag out the extension ladder before the cold weather. There are other chores, but none that would make their home a fortress against the approaching evil. *Coming*, it had said. The air reverberated from more thunder, sent splintered wood from the broken well cover tumbling down in tiny dirt avalanches. He reached to pull phantom sheets over himself. They were wet and still warm from Petey's blood. The road was far away.

"Christopher," he whispered.

He tried not to hear the sound of his wife thrown to the bed, the metal on metal squeal, the hammering headboard. He tried not to hear his daughters.

A dog barked and Miller gasped, choking on spit. It was a bark as familiar as any voice, one that greeted him when pulling into his driveway, and when it was time to charge around the yard like a maniac. He brought two fingers near his mouth and almost whistled before realizing he could not survive being pounced on by his sliced-open dog. Not then, and not ever again. Lie down and stay dead, Petey, this is no place for you. Your new home is in the peaceful spot out back of the house. When the dog barked again it was more resigned.

"Christopher," he repeated, and then began mindlessly shouting his name. "Christopher!" His pleading helped drown the sounds of bed springs being tested under a pounding weight. It muffled the sound of slapping, and the dull thud of a punching fist. He shouted Christopher's name until the broken lamp cord was wrapped around his throat and pulled tight. Or was it a cord? He felt what could be long fingers powered by muscles beyond the strength of any human. His eyes were bulging when the power truck's yellow light danced back across his vision. It swirled on leaves and low brush, and he knew it wouldn't pause because the men inside the front cab had important work involving dangerous wires. He grabbed what held his throat, and sucked at the air.

"Please," he huffed, repeating the word until his air was spent. Before his eyes began to roll up white, he saw the group of Cyclops creatures in yellow helmets coming to where he sat guarding the girl. Despite their single glowing eyes, they seemed human and full of questions that made no sense.

"Are you hurt?"

"Can you stand?"

"What's your name?"

***

He rises from the kitchen table and opens the refrigerator. It's nearly empty because dear old Henry has had more important worries over the past eight days. He takes a half-empty can of dog food from the top shelf and scoops it into a bowl.

"You did good out there."

Miller isn't the least bit surprised by Christopher's voice.

"I'm a hero." He chops the smelly meat into pieces that toothless Sasha can manage. "Maybe I'll get the key to the city."

Christopher laughs, a wet sound, as if he has a bad head cold. Miller turns to see him sitting, chair pushed back, muddy sandals propped on the clean table cloth. "This berg's too small for a key. Maybe you'll get a latch to a screen door that we can have bronzed. We'll pick up a chain, make it a necklace."

Maggot growls from under the table when the front door opens and then ticks shut. Henry's slow footsteps come down the hall and into the kitchen. He barely looks up as he lifts a cold hand and holds it against Miller's face. The gesture is so tender and personal that Miller shudders and nearly jerks away. Then Henry shuffles past and draws a glass of water from the faucet, not seeming to notice the rudely perched man at his table.

"She'll live." Henry's pale face looks a hundred years old. He brings the glass to his lips, but hesitates and doesn't drink. Instead, he lowers it back into the sink where it spills across the clean metal surface. Henry brushes past Miller in an arthritic gate, out into the hall to the base of the stairs. He pauses to catch his breath, and looks back to the kitchen. Miller can't hear the words, but easily reads the old man's parched lips forming the word goodbye.

Henry mounts the stairs one at a time.

Five minutes pass before there's a final click of a light switch and the sound of bed springs. Another five minutes slip by before Christopher gets to his feet, cracks his knuckles like a high-stakes gambler about to deal from a marked deck, and turns toward the staircase. He whistles a happy tune from an old Disney movie, long nose clogged, but he's as cheerful as ever.

Heigh-Ho, Heigh-Ho, the tall man with white hair is one of the Seven Dwarfs, and off to work he goes.

TWENTY-FIVE

Miller counts steps with an imaginary abacus held in front, color beads shifting up and down, right to left. It's a childhood Christmas gift he used as a toy for non-counting games. At some point he broke apart the bamboo frame to scavenge the wire and discs. His chin rides his chest, a resonant hum filling both ears as if he's underwater. There's pressure from all directions, but forward has least resistance. The road is a portal that offers numbing rhythm. Faster and his teeth chatter. Slower is more of a deep message. Erections often accompany the change of speeds, but they eventually wither from the blessed numbness.

"You feel it?"

The voice robs Miller of his pleasant stupor. The question repeats, and he's especially furious the invasion comes from outside his head. Fucking Christopher. For the inner voice Miller accepts partial blame, but goddamn Christopher to hell for making him lose cadence. You fuckwad. You murderous, smelly, stick-figure fuckwad. Why don't you fall down and die? He tosses aside the imaginary abacus to look at his hands. They seem capable of digging another shallow grave, maybe leave 10 stupidly pointed toenails exposed for wildlife to nibble. Miller scans the surroundings. It's daylight, and much warmer. His back and armpits are wet. There are bird noises, and no cars. His fists are clenched, and his teeth grind, but the anger dissolves the way a nightmare is forgotten. Some nightmares, anyway.

"Well, do you?"

He still wants to tell him to shut his face, but his throat is dry. Too dry to even swallow until he works spit around his tongue, forces it down. "Do I what?"

Christopher is smiling, full of new energy, and Miller hates him more. He's pointing like an idiot at a highway sign indicating they're one mile from Jefferson, Ohio. "It's the feeling of being close

140

to greatness."

They'd left Henry's house before family or friends arrived, and Christopher had turned them north without giving a reason. Miller was bothered by the change, but is pulled along in Christopher's wake, bone-weary from the night in the woods. His pack is light, and they should have taken cans from Henry's pantry. Christopher's pack looks empty, nearly flat against his back.

Miller hopes it isn't Toby who finds his grandpa, but it's out of his hands and he pushes away the thought. Christopher has a cold, he thinks instead, and the idea cheers him. The man whose bones mend faster than a Saturday morning cartoon character has caught the sniffles while attempting to steal the soul of a lost girl. Miller chuckles despite his bleary eyes and the beginning of a headache. The girl won, you fucker. An innocent little girl beat the mighty incubus, swatted away the Angel of Death with a sweet pea scented palm. She tumbled down the rabbit hole, was bloodied and broken, but refused to give up the ghost. Is that why you're sick? The tasty treat stayed out of reach of your ridiculous pointy fingernails, and it put you off? Or is she alive because you're sick? Chicken or the egg stuff, perhaps.

"I know what you're thinking," Christopher says.

Miller's heart skips. He waits, says nothing, erases images of chickens and eggs, wants to share nothing. He misses the comfort of Mary's hiking shoes. His ankles are sore, the road less yielding in sneakers.

"You're thinking this town's claim to fame is that it's named after Thomas Jefferson. That he slept here, penned a few lines of the Declaration of Independence in some frontier beer hall?"

"I was sleeping."

"Sleep walking through life like most of humanity." Christopher reaches to rub Maggot's head. It makes the dog's blunted tail whip back and forth. "Jefferson was small beans compared to the genius hailing from these parts."

"My feet hurt."

"That's not good," says Christopher. "You know what they say about soldiers hiking on their feet?"

"It's an army marching on its stomach."

"Hiking, stomach, whatever. But do you know who I'm talking about?"

Miller's head throbs from dehydration, but he's encouraged

watching Christopher wipe his nose, and by the occasional wet cough that rattles deep. "If you're asking if I know who put this town on the map, I'm guessing it was a once-famous serial killer. A minister who molested and then buried hitchhikers in his basement."

Christopher wags a finger. "That's terrible. And I'm disappointed."

"My feet hurt bad."

"I know just the thing." Christopher tugs Miller's shirt, then leads them across the road and away from slick pavement. The trio hops a shallow ditch and they fend through brambles and low branches, out into an open field. It's a spot where the woods end and a stone wall draws a straight line along the edge of lush acreage. It's a dairy farm with ancient, rusting machinery, and a cluster of toppled milk cans outside the main barn. The metal roof displays giant letters of a faded Purina advertisement. The soft dirt is good on Miller's aching shins.

The farm shows no life signs, no chickens or yapping dogs, and no manure smell from the paddock. The clapboard house is a lonely enclave tucked under a stand of century-old trees, missing the dented pickup or rusted Chevy out front.

Visible is the interior of the second floor hay loft, and Miller envisions the luxurious possibilities.

"We're paying homage." Christopher uses his hands, pronounces the word homage with a French accent.

Maggot pants hard at the field's upslope, his nose to the ground, always searching. They crest the knoll to a panoramic view over a wooded glen sliced by a shallow stream. Christopher stops to take in the scene, but it's more an excuse to recover, arms crossed behind his head, back arched, looking but not really. The man's lungs are wind through a crowded space. He coughs and spits cloudy phlegm, then smiles at Miller and shrugs. He's the man who wakes up in bed after a tornado has destroyed the house around him. Or the driver whose car has rolled a dozen times in a high-speed crash, then steps out unscathed to straighten his tie. Or at least he was. Now he's vulnerable. Miller thinks he'd now emerge from the wreckage with a shattered pelvis, a blinded eye.

"That hay barn looked good. I'd kill to sleep on something dry," Miller says, and immediately regrets the words.

"The Spiraltron." Christopher annunciates the word with

gusto, in three long syllables. He points down the hill to an unpainted wood structure camouflaged by the surrounding foliage. "Not the original, of course, but this hallowed ground makes up for it."

"Seriously? This is where your genius lives?"

"No, he was born on the property." Christopher strides down the hill, and Miller follows. "Locals built it to honor Victor Bent, the first human entrusted with the gift of alien knowledge."

"He claimed he was abducted by Martians?" Miller looks over his shoulder at the slope they'll have to climb back up.

"Don't be ridiculous. They were from Venus. As Victor told it, he was transported to the mothership while meditating out in the Mojave Desert. They knew he was a special man."

"I'm sure they were right."

"Look at this!" Christopher is giddy despite the congestion and hacking cough. He's practically skipping as they approach the weathered plywood dome that's easily two stories.

"It looks like some kind of haunted observatory."

"You won't be such a negative Nelly once inside," says Christopher. "The torrent dome is ill sanctum for pessimists." Christopher puts a palm to the side of the building. "Venusian ingenuity, my friend. The Spiraltron is a portal for rejuvenation. The miles peel away inside one of these babies."

"I'm not going in. Let's head back to the hay barn, have some beef stew. There's one can left."

Christopher ignores Miller's antipathy, drops his pack and pries at loose plywood. Maggot keeps getting in his way, crowding close, sniffing at the gap Christopher creates. "Locals did splendid work duplicating Victor's original. It's smaller, but the principle remains. They tacked hand-painted signs out on the highway, planned on charging admission. Smart folks. Put it all the way down here to charge for a hayride."

"World's largest ball of string was already taken."

"Sarcasm is unbecoming." Christopher tears away splintered pieces of exterior wall.

"How's it supposed to work?"

They kneel to peer inside. "It uses negative ion fields to revitalize human cells." Christopher's voice echoes from the interior. Maggot's head turns sideways, ears cocked.

"Oh, of course. A fountain of youth."

"Exactly right," says Christopher. "It indefinitely extends human life."

Miller glares. "And how old is Victor?"

"He's dead, but that was poor genetics." Christopher squeezes through the opening, then pokes his head back out. He holds it wide enough for Maggot, then awaits Miller. "This thing has trippy acoustics. How's your singing voice?"

Miller leaves his pack to follow the dog, the only illumination from warped plywood sheets losing their light-tight seal. Maggot begins wildly barking, spinning circles, and it seems as though the structure's entire contents all at once goes berserk. Frightened animal sounds reverberate from every direction, and live things scramble over their feet. Miller retreats in a panic but can't locate the loose wall seam.

"What is it, boy? Did you find an alien?" Christopher backs into Miller, pinning him face-first to the wall. "Show them we mean no harm!"

There's angry chittering over the barking, and the musky odor of a wild animal den.

"Damn, I don't think they're aliens," Christopher shouts, but still has Miller immobilized, unable to turn. "Just some raccoons, unless they're trying to fit in with a disguise. Stand down, Maggot! Stand down, boy!"

Miller works free when Christopher moves to retrieve the dog from the cornered animals. In the dim light they watch a mother coon herd five cubs to an escape hole.

"Who's my good dog?" Christopher bellows, and Maggot forgets the raccoons, covers his owner's face with slobber. "Who's my mighty hunter?"

Miller brushes his hands, and then carefully extracts a fat splinter from his left palm.

"That'll get your heart pumping." Christopher stands surveying what's been a home for more than raccoons. There's a pile of abandoned sleeping bags and other camping gear. He prods a batch of dirty mess kits with the toe of one sandal. There's a gas lantern, and a mound of empty water bottles. Small nests have been built around the edge of the floor, and mud wasps have converted much of the ceiling into something resembling a cave.

"Can we go?"

"You need to give it a chance," says Christopher, wheezing. He begins shoving debris from the middle of the room, mess kits clattering. "People pilgrimaged thousands of miles to Victor's original dome. He held conventions for fellow contactees to describe their own alien experiences. The three times I went were a total blast."

Miller uses his shoe to brush a spot clear of desiccated scat, then sits cross-legged. "So he was surrounded by other nuts in tin foil hats?"

"He was a pilot," says Christopher, also dropping to the floor. He pauses to sneeze into the crook of his arm, and then maneuvers to be in the exact center of the room. He grunts when he stretches forward to unbuckle both sandals and rub his dirty feet. Maggot lies down with his head in Christopher's lap. "He was an inspector for Lockheed, and an author. His book was called something like Mothership Mojave. Is that the coolest? It's still available on Amazon, but I bought a signed copy in-person."

"I'm not feeling younger."

"A little patience." Christopher lies back, and Maggot gets up to turn a few circles before collapsing between his legs. "Relax, and allow your pores to absorb the ions."

Miller also lies down, folds his arms to cradle his head. They are hip to hip. The wood is hard on his butt and shoulders, but at least it's smooth. He yawns while Christopher talks.

"Victor was quite a showman. He'd climb onto this tall platform, peer into the heavens, and begin what seemed to everyone a one-sided conversation. The first thing he'd say was, 'Who am I talking to?' And it would get all quiet down below."

"Aliens never answered?"

"Well, Victor heard them loud and clear."

"You truly believe this guy talked to aliens?"

Christopher ponders. His breathing is forced, noisy. "I think it was a one-time thing for Victor. But he had to keep it fresh, or people would stop coming. They'd start questioning why aliens would travel all this way and then hang around for years not communicating. To some it wouldn't make sense."

"Aliens would have better things to do," says Miller. "Colonize West Virginia. Open a Taco Bell franchise."

There are animal noises on the other side of the wall, and Miller remembers he's left his backpack. If a raccoon can open a soup can, then more power to it.

"It's a world full of skeptics," says Christopher, who then moans and makes purring sounds that are practically sexual. "Oh, I'm feeling ionic effect," he adds, and there's no mistaking the awful sound of fingernails digging into the wood flooring. "Praise be to Allah. God is great, my friend, truly great."

Miller tilts his head away from the ceiling and watches Maggot licking one of Christopher's feet. "You were with Victor when he died."

Christopher struggles through a coughing fit, and then works to clear his throat. "He'd been sick. His ticker had a few bad gears. I dropped in to see him at a hotel in Santa Ana, where he'd been holed up alone for months. Books and trash piled to the ceiling. At least a hundred pizza boxes. Place smelled like anchovies. The only person to keep interest in poor old Victor was the tax man."

"You had no problem finding him."

"It was the late seventies by then, and the world had gotten too cynical for a man like Victor. The conventions lasted twenty-plus years. Guess what the new owner wanted to convert the dome into?"

Miller doesn't have a clue.

"One of those discotheques. Music, lights, and booze, with a big paved parking lot." Christopher sighs dramatically. Maggot stops licking, curls into a ball. "Victor was chosen from billions of people to share the Venusian knowledge. Anyone else would have been a laughing stock for claiming to ride in a flying saucer, but he pulled it off."

Miller pictures the clutter, the reams of half-written manifestos from a tormented mind. "So you came from behind and touched his cheek? Is that how Victor died?"

Christopher pauses as if remembering. "Not true," he says. "I stopped at a toy store and bought a Halloween mask."

"A man from Venus?"

Christopher shakes his head. "They only had Martians. You know the kind. Giant forehead, tiny little mouth."

"Close enough, right?"

"His ticker froze when he answered the door," Christopher whispers, perhaps out of respect for the memory. "Dropped dead at my feet."

"But he was smiling," says Miller. "Because the aliens had

finally come back for him."

"How'd you know?"

***

Miller is balanced on sleep's precipice, filtering through the last conscious thoughts of another long day. They raised the girls on fairy tales and a healthy mix of skepticism. Yet here he is, being led by a psychopath who'd perfected a few spectacular magic tricks.

Human beings did not move clouds any more than their pointed fingers slew birds in flight. It was hypnosis. The power of suggestion to a traumatized brain. He'd been tricked to believe he'd found the stricken creature. The wings felt real, the body still warm. When it was brought back to life, it pecked his hands exactly how he imagined a bird's beak would feel. Had he ever been pecked by the girls' birds? He thinks not. He certainly never held one. He rubs a hand over his stomach, recalls the mass of parasites feeding on the contents, poised to eat vital organs when his half-digested lunch was gone.

He pictures Christopher in a medieval castle's bleak dungeon, huddled over iron vats of boiling potions. Glass containers line the shelves, a little eye of that and a few tongues of this. Christopher is the dark chapter of the fairy tale he edited from the girls.

And then Miller recognizes that he is dreaming.

He's being transported. An elevator dropping too fast, he bites down hard enough to bloody a lip, braces for impact. But his body eventually slows and comes to rest in a position similar to when he'd settled next to Christopher under the dome. If it's truly an alien spaceship that's whisked him away, then Venusians travel in pitch dark. They do, however, build ships for comfort, perhaps due to the vast distances of their voyages. Every muscle and joint in his weary body reacts to wonderful softness, his head and neck supported by pure satin joy. Gravity is light because of the cushioned embrace, which is stark contrast to the wood floor left behind.

The smell also contains contrast. It is an alien laboratory of chemicals, mixed with the earthy odor of fresh cut lawn and newly tilled soil. He pictures aliens scooping samples in a farmer's lonely Iowa field, jarring it in their formaldehyde equivalent for later study.

He lifts his right hand and discovers gravity exists aboard the vessel. When the hand hovers too high it brushes something equally soft as his pilot seat. He touches both palms to a wall much closer than expected, and fights back a claustrophobic surge. The soft walls are at his sides and beneath his feet. He reaches above his head to find the silk cocoon is complete.

"This isn't a spaceship," says his inner voice. "And you are by no means flying across the sky."

He pushes up hard with both hands, but behind the padding is something that doesn't budge. The sense of being trapped jumps to a whole new level, and he pounds his fists until his muscles cramp.

"You're going to wake the neighbors carrying on like this," the inner voice says.

He is breathing hard when he gives up the fight. Body heat turns the cool air humid. He puts fingertips to the fabric, draws an index finger along one seam, and there's a vague memory of showroom caskets arranged by price. A smiling funeral home director described models, and Miller was suddenly a contestant on a gruesome TV game show. The man with a trimmed mustache and beard showed flashes of unnaturally white teeth. Miller watched the small round mouth form words that tumbled into his own numb mind. Hearse and transport. Fancier words such as cosmetizing and everlasting became insect-like once freed, emitting a buzzing sensation inside Miller's head. Death was the hiss of a snake, tranquility a storm. Miller nodded each time the mouth paused, its pink tongue darting out to taste the pale crust in one corner. Miller was assured his loved ones would be at peace, which was an obvious lie. The word peace was the ring of hammer on the head of a nail. Miller fought the impulse to slap the round little hole, to stretch it open and catch hold of that goddamn tongue to keep it from making any more words.

"Lizzy is afraid of the dark," Miller says in his sleep, the sealed coffin muffling his voice.

***

Maggot barks, scratches at the wall. Miller rubs his eyes, gets his bearings in the dim light. The claustrophobia is gone, but his back is on fire from the plank floor. Christopher is sitting up beside him, ignoring the dog, intent on something in his hands. Miller watches him reach up, run fingers through his hair and come away with a second clump that he holds in front of his face. His head tilts over what looks like shower drain debris, a mess of dangling white strands. He puts it to his runny nose, sniffs, then lowers his hands.

There's the wet splash of Maggot peeing on the wall, whining because he anticipates a beating. The dog shuffles from the mess, head down, moves to where the coons found escape, works his nose into the hole.

Miller again eyes Christopher. "You're sick. You came to see if this thing would help, to see if it was magic."

Christopher is silent except for his boggy lungs, and Miller settles back, stretches against the hard floor to rest a little longer.

TWENTY-SIX

A mammoth convoy gives birth to trash and dead leaf tornados. Eighteen-wheelers send underfoot tremors that threaten to split open the earth. Maggot cowers, emits anxious yelps with each air horn blast.

Christopher is unaffected by the proximity to danger, mood rising toward a manic state despite his burgeoning maladies. He makes a game of the trucks. "That one's filled with peanuts."

"We should look at a map before we get killed."

"Or maybe those candy bars with peanut butter and chocolate. Peanut butter is the bomb. Can you imagine being allergic? Damn, I'd kill for a PB&J and ice-cold milk."

Miller concentrates on maintaining a fast pace. They stayed straight when the road they were following swung left. The new road crossed a steel suspension bridge and immediately widened. This highway has signs forbidding pedestrians, let alone ones with skittish dogs.

"Fish sticks," Christopher calls over his shoulder, pointing.

"Why fish sticks?"

"Picture on the side, but I guess they could be trying to throw people off."

They pass beneath a giant green and white sign listing Cleveland exits.

Christopher is looking all around, nodding. "Ever been to the Eiffel Tower?"

"It's not in Cleveland."

Another truck whizzes past with its horn blasting. Maggot bumps Miller's right leg and nearly sends him into traffic surging from behind.

"Your dog's not thrilled about this road."

"I've never been to Gay Paree," Christopher says. "But I'd

love to visit the Louvre, cruise the Seine, and definitely climb the Eiffel Tower. I read that only one person was killed during construction. And it was when they were fitting the elevator, not putting up beams. Imagine only one death while erecting the tallest building in the world. A whole city of men perished digging the Panama Canal."

Miller steps over a mummified cat. Maggot whines and doesn't take his eyes from it as they pass. "Panama was a different environment."

"Mosquitoes and snakes, oh my!"

Miller uses one hand to try calming the dog. Glass litters the breakdown lane, and he worries about Maggot's soft pads. "Mary and I didn't travel much. She mentioned Paris, I guess. But then came the girls."

"People say it smells like piss. Probably one of those trendy American rumors that dumps on anything French," says Christopher, who gesticulates with both hands, then wipes his snotty nose. Two small bare spots at the back of his scalp are visible until wind rearranges his hair. "Those people should stroll the Lincoln Memorial on a holiday weekend."

"We've been there," Miller says, and nearly tells him about Lizzy getting carsick, and having to spend an extra night in a motel to give her stomach a chance to settle. They smuggled Petey, but didn't feel guilty because of the dirty ashtrays. They had a pool mostly to themselves. Celia did cannonballs. They ordered pizza delivered and watched a black and white movie. They played Candy Land, and turned the air conditioner up high and snuggled under blankets. They were happy. Miller keeps it a secret.

"The Eiffel Tower has lots of jumpers," says Christopher. "Although the story I read claimed the first suicide was a guy who hanged himself from one of those huge beams. Sort of a waste of a tall building, don't you think? Like filling your prescriptions and then slitting your wrists. Or buying a gun and sticking your head in the oven. People do that, you know. It's like their brain isn't running on all cylinders. Plans go cockeyed."

Miller only grunts, wanting away from this highway more than ever. He needs the road to bring relief, not memories.

"I love reading that stuff. Four hundred souls have leaped from the Eiffel Tower. A drop in the bucket considering the big picture, but damn. The most intriguing was a Brazilian girl. Went up with her brother, but was upset about something or other. He was clueless to what bee got in her bonnet. He tried pulling her back, but she was full-on committed. It's the way you've got to be. Set your sights and holler *bonsai*. Her body landed on a first-tier restaurant roof. Some thought it was a bomb. The glass roof cracked and, voila, there looking down was this recently pretty young thing with caramel skin. A few diners bolted for the doors, but not most. Nah, they kept chowing down, some with a raised hand signaling the *sommelier*."

"That's why you want to go?" Miller asks. "In case you get lucky?"

"And there you are with more cynicism. I'm talking vacation, and you feel the need to bring up work," he says, turning to wink at Miller.

Christopher leads them down a curved exit ramp. It's relief away from traffic. They're soon on sidewalks and crossing small streets, Miller and Maggot trailing as if Christopher knows the way. A few blocks and there's a park with a view of water so wide and far it could be an ocean.

"Lake Erie," Christopher says, as if reading his mind.

Miller drops his pack on a graffiti covered picnic table. Famished, he pulls out the beef stew and places the can over a cartoonish drawing of a penis. Before he finds the opener, the wind shifts and the air goes rank.

Christopher nods toward the adjacent industrial complex. "Sewage treatment."

Miller blinks tears. "Great picnic spot."

"One of my favorite places." Christopher drops his empty pack on the table, then stretches his arms over his head. "Listen, I have a few quick downtown appointments."

"I'm not waiting around," says Miller. "My legs need an hour or so, but that's it. You can catch up."

Christopher goes through Miller's pack, finds Maggot's food. "No, this is for a few days. We have temporary asylum, a clean and dry place to stay. Not the fanciest digs, but better than your ant-infested hay fields. Who ever heard of biting ants?"

"I can't."

"Such a baby. It's only a few days, you'll be fine." Christopher holds up a hand, lowers his head, and then suffers a sneezing fit that lasts a full minute. Maggot backs away, makes the same nervous whine as on the highway.

Miller's eyes close and he turns to face the sun. He takes a deep breath and his stomach rolls over from the smell, any appetite long gone. He rubs his thighs, massages his knees. His legs will tell him when it's time to move.

"Prettiest park in the city," Christopher says. "Look, I promise absolutely no bar fights, if that helps. Just some good old rest and relaxation."

Miller pulls his shirt collar over his nose. "You know I can't stay."

"You can walk Maggot five times a day. He can take a shit on half of Cleveland, and you can do whatever you have to do. There's hot water and a bed. A little privacy would be nice, right? I'll be out and about to take care of some commitments."

He cringes at the idea of Christopher's commitments. And the idea of stopping for days makes his chest constrict, his back and armpits go damp. He opens his eyes to watch squawking gulls come in from the lake, most landing on the adjacent roofs, a few gliding over the park lawn to inspect a tumbling McDonald's bag. Maggot growls, ducks out of from beneath the picnic table to begin a slow stalking hunt. The dog creeps forward nearly on his belly, then freezes except for his ears and quivering tail. His approach resumes when confident the birds are oblivious to his advance. It's impressive for an otherwise inelegant dog, almost lioness-like.

"You can leave if it gets to be too much." Christopher shoves his pack aside and climbs over the bench to sit next to Miller. Maggot has achieved striking distance to four gulls bickering over a French fry container. "Hell, I'll buy a TV so you can watch the Travel Channel. You know I'm a problem solver."

"You're an asshole," Miller says, but half smiles.

"And you're Mr. Cheerful."

Maggot's muscles twitch, his damaged tail straight out behind. He readies to pounce on the preoccupied birds.

"Call him back," says Miller, but the dog's haunches come un-sprung and he propels forward, mouth wide and teeth shining. The gull in his sights nearly escapes with a simple last second hop, but Maggot manages to clamp down on a webbed foot. The bird goes into full survival mode, wings drumming against the attacker, long yellow beak pecking and trying to bite back. The gull's three companions take flight, head out over the water in a straight line. Miller feels Christopher's arm across his chest, as if to hold him back.

"It's good for him," says Christopher. "Sometimes nature needs to run its course. People are always interfering, gumming things up. It disturbs the delicate balance."

The bird isn't going down without a fight. Its beak has a tight hold on Maggot's upper lip, the shoulders of its powerful wings beating the dog's knobby skull. Maggot is hunched forward trying to get a paw on top of the bird, maybe to pin it down or maybe to get free. When that fails, he begins thrashing his head and backing up, the wings hammering harder as if the bird senses the upper hand.

Miller looks at Christopher, who's shaking his head and frowning. The bird's white feathers are splashed with bloody drops, as Maggot falls onto his back and uses all four paws to try prying the bird from his face.

"I expected the hunt to go a little smoother." Christopher raises one hand and points a skinny finger, just as he had at the small bird over the field. The gull instantly goes still, and Maggot twists out from under the limp body. He scrambles to his feet and barks at the motionless body, moving in a wide circle until certain it isn't coming back to life to resume the assault. Satisfied, he scoops the bird in his jaws and trots back to Christopher with his trophy, tail swishing and ears cocked high. The dog crowds between his legs and drops the bird in his lap.

"That a boy," Christopher croons, using both hands to scratch the dog's ears hard and deep. He leans close to let Maggot lap at his face. "My big mighty hunter. Who's a good boy? Who's a good boy?"

Christopher eventually pushes the dog away and cradles the gull to his stomach. Maggot backs up and sits, prepared for a game of fetch. But Christopher gathers the bird's wings against its body and bends forward as if to smell or maybe speak to it. Then, with the flourish of a magician setting free a trained dove, he uses both hands to toss the white corpse into the air. Maggot spins to catch the bird, but its wings spread and begin wildly flapping. The bird rises and then veers toward the open water, and doesn't look back.

***

Temporary asylum is a brick building with rows of identical narrow windows. It looms fourteen stories over a ghetto neighborhood. The steel elevator is urine and cigarettes stink, and there's been no consideration for superstition. A scratched plastic button with the number thirteen is sandwiched between fourteen and the one Christopher's thumb jabs. Both men heft plastic grocery bags out of the elevator, the sound of slammed doors echoing down the concrete hall. Gang tags color the otherwise naked cinderblock walls. Swirling script leaves no doubt the twelfth floor is Murda Boys turf. Maggot trails, toenails typing a storm.

Sagging furniture fills the apartment, is overlooked by praying Jesus images taped to walls like no trespassing signs.

"Home sweet home!" Christopher sweeps dirty dishes into the sink to make room for the bags. "You look a little unsure about this, but don't jump to conclusions. The neighborhood is a tad run down, but these are the salt of the earth people. What's a good word? Authentic, or maybe genuine? Take your pick. I love coming back."

"I haven't seen any people." And it's true. There had been radios and voices from houses and alleys, but once beyond the stripped automobiles outside the tenement, residents are burrowed away. Televisions switched off, the inhabitants attempting to listen, or are taking cover to wait something out.

A knock draws a startled bark from Maggot. Christopher abandons the groceries and doesn't bother with the peep hole. A man cradles an older model television to his fat stomach. He hesitates in the doorway, lips moving, maybe a silent prayer. He carries his load to the living room corner, quickly twists the coiled black snake into the female plug. He leaves the remote on the unit and speed walks to the door. He crosses himself at the threshold and leaves. A Spanish game show plays when the tube warms.

There are no darting roaches or mice on Christopher's tour. No live ones, anyway. Small cadavers are plentiful throughout, and Miller imagines none of the mice bodies have gone cold. There are two identical rooms with bare twin beds and wooden chairs. The yellow tiled bathroom has no shower curtain. The toilet water is brown. The mirror has a fist-shaped crack.

"Which do you want?" Christopher can't stand still, shifts foot to foot. He coughs without covering his mouth.

"Does it matter?"

Miller takes the room on the left and falls into bed still in his newish sneakers, not ready to accept the walk is paused for any length. Claustrophobia has dropped the ceiling and pulled the walls closer, but is manageable because of fatigue.

Maggot puts both front paws on the mattress, looking to share, but Miller pushes him away. He dozes, listening to television contestants answer questions. A winner howls. There are commercials with rapid fire dialogue, and then the television is switched off and the apartment is silent.

TWENTY-SEVEN

It's night when Miller stirs. He fumbles for the wall switch, then gets up and turns on every light in the apartment. Christopher is gone and Maggot sprawls across all three couch cushions chasing something in his sleep. There's a new leash curled on the kitchen counter. The clock above the refrigerator says it's almost two, as Miller bends over the sink to peer down at the street corner, looking for people, anticipating roving gangs. Could it possibly be safe? Looking back at the twitching dog, it's not really Maggot who needs the walk. The apartment is a shrinking cage, and it's getting worse. Invisible things have begun crawling up his legs and across his back and arms. He can't scratch them away. He'll walk or go insane.

"Maggot." The dog lifts his head, sniffs for food. "Come."

Sliding to the floor, Maggot performs a languid, joint popping stretch. He trots to Miller and sits, eyes practically translucent in the stark light. There's something disturbing about the dog. Nothing he can pinpoint. Not that the dog seems dangerous, but there's something not so dog-like behind those eyes. Conspiring isn't the right word. Plotting is too strong. It's more like there are bad thoughts coagulating inside his bony skull, a swirling malignance set to bloom. People would probably say the same about Miller, would recognize the infection. Being close to Christopher has affected him and the dog.

Shaky hands fasten the leash. The dead owner's tag is gone. "A walk sounds good, huh?"

Spanish music seeps from door cracks despite the hour, Maggot pulling the lead to investigate the accompanying strange food smells. Even though it's only a hallway, the walking relieves some of the pressure, and the beginning of a headache recedes. Blood flows to Miller's warming muscles, his mood lifting until they reach the coffin-like elevator. He can't step forward when the door slides open.

157

There's a million volt barrier, a guillotine's oblique blade suspended from distressed rope. Maggot sits and whines, anxious, until the door closes in front of them. At eye level the word FUCK is spray painted in box letters.

He turns to an unmarked exit for the stairs, braces the heavy door for the dog. There's an acrid, burning chemicals stench and a blue haze. Maggot rebels, tries scooting back through before it swings shut, but Miller holds tight.

"It's okay." His voice is hollow in the cinderblock stairwell. From below comes a repetitive ker-plunking noise they walk toward, Maggot's toenails skittering down the dusty steps. The acute sound increases with each floor descended, a hammer on tile cracking, twice quickly, then a softer slap. It becomes almost painful. The source is on the sixth floor landing, a space no larger than his new bedroom.

"Hello," says a boy, maybe ten, wearing only tan shorts and grungy socks. In his hand is an orange billiard ball. It has a white circle with the number five on opposite sides. The boy sits with his bare back to the wall, knees drawn up. He again tosses the ball that strikes the floor, then ricochets off the wall. He catches in the same hand, his extended black arm flecked with cement dust. "You just moved here."

In one corner is a rag pile that's actually a human being. Maggot has enough leash to sniff it, prodding the partially obscured face, but the bundle doesn't move.

"I'm visiting."

"You're staying with the other white dude." The boy looks him up and down, then tucks the ball in his lap and reaches behind his back. He produces a glass pipe and disposable lighter. The umber mouthpiece goes to his lips as he flicks the lighter, yellow flame embracing the charred bowl. Smoke swirls as the glass heats, and the boy draws a cloud into his lungs, suppressing a cough. He traps the smoke inside his scrawny body for a half-minute, before smoothly exhaling. Miller remembers when Lizzy first learned to hold her breath underwater, perched on chubby knees in a kiddie pool, pinching her nose and bravely leaning forward. The boy holds the pipe to Miller. A peace offering.

Miller shakes his head as the bitter tendrils touch his face, invade his nostrils. He looks longingly toward the next flight of stairs. He could easily step around the boy and keep going.

"He's the boogie man," says the boy, returning the pipe and lighter to the space behind him. "Grammy says to stay away, but she don't say why. Are you two faggots?"

The question is more jarring than watching him with the pipe. Miller fumbles words. "We met on the road. This is his dog." It comes out high-pitched, defensive. "It's not like that."

The boy begins to polish the orange ball, the narrow tendons under his charcoal skin dancing. He looks up with eyes so bloodshot it seems all the tiny vessels have simultaneously burst. They are the eyes of the badly beaten, but weren't like this a moment ago. They were milky white.

"You suck his dick until he shoots off," the boy says, then smiles. His front teeth are stained. He sounds drunk. "Grammy knows all about you, but she don't tell me nothing. I ask, but she don't say. Everybody hides from the boogie man. What the boogie man gonna do, Grammy? He only one dude, so what he gonna do? She knows, but don't say."

Miller moves to step around the boy, but Maggot won't come. Miller turns to see the dog's hind leg lifted, drenching the rag pile in a yellow stream. "Dammit!" He yanks the leash and the dog paints a wet zigzag on the wall over the man or woman.

The boy begins laughing, and then a door is pushed open somewhere above, hinges crying in the gloom.

"Faggot wanna touch my balls?" The boy holds out the nicked orb, then snickers. "You can touch all my balls. I let you stroke 'em nice."

"I'm sorry." Miller winds in Maggot's leash. A single set of heavy footsteps comes from two or three floors above. It's a familiar slapping, but the acoustics make him uncertain.

"Grammy doesn't wanna talk about the boogie man." The boy's arm whips forward, sends a perfect strike to the head of the slumped body in the corner. A tattered scarf is knocked aside to expose open eyes, half its face. The body doesn't stir or make any sound.

Miller drags Maggot past the laughing boy, who is pointing at the rolling ball. "Fetch, faggot. Fetch my hairy balls!"

Miller lunges down the stairs three at a time until he realizes Maggot is lagging, that he's choking the dog. When they reach the stairwell bottom, he pauses before opening the door. Over Maggot's

panting he again hears the boy's slurred voice.
"Are you the boogie man?"

TWENTY-EIGHT

Miller leads Maggot through heavy glass front doors, into night air reeking of garbage and recent fire. It's the burn-day smell of his grandfather's farm, where flammables were stuffed inside 55-gallon barrels and left to smolder through Sunday church services. The drums were loaded on a riding mower trailer and dumped in a gulley beyond the back corner of a hay field.

But this neighborhood sounds nothing like those bucolic fields. Streets are empty, but emergencies thrive. The night is filled with police sirens and fire engine horns, reversing truck beeps, and a car alarm symphony.

A few of the cars abandoned on the street have been reclaimed by squatters, piled to the roofs with clothing and plastic bags. Cigarette smoke wafts from cracked windows. Some have music playing from what sound like transistor radios.

Miller tries imagining the life lessons he could have shared with his daughters, but who is he to judge? He'd been disturbed by the girls' choice of Halloween costumes two years ago. Mary allowed them to be hobos, with Goodwill clothing they'd taken scissors to, and dark makeup on their cheeks smudged into beards.

"It seems wrong," he told his wife. "Like blackface."

"It's from one of Celia's books. You don't understand."

No, he hadn't, nor did he really try.

Two women he assumes are prostitutes are circling the block. They walk arm in arm, probably for protection. He's about to be intercepted before reaching the corner, considers crossing the street. But one girl spots the dog and bends to call out, her bare thighs parting as she squats. Even in the shadowy street light he can see up her short skirt. There is a narrow slash of color, the shiny material drawing his eyes. Maggot pulls at the leash, anxious to go to her, and Miller is embarrassed for his erection as he stumbles behind the dog.

"What's his name?" The girl rubs Maggot's sides and lets him sniff around her knees.

"Petey," he lies, not wanting to explain the terrible choice, but feels rotten using his dead dog for cover.

The other girl is older, stands tapping an uncomfortable looking high heel, and pulls a cigarette pack from a glittery purse. "C'mon, he don't want a date."

"I used to have a dog," says the girl stroking Maggot. She has straight black hair that's darker than her mocha skin. Her shoulders are soft and round, breasts barely concealed under thin yellow material. He can see her dimpled areolas and stiff nipples. Her mini skirt is red and she wears short, spiked-heel boots. Her naked legs are glossy from lotion, thighs now spread wide around Maggot's wagging body. Her smell overcomes the stench of burned garbage, strong but sweet, a mix of fruit and flowers. He allows her smell to fall over him, and it brings faint memories of Christmas holidays from when life mattered.

He expected a face hardened by a life he can barely conceive, but her eyes are bright and clear, filled with the joy of someone receiving a dog's love. She has the eyes of a kid, he guesses no more than seventeen, and the surge of guilt is sickening. She can't be more than a few years older than Celia.

"Be careful," he says, knowing how stupid it sounds. Be careful of what? Slobbering dogs? Middle-aged men with bulging erections?

"I can tell he don't bite." She kisses Maggot's ear, lets him nuzzle her neck, and then stands back up and presses her skirt. She makes delicate noises while doing this, a petite hum or something. Lithe fingers adjust her top, then accept the other girl's cigarette. The filter disappears between full lips, the muscles in her jaw moving to draw the smoke. Around her neck is a red band of velvety material that makes her throat appear slit.

The girl laughs and coughs when Maggot jams his nose into her crotch. She deflects his head one handed, angling her hips from the probing. Her long nails are painted white and have ornate decals.

"I'm sorry," Miller mumbles, pulling at the leash and stepping around the girls. "I'm so sorry."

"Goodbye, Petey." The girl waves her fingernails, and his heart breaks a little more.

***

A few blocks and the blight is complete. Behind boarded windows is a former working class neighborhood in full-on decay. Chain link fences surround square lawn plots gone wild. Maggot shits on a cracked cement driveway sprouting daisies and juvenile trees.

Beyond is a school with taller fencing and barred windows. Its dented metal doors have dangling chains fit to haul ship anchors. A different gang has claimed these ruins.

He maneuvers Maggot around a glittering carpet of broken glass, searching for his walking rhythm on the uneven pavement. He pretends this brief journey is one way, and that he's back out on a lonely road that might continue forever. It offers a rush, a lifting of something heavy from his shoulders. Why not keep going? He owes Christopher nothing. There's no reason to go back.

"What about him?" says the inner voice, and he glances down at the dog that's trotting to keep pace.

"I don't know."

"Of course you don't know. Why plan when flying by the seat of your pants is going so well?" The voice is thick with sarcasm. "Drop the leash and he'll find his way back to that psychopath. Or bring him along. He's a happy clam not getting his ass kicked. Now, sport, let's discuss *your* situation a little more."

"I want to walk."

"It's a pretty night. Call girls out in force. A few gunshots over yonder. Reminds me of Detroit in the springtime. Hey, you think people from Cleveland vacation in Detroit? Or is it the other way around?"

"Leave me alone."

He continues along the empty street, away from the apartment building. The downtown city lights are to his left, and the dark skies to his right must mean the lake. Straight ahead is freedom.

"Maybe you've got this under control," says the inner voice. "A guy and his dog on the open road has a romantic ring. Like riding the rails. You're one freight train from a Woody Guthrie ballad."

He tugs Maggot away from an upended couch in the middle of the street. "You said you knew a secret about him, but weren't ready to tell me."

"Oh, yeah, and it's a humdinger," says the voice. "You think you're ready?"

"Yes."

"He's a Democrat."

Miller keeps walking, doesn't respond.

"A Libra?"

"Fuck off."

"Hey, now." The voice feigns hurt. "I'm not the bad guy in all this. I'm sure as hell not the one currently playing hide the salami with a couple of cheap hookers."

Miller stops. "What do you mean?"

"The hot piece of chocolate you were checking out back there? Her skin was silky smooth because she's only fifteen. You served up that pretty little thing on a silver platter."

"You're lying," Miller says, knowing he's not. He closes his eyes, can almost see Christopher pinning her compact body to the bed. Even though she's young, she's been around long enough to deal with her fair share of lousy things. But Christopher's brand of misery is a whole new ballgame.

"She sure set you atingle, you filthy perv. And you left her to him."

Miller turns and runs back down the black street, Maggot loping along, biting at his leash, loving the exercise.

TWENTY-NINE

The apartment door is ajar, and Maggot noses it for Miller to view the empty living room and kitchen. Miller unhooks the leash and steps inside, expecting muffled screams, pleas for mercy. Maggot bounds to his couch spot, circles twice and collapses.

"Christopher?" No need to shout. He'll be heard or felt, or whatever it is that connects the two men.

And then he smells the perfume, a mix of fruit and flowers, and blind rage surges, makes him want to roar. His fists clench as he follows the scent down the hall, and kicks open a door for the first time in his life. He steels for a gory, blood spattered scene, dismembered body parts hung from the ceiling on sausage twine, slowly rotating in the breeze from swarming flies.

But there is no blood. The room is filled with sex sounds, not murder. Christopher sits naked on the wood chair, the older girl also nude, straddling, hips making wave motions. Christopher winks at Miller, flashes a coy grin, then turns his eyes to the bed. The velvet neckband girl is on her back, legs parted to display a shaved mound, long thin arms at her sides, palms up. Her clothes are a colorful bundle on the bare mattress near her head. Her eyes are open, and he cannot look away. Those full and precious lips move into a slight smile, expose small perfect teeth. Her nipples are little bulls-eyes. Miller has only seen naked black women in porn flicks, is caught up in curiosity until her legs move farther apart. She entices without words, his dick full and aching, the wet sliding sound from the other couple enveloping them.

"Yes, baby," says the girl in Christopher's lap, husky, taunting, and Miller believes the words are meant for him.

He stands over the end of the bed pawing his shirt buttons, tantalizing smells reaching and pulling. The girl's eyes close and her back arches, hands rising to her modest bosom, fingertips drawing tight circles, working the twin hard beads in a way that should hurt.

"Love me." Her words are barely a moan.

The damp thrusting from the chair elevates to a harsh slapping, as the screwing turns frantic. Miller's knee weighs down the bed, but he's distracted when the kinetic din is infused with choked-off gurgles.

"I love the smell of dirty slut in the morning." Christopher mouth twists into an idiotic smile, upper lip a mess of crusted snot. His hands clench the girl's neck, her ashen features upturned, bulging eyes ready to explode, and for a split-second Miller see Lizzy's laughing face full of pink bubblegum. The girl's hips no longer move on their own. Instead, she's suspended by his powerful grip as his crotch pistons. She is being simultaneously bludgeoned and hung.

"Do it, Miller. Stop being a faggot and screw your little princess."

The words cause him to retreat from the bed. He struggles to recall who also called him that word.

"Love me," the girl repeats, and now Miller sees she really is a child. He looks down at his strained pants and hates himself, imagines he could rip the revolting appendage from his body. He turns the anger back to Christopher and lunges for the chair, grabbing one sweat slick arm and wildly swinging a fist. The prostitute's tongue is out and flapping with each thrust from below, and it brushes the side of Miller's face as he throws more punches.

"Love me," the girl from behind says, louder, pleading.

Miller continues pummeling until Christopher stops thrusting, face contorting in orgasm. When he's done, his grip releases and the girl sinks to the floor in a limp pile. Miller collapses over the chair, head bowed as if in prayer. The smell is dank sex, sour sweat, and perhaps something from a long buried coffin. White hair strands across Christopher's thighs are broken cobwebs, bits of scabby skin beneath the chair huddle in drifts. He is shedding, or coming apart.

Christopher puts a hand on Miller's back. The touch is tender, non-threatening. "What we've got here is a failure to communicate," he says, and Miller senses the asinine smile.

Minutes pass. Somewhere a toilet flushes and a baby cries. Christopher pushes Miller away, goes to the window. He places a small object on the sill, arranges it like a keepsake. It glints. A knife or old-fashion straight razor. Miller drops to his butt, facing the bed. In his left hand is a strip of soft material he carefully unfolds. It's the young girl's red velvet neckband. He looks up, already knowing her throat has been slashed.

THIRTY

Her face is in frozen tranquility, as though she's slipped into restful sleep instead of having her throat cut. A child at peace. It's a look Miller knows from worrying over his own girls, slipping into their room to inspect for signs of life.

The mottled pink cheeks appeared feverish but were always cool—not cold—to the touch. A routine as regular as brushing teeth, he'd lumber out of bed if he'd dropped off during the late news. It was fear of missing a single night, and the certain consequences. Let down your guard once.

Lizzy and the girl with the same fine veins across their eyelids, intricate designs sketched on fragile skin; the identical way of sleeping with parted lips, although no stuffed bear was tucked beneath the prostitute's chin.

He attempted to recruit Mary into his obsession, wanting to share worry that one of the girls might stop breathing, and then rejoice by discovering they had not. She would have none of it.

"The girls are fine. They're healthy and happy. Stop making yourself crazy. And please quit trying to involve me. Find a good book, honey."

But somewhere in the world a child had died from a bad dream or an unexpected sneeze. If it happened once, it would happen again. He hit a nerve calling her callous. Talk about someone turning cold. Mary was plenty frosty for a solid three days.

He kneels beside the dead girl. If he'd been more careful. If he hadn't let his guard down. If he'd known the extent of the evil. Danger wasn't something to check up on, but to build a fortress against. Brick and mortar, not silly rituals. Steel doors and shatter-proof glass. It was his fault they didn't survive what came out of the night.

Daylight brought easy to spot perils. Celia climbed to the very top of the tree now towering above Petey's unmarked grave. She shimmied up the main trunk until the wood was only a few inches thick. The canopy began to bend, bobbing with each of her motions as she adjusted for a view toward town. She was a skinny 11-year-old, threatening to be taller than her mother. Her new height qualified her for the amusement park rides that spiraled upside down at crazy speeds. He was nominated as roller coaster chaperone, his marshmallow belly pinned under the safety bar. Mary with Lizzy on the gentle kiddie rides, clanking around on lazy caterpillars and spinning in giant teacups that remained comfortably near ground level.

He reaches to touch the dead girl's cheek. It's cold and smooth.

Christopher is busy dressing. "I know this looks bad."

"She was a kid." Miller's voice is calm, though he's quaking within, his body wanting to rattle apart. "You murdered them."

"I don't blame you for jumping to conclusions."

"Are you serious? Jumping to conclusions? You're a cold-blooded killer." His fingertips caress an earlobe. She has tiny crosses for earrings. Did Celia have pierced ears? He tries remembering the battle, the desperate argument about everyone else having double-piercings, and nobody's stupid ear had fallen off. She called him a monster for being so mean, but she had no idea what a real monster was. Not yet. The storm was still far away. And then he remembers Mary snuck her off to the mall, did a Mary thing, and he's glad. Fingering the dead girl's gold cross, he has a perfect image of the little red and black ladybugs Celia wore in the picture he gave the undertaker. "This is a child, you bastard. A dead child after you slit her throat."

"Well, you hit me," Christopher says.

"This is a joke to you? A fucking joke? You're some sort of devil. No, you *are* the devil."

"I didn't murder them," Christopher says, and Miller hears him zip his pants and then pause. "I mean, I did, but it's more complicated than that."

"I watched you kill them."

"I saved them," says Christopher. "I saved them from something a hundred times worse."

"You strangled her. And you cut this girl's throat. Nothing

you say will change what you did."

"Okay, fine. In retrospect, I got a little carried away." Christopher's voice has turned defensive. "But it was nothing compared to what their pimp had waiting."

Miller touches sleek hair. It's coated in oily sheen, but stiff. He's never felt a black person's hair. It's coarse as hay in the fields where they've slept.

"They were both HIV positive," says Christopher. "My girl was bothered by swollen glands in her pits, was losing weight. Other things. They went to a free clinic, were tested, and bingo. Their pimp discovered his best moneymakers screwed up royally by swapping needles. And the bastard sets a pretty harsh example when driving home a point. Guy does things hard core."

"You lie about everything."

"See for yourself. Take a gander at those track marks. Kid was still a rookie, but starting to roll pretty heavy. Only takes one bad needle, my friend."

Miller lets go of her hair and reaches across her naked chest. He gently grasps her wrist, turns the arm to expose a fine line of pin pricks running up the inside of her elbow. Dark bruising surrounds a few that are puffy and appear infected.

"It was gonna be a whole production," Christopher says. "Teach his other girls a lesson they would never forget. He's a real psycho, goes all Viet Cong on girls who fuck up. Carries a set of pliers to yank teeth and rip off fingernails. Gives me the willies. Some mighty fucked up *hombres* in this world."

Miller allows her wrist fall to the stained mattress. Christopher stands fully dressed, peering out the small window. It's morning, and hours having passed since Miller thought he was coming to the rescue.

"We could have saved them," Miller says. "We could have gotten them help."

"It's not like that. This isn't the Peace Corps, and we aren't Boy Scouts. There's no teaching people to fish so they can live happily ever after. You can't interfere, or things are thrown out of balance."

"Balance? You call this balance?"

Christopher continues staring out the window, his body blocking most of the light. Miller turns back and puts his head against the edge of the mattress. He breathes in the fruit and flower smell coming from the dead girl. Her scent is still lovely. Like Christmas.

"I miss my family so much." Miller words are muffled by the quilted surface.

"I know you do, my friend," says Christopher. "I know you do.

THIRTY-ONE

Police will end the nightmare. There is no escaping dead bodies in an upper floor cinderblock apartment. Someone witnessed two whores disappear into the devil's den, and not come out. The young one must have screamed seeing the blade. Double murders give off a certain vibe. Fear of the police and white-haired bastard shoved aside to dial.

"9-1-1, where is your emergency?"

"The devil is everywhere."

"Do you need an ambulance?"

The caller paused. "We need God, but I guess some cops will do."

One phone call isn't too much to hope for. It's civic duty, after all. Street walkers are still somebody's daughters. Or sons. Miller anticipates the urgent banging and order to open the door. Hell, it'll be more than a pair of patrolmen, they'll have an armed brigade. There won't be time to react before the battering ram is followed by the swift boots of a ninja-like SWAT team. Weapons raised, they'll first send a broad-shouldered German Shepherd with grizzly bear jaws down the hall.

Miller's own fear of police was instilled by a single, long ago incident, the product of a boy's momentary lack of judgment.

He'd been arrested once in his life before meeting Christopher. He was put in adult handcuffs that he could have easily wriggled from, yet they were iron clamps riveted to bone. It was the day after he turned nine, a chilly fall afternoon with leaves dropping from a clear blue sky, the Eagles pre-game show on TV. Gravel crunched under his sneakers as he stalked around the garage, new pellet rifle tight in his hands, loaded and pumped full of air. He hesitated at the back end of the brick wall, searching the chaos of blowing leaves for a target, bangs already in his eyes despite a back-to-school haircut. He lifted the weapon, tucking the plastic stock firmly to his shoulder exactly as Dad had shown. A real rifle kicked and bruised if there was any gap.

He peered down the barrel, left eye closed, and right index finger off the trigger but ready. He leaned against the coarse masonry, felt sharp edges through his sweatshirt and the waist of his Levis. The rifle sight first found the dog house, then swept across the yard to Mom's laundry line and its dozen wooden clips with rusty springs. He considered each before moving back to the trees separating their property from Mr. Cooper's junky old place. Plenty of targets over there, for sure, but Mr. Cooper was always home tinkering with his beat-up mowers.

He brought the sight up to his mom's outdoor thermometer, but she'd slaughter him for even thinking about it. She picked it out of a catalog and spent forever adjusting it to the right spot. It was the size and shape of a dinner plate, with some kind of purple flowers and big numbers she could see from the kitchen window.

That's when the red bird fluttered. A cardinal, he knew, probably named after the baseball team. It was on a limb in the thermometer tree, fixing its wings and doing whatever birds did when they weren't flying. It had a pointy, dunce cap head, and was wearing a robber's mask. The cardinal was a little higher than Mom's thermometer and maybe twenty big steps away. A really hard shot, especially with the bird hopping along the branch. He pressed the rifle to his cheek, smelled gun oil that made the metal parts slick. His heart raced, body suddenly warm and tingly as he aimed the notch on the end of the barrel at the bird's puffy chest. He curled his finger around the trigger and took a deep, even breath as Dad had instructed. You were supposed to relax, not be herky-jerky. You squeeze a trigger slow and easy, never rushing.

The bird skipped a few more times, then stopped and tilted up its head. It let out a burst of loud noises that made him flinch even though he'd watched its beak open, knew some kind of call was coming. A long whistle, then a bunch of short, fast sounds that echoed around the yard. A single sweat drop ran down the middle of his forehead, and he fought the urge to rub at it. He instead blinked away the tickle, and flexed his jaw to make his ears pop. The bird jumped sideways and repeated its call, wanting something, food or maybe it was lost. He kept his concentration, tuning out distractions like Dad told him. Focus, as though the only two things in the world are you and the target.

He began squeezing the trigger when the bird stopped to make another call. There was an instant of worry when the movement wasn't smooth and the trigger seemed to stick. But then came the crack of high pressure air being released. The pellet moved too fast to see even though everything had turned into slow motion. The bird disappeared as if it had gone invisible, and he relaxed his trembling grip. He blinked more to refocus, searched the other branches. There was nothing, only a few brown leaves twisting at the end of their stems.

But then there was commotion on the ground beneath the branch. Something jigging up and down like corn being popped. He pushed from the garage and approached the flopping creature with the uncocked rifle held out in front. The bird went still by the time he reached the tree. It had settled on its back, yellow beak gaping, frozen in mid-call, or maybe it died crying. Did it matter? Square in the middle of its chest was a round spot that was a deeper shade of red.

"What the hell is wrong with you?"

His father was right behind him, and he shrank away with a girlish scream, the rifle dropping from his hands. It was the last time he touched the gun. It was the last time he wanted to touch it.

Before he could try to explain, his father's open hand slapped the top of his head. He saw black dots and flashes of white as he fell to his knees. His father grabbed the back of his sweatshirt at the neck and forced his head down to face the corpse.

"Look what you did." His father's voice was full of disgust.

And then he was on his feet being marched back toward the garage, clutching at his throat to pull the material loose enough to breathe. He was sobbing and trying to say how sorry he was, when his father opened the rear door of the station wagon and threw him in head first. The door slammed so hard the pressure stabbed his ears. It was the first time he had ridden in a car unbuckled, was flung around the interior, banging across the huge back seat when they roared from the driveway in reverse. He was dumped onto the floor when the tires screeched to propel them forward and around the curve that meant they were headed toward town.

He climbed back on the seat and watched power lines ebb and flow through tears, brown picket fence of telephone poles rushing past. They were going too fast, would crash any second, and it would also be his fault. When his father stomped the brake pedal, he tumbled back to the floor sideways, pinned behind the front seat. The door opened, and he was dragged across a sidewalk and up the front steps of the big stone police building. A thousand times he had ridden his bike past this place, but had never been inside. It was where criminals and really bad kids were brought after their villainy. He never imagined being one of them.

He stumbled through the front doors behind his father, was shoved backward into a plastic chair. His father put a hand on the wall over his head and leaned down into his face. "Don't you dare move."

He nodded, snot bubbles forming and then bursting, splashing his hot cheeks.

He watched the floor, old cracked tiles with a skinny black rug running down the middle, and listened to a typewriter make clicks and bell sounds. After a while he heard his father's voice, but didn't try to comprehend what he was saying. He knew his father was confessing the sins of his son, and couldn't bear the weight of the actual words. Then a shadow fell over him, and he looked up at a police officer's scowling face. He wore a blue uniform and had a wide black belt with a gun on the side.

"Get to your feet."

Both knees wanted to quit. He was trembling like crazy, face wet and hair plastered. He had to pee and maybe even poop. His guts were a mess. "I'm sorry," he tried, but the words were mush. He'd done the worst thing in his whole life and had no way to explain. He could promise a million times to never do it again, but it didn't matter. He'd been trusted with the rifle, and then killed something in cold blood. Nothing could make the bird alive. Dead was forever.

"Put your hands out."

The policeman unsnapped a black leather case attached to his belt and removed silver handcuffs. They were huge metal things with sharp teeth meant to ratchet together. They were like nothing on TV.

"I'm sorry," he was able to mutter.

The policeman grunted and dropped one heavy cuff over each of his wrists, and then clicked them all the way closed.

"I didn't mean to do it."

***

"Take the dog for a long walk. Get some color back in those cheeks." Christopher bends over the older dead girl, tries pushing her eyelids shut. He sucks in a deep, noisy breath, and winks at Miller. "Love means never having to say you're sorry."

Miller doesn't return the smile. He leaves the bodies to Christopher and goes for the leash. Maggot dives from the couch, tail thumping up a storm, ready for more shitting and running.

The elevator is a piece of cake. Murder is a clear antidote for certain anxieties. It's early morning when he pushes back through the front doors. There's the steady thwack-thwack of a girl jumping rope on the cement landing. He doesn't want anything to do with her, dreads what new atrocities lurk, so he tries hurrying past to find a spot for the dog to piss.

"Hey, mister, mister. Hey, mister, mister." Her voice matches her body's rhythm.

Maggot bullies the leash toward the girl. She wears a flowered, knee-length dress and patent leather shoes. Not play clothes, so maybe it's Sunday before church. Sunday morning and the smell of dirty whores, he thinks, rubbing his eyes. Her hair is in wiry pigtails sticking out at odd angles, tied off with pink ribbon.

"Hello," he says, allowing the dog close enough for her to pet his head. Maggot is all tongue and nose, vacuuming in the scent of this new human. Her colors, chocolate and pink, make her look like a piece of candy. He glances up at the tenement windows and frowns.

"Your dog is friendly."

"He loves everybody."

"He's a funny color." She rubs the knob at the top of his head. "Like he's not any color at all."

The bright morning sky gives his coat a bluish cast. The girl takes an ear in each hand and lifts just as he cocks his head, giving the dog the world's dumbest look. Miller remembers having a camera, collecting memories of his family and putting them in albums.

"What's his name?"

He swore to never again call him Petey. "We call him Maggot."

The girl giggles. "How old is Maggot?"

"I don't know." He is uncomfortable talking to a child who is alone, aware he's on the bad side of advice about not talking to strangers. He looks back up at the windows for witnesses. "We got him when he was full-grown."

"I'm seven years old," she says, and Maggot is in ecstasy as the girl uses her short fingernails on his chest. He melts to the cement and surrenders his belly. His one back leg spasms when her fingers find certain places. "Do you have kids?"

"Two," he says without hesitation. "But they live far away."

"Did you ride an airplane to get here?" The girl looks at the sky, where there are only clouds.

"We walked," he says, following her gaze. One of the clouds is the shape of a toddler's toy airplane, with a stubby fuselage and puffy wings. He vaguely recalls his girls watching a cartoon with talking airplane characters. Mary allowed them to eat cereal on the couch, an old fleece blanket across their laps. He lost his temper when Lizzy spilled milk. And the yelling caused Celia to spill hers.

"That looks like Jay Jay the Jet Plane," says the girl, pointing. "Look, it's Jay Jay. Did you do that?"

He remembers because it was such a bizarre cartoon. The airplane was a boy with a human face. Mary pulled one off a store shelf, and they laughed at its creepiness. She threatened to buy one for his next birthday.

The cloud fully transforms into a blue body with oversized black wheels. Even the face is recognizable, with a button nose and toothy smile. Yet it is still a cloud if you are not staring directly at it.

He looks down to find six other children have appeared, and more are filing out of the front doors behind.

The rope jumper points to a cloud beyond the airplane. "Can you make a kitten?"

Other kids are murmuring, small happy noises over his creation.

He concentrates on the new cloud, pictures a cat from a pet food commercial. Two triangles form at the top and take the shape of ears. Next are the eyes and nose, and then a line forms the mouth. A cat body extends out from the head, and there are ohs and ahs from the swelling group.

"You're a magician." It's a boy at his hip. "Can you make a race car?"

"No, make a clown!" A tiny girl bounces on her toes, hand

pulling the end of his shirt. Maggot is sitting up, leaning into the girl with the flowered dress. She has one arm around him.

He chooses a cloud away from the others, decides on an image, and squints in concentration. The cloud begins to move within itself, the vapors boil and rearrange. A portion extends up and away from the main section, and he hears guesses that it's a balloon. But the shape is not round, has a sharp angle at its peak. Another portion of the clouds snakes out below and curves in on itself.

"It's a lollipop!"

"It's a yo yo on a string."

"It's a dog flying a kite."

He is energized by their joy, delights in their guesses. He is jostled more, and feels their heat and excitement at something they've never before seen. He risks looking away from the cloud, knowing it will begin to drift apart, but needs to see their upturned faces. They are round, with wide eyes and enormous smiles. Many are missing front teeth. There are fifty faces, maybe even sixty. And more are running from the building to join the commotion, a flood of beautiful children.

"It's a flying saucer," shouts a boy. "It's shooting a ray gun at a squirrel!"

They laugh at the idea, and he realizes some are clapping. He again concentrates on the cloud, forms the animal body, turning the main portion fat and tinting it brown in his mind.

"It's a dog!"

"It's a Godzilla!"

"It's my Aunt Keisha."

More laughter.

The cloud continues its metamorphosis.

"It's a bear," says a girl, and dozens of children howl agreement. Some say they knew it was a bear first.

"The bear is riding a bicycle!"

"It's called a unicycle, stupid," says a slightly older voice. "It's only got one wheel."

There are cheers when the bear begins to pedal.

"What's it holding?"

"An umbrella!" shouts a girl, her voice filled with glee. "A bear with a pink and white umbrella!"

More than a hundred children witness his creation, black and brown faces with bright eyes. The laughter is music. He wipes tears on a sleeve. Some are pointing, and some hold little brothers and sisters up by their armpits. He is a magician, and again sets the cloud free when he turns in a slow circle to look down and across the sea of jubilance. The children crowd him and touch his dirty clothes, some trying to hold his hands.

He chooses another cloud, begins concentrating on an image of a tightrope, but the noise of squealing tires pierces the air and chokes off the glee. He is confused, momentarily certain he is hearing the typewriter from his police station memory. But the metallic tat, tat, tat pecking sound is too loud, and there are screams and other sounds of panic. The children stampede, some bumping into him hard, and he hears Maggot yelp as the leash is torn from his hand. Tires again squeal out on the street, perhaps 30 feet away. The tires have left their own cloud of blue and gray smoke that rises from the blackened pavement.

It becomes quiet. Maggot leans trembling into his left leg. On the hard ground in front on them is a child's jump rope with yellow handles. The rope is a meandering line along cracks in the cement. The little girl in a flowered dress still clutches one of the plastic handles, but her hand is going limp. Her blood leaks out and searches for the cracks.

Above, the fat brown bear continues to ride its unicycle across the morning sky.

THIRTY-TWO

Miller runs from the dying child, blindly crosses the street, and angles left. He hears Maggot bark, but no scratching toenails follow. The overgrown yards and crumbling homes are the ones he passed last night. He sprints around the upended couch and littered glass, is another two blocks free before a stitch threatens his escape. He pumps his arms harder, until his sneaker splashes down in an uneven dip that pitches him forward, face striking the pavement before his hands. He slides on bare skin, right knee letting go like a popped-cork. He tries getting up before his equilibrium can stabilize. He stumbles to his hip on bent wrists, trying to protect palms that are scraped raw.

"Christopher didn't kill the little jump roper," says the inner voice. "He was upstairs playing house with a pair of dead hookers. He's in the clear, sport, so you know who that leaves?"

He makes it to his feet, steadies himself on rough seas. He swipes an arm across his forehead, smears blood oozing from a swollen gash. Again his balance threatens, but he resumes a jog despite a knee joint that's stuffed with burning shards.

"You were looking for a career change. Bet your high school guidance counselor never wrote it up this way, huh?"

He has the gate of Quasimodo, right arm rowing air to propel forward. One blood-filled sneaker makes wet kissing sounds.

"We need a new nickname for you, sport," the voice says over his gasping breath. "Pull over and take five. Give me a chance to think. You don't wanna be in a rush to pick something that's gonna stick."

Through the jolting misery comes familiar warmth, a heat within his muscles that arrives in late stages of long walks. There's also mounting relief from putting distance between him and the heartache left behind. A second wind arrives despite blood pouring from his nose and chin, and the wrong angle of his right knee. He passes burned-out cars and rubble-filled yards, the early sun flashing behind telephone poles that have shoes knotted together and tossed over the wires.

He hobbles across a four-lane road into a different world. There are children on bicycles, a parked ice cream truck that is empty but not graffiti splashed. Dogs still bark, but their sound is curious not savage. There are trimmed hedges and trees with leaves that have just begun their change, instead of heaps of rotting garbage turning gray. A white minivan approaches, and the man behind the wheel begins a wave. His half-smile turns to a grimace; the eyes that meet Miller's go wide in recognition of the crazy man's damage. The van's engine roars behind Miller, hurtles toward a safe distance.

"Killer," says the voice, and he nearly stumbles. "Your nickname is Killer. I was making it too complicated, when simple is best. Isn't that right, Killer? Has a nice ring. Killer Miller, dig a grave and watch him fill 'er!"

He lumbers through stop signs at the end of each block. Cars sometimes honk, and he is cursed by a teenager on a skateboard.

"That little sweetie pie wanted to pet your nice doggie," says the voice. "Hell, he's probably lapping up her blood right now. Hanging with the devil has screwed with you and the pooch. Goes to show change isn't always a good thing."

Houses grow larger, lawns deeper. He runs past a yellow sign meant to alert drivers to playing children, but is relieved the street is empty. He doesn't want to kill any more innocent kids, doesn't want to leave behind any cancer or plague. And there's no telling the nightmares he'd cause, or how soon the police would be tackling the hemorrhaging madman, locking his hands in those metal cuffs.

"I'm sure they'll have a special straightjacket for Killer Miller."

The stitch returns worse than ever. He vomits a brown stream to one side, then cups a hand to blow his nose.

"They won't need a bloodhound to track you. And speaking of looking for you, guess who's wondering where you've gotten to? Need a hint?"

He has a sudden vivid image of Christopher down on all fours, head bowed to sniff the ground. Maggot is whining and uneasy, upset by his master doing dog-like things. Christopher is on a scent that is sharp and as clear as sliced cheddar. His nose to the pavement makes sucking noises, body weaving but never losing the trail. Miller feels him back there, can hear the damp snorting, the shuffling hands and knees on the rough surface. Christopher's progress is slow, but Miller knows nothing could make him stop. His regal nose is being rubbed raw against the asphalt, the road is sandpaper on thin skin. He'll keep coming forward, unrelenting, until he is only bloody stumps. And then he will wriggle like a worm or a snake, using his chin to inch toward him.

A car bumper strikes Miller's hip and spins him one full rotation. He bounces and lands in a sitting position on a grassy patch next to a newly painted fire hydrant. His ears chime and he expects car doors, and worried voices telling him to lie down, sir, the ambulance is on the way. He instead catches a glimpse of the rear of a car, a Lexus or other expensive make, with two bumper stickers. One reads HILLARY, the other has a pink heart and says SOCCER MOM.

Good for you, he thinks with genuine relief. Get far away from the monster, and don't check the rearview. God knows you don't want that image creeping into your dreams. He prays the soccer mom is able to rationalize her split-second decision, wishes for a way to let her know it was the right thing to do.

He gets an arm over the hydrant and leverages his weight against the stubby cylinder. Blood slicks the surface, but he manages to get both legs under him. At least the new red paint matches and won't need a touch up. Minutes pass before the dizziness recedes. He looks around the intersection to get his bearings.

"Find the bloody trail and go the other way," says the voice, and he sees the drops reflecting the clear sky. "Damn the torpedoes, full speed ahead!"

He lunges from the hydrant, hip grinding in its socket with each step, his tennis playing days a thing of the past. But he knows he is close, can sense his destination through static that has turned his vision into a bad TV channel. He blinks, wipes at the blood, rubs his eyes hard.

"You're almost there, Killer, just one more street. Of course, there's the little matter of a tall fence."

He limps to a halt, stands in the middle of a street facing a shimmering expanse. The road has come to a T intersection, a dead end that for him is deliverance. Yards left in his walk that will become a swim, and then a peaceful descent to a watery womb. The sole impediment is a 10-foot chain link fence that continues into the distance in both directions.

"Let's not dillydally. He's coming, Killer, and this fence ain't climbing itself."

He crosses to the gravel shoulder to inspect his burden. On the other side of the fence is a rocky knoll dropping to the water's edge. There's no way under. A weedy strip covers the bottom six inches of braided metal, and there's a bar that runs the length. He kicks, but it's no good. Grabbing a spot over his head delivers an electric jolt. He recoils before determining the pain is injuries from his first fall. He again reaches, toes his left sneaker between links, and hauls upward. He grabs higher with his right hand, looking down to find a spot for his other shoe. His injured hip catches fire, and he nearly blacks out as his left hand finds the top horizontal bar. He risks waiting a few seconds to see if the pain passes, but it does not. He forges on, knowing what's catching up, certain Christopher will at any moment reach for the back of his shirt.

Both arms are across the bar, and he takes a few more seconds to slow his heart. With a hardy grunt, he heaves his torso over the summit, but his hip doesn't allow a pivot below the waist, and his momentum is unstoppable. Instead of his legs swinging around, he goes headfirst.

The last thing he sees before slamming down is blue water sparkling in the distance, out where the mighty lake runs deep and cold, and where he imagines peace is everlasting. He tries to swim before losing consciousness, but the water where he's landed is rocky and only a few inches. Somewhere close a dog's bark is meant for him.

THIRTY-THREE

The aluminum boat that rocked too easily is a dream constructed from childhood memories. Any attempt to stand and it threatened to shoot out from under your feet. His father would never again set foot in the damn thing, having slogged out of the water and up the duck shit coated bank. So much for an afternoon fishing with his son. He'd used curses brand new to the boy, who pulled off the miracle of miracles by not laughing, thus avoiding either a mighty wallop or his own headfirst trip into the mud.

Grandpa's pond was his private oasis, and that was fine. He borrowed tools from the barn, a wrench to tighten the oarlocks and a screwdriver for where Grandpa had tried fixing the broken seats. He lugged the boat out of the water and capsized it in the grass. He painted it all black from half-used cans, let it dry, then rolled it over and used white on the hull for a Jolly Roger. He took his time, copying from a comic book picture, and was careful to check the weather report to make sure rain wasn't coming. He rode his bike back to Grandpa's the next morning, surveyed his artwork, and then pushed the boat down the slick bank.

He stepped back in the beaten down grass, and for the first time in his life felt like he had something nobody else did. That pond and boat were the best thing in the world. For a few minutes he was captain to an incredibly awesome pirate galleon here in a secret dead man's cove. But by the time he'd bagged up the cans and rags, the black paint began to run. It washed from the aluminum frame into a dark film slowly blooming outward on the water's surface. He sat hard in the painted grass, a line of mallards paddling over to inspect his failure.

He probably cried. When he came to grips with the fact that there would be no galleon, he headed back to the barn for a solution to a different problem. Even the slightest breeze was enough to push the lightweight boat. One strong gust and the whole thing would be skimming across the pond, knocking up against the bank before he could get his worm back in the deep spot with a second cast.

The old hay bailer had a giant ball of twine that would work for hauling an anchor. He used his pocket knife and wound at least 30 feet of hairy string onto a paint stirrer.

A suitable weight was more of a challenge. A big rock was no good because it couldn't be tied off right, and would work free when pulled up. He picked through rusty tractor parts in dusty light coming through cracks where Grandpa had nailed planks to fix a big hole.

He was sweat slick and coated in chaff when he pulled the perfect anchor from the corn crib floor. It was an iron cross, two feet high and one foot wide. It had an oval plate welded where the cross intersected, but no markings or words. He cradled it to his stomach, leaning back for balance as his sneakers shuffled out into the hot sun.

He tied one end of bale twine to the lone cleat, the other to the cross. He rowed his former pirate ship out to the center of the pond, which was the shape of a squished circle and bigger than a kickball field. He stowed the oars and stepped across the front bench to heft the anchor onto the bow. He set the cross upright, turning it into a cool-looking hood ornament before tipping it over the side. It hit the water flat, splashing his face and chest. The cross sank out of sight, jerking the twine and making it hum across the aluminum gunwale.

The tough brown string coiled around his ankle where he'd stepped through a noose. Even though it happened in about two seconds, there was plenty of time to realize his stupidity. There were a dozen more snares formed all around from unwinding the stick. Stupid, stupid, stupid. There was no chance to grab the twine or to brace, only an opportunity to fully comprehend the rotten event about to occur. Acid was poured on his leg when the slack ran out, or a giant pterodactyl had swooped down and snatched hold. He was wrenched upside down, head thudding the seat, as he was dragged on his butt, and then he went over the side and splashed down.

He'd been too surprised to get much of a breath before going under, only a reflexive gasp. He looked longingly at the fading light, waiting for the anchor to thud down on the muddy bottom, but it never did. The twine was cut too short, or he'd wrapped the cross too many times. Instead, the unstable boat capsized and was held firmly at the surface by trapped air. The cross wafted below his throbbing ankle, the twine surely about to slice through skin and bone.

It'll cut off my foot, he thought, and then realized it meant he'd be set free. He saw it happen with one of Grandpa's leg traps. A beaver was damming the spring that fed the pond, turning a low spot in the woods into a bog.

"Kills trees and causes an awful mess," Grandpa told him. "Makes you wonder what God had in mind by designing them critters."

They were walking back along a narrow animal path to check the traps when Grandpa reached a hand to his shoulder, leaned down close to whisper. "Worst thing is their big chompers. Makes 'em look a little like Grandma when her mood takes a turn."

The beaver had sprung the trap, metal teeth slamming closed on one rear leg. Maybe the trap had cut clear through, or maybe the beaver chewed himself free. Either way, one leg was all that remained.

"Will you looky there." Grandpa sounded like he'd never seen such a thing. They followed the blood trail for 100 yards, probably out of curiosity, but the red dots ran out. Grandpa looked up, maybe checking the trees. The boy hoped the beaver would grow a new leg, the same way lizards grew new tails.

Suspended in the water, his ankle was out of reach even if he could chew his way free. His body drifted for what felt like minutes, slowly rotating as his scant air exhausted. He didn't flail or cry out. What lurked in the muddy water barely out of sight wasn't scary. Fading was the discomfort from his burning ankle and sore head, the embarrassment of his fatal stupidity.

Then he looked up and nearly laughed. The ducks had returned to investigate the commotion, were paddling along with big orange feet, giving him a submarine view most kids would never see. The ducks were fuzzy footballs, silly wind-up feet making them turn tight circles. Some dipped their heads under to say hello.

He shut his eyes, and let his muscles go limp. His last air became bubbles headed for the surface. He wasn't afraid of allowing in the water, even knowing it would hurt at first. Like diving into an icy pool, you're convinced in those first seconds it will never get better, the shock is forever. But this underwater place was too good, too peaceful to leave. No red-faced policeman with handcuffs, no teasing kids shouting Deadeye Miller and Bird Slayer, and no father poised like a beaver trap. The water would hold him and keep him safe.

He was bracing for a deep inhale when some kind of underwater vine wrapped around his neck. It choked off any chance to let in the water, and tranquility turned to panic. He kicked and thrashed, but whatever had him was too strong. He was pulled backward, water rushing past, and the cross climbed to follow. The grip tightened when he grabbed at his throat, and black dots crowded out his vision.

The sensation was of being lifted and then cradled in a grown-up's arms. His lips parted and his mouth was prodded by fingers with pointy nails. His tongue was forced aside, and then the fingers withdrew to press on his forehead and arch his throat. The sun on the other side of his eyelids was eclipsed, and he understood he was being kissed in a way his father sometimes kissed his mother. It was a dirty movie kiss, where mouths jammed together and looked like they were eating. It made him sick to his stomach, but he didn't want to throw up in someone's mouth. He fought the impulse and let the kiss happen, tried imagining eternity under the deep water.

THIRTY-FOUR

Miller lies on a rock-hard mattress watching Christopher slink around the room, lifting dust sheets and pulling out drawers. If he's looking for something he doesn't find it, but Miller senses Christopher is killing time.

"Welcome back to the world of the living!"

Christopher comes to adjust pillows, smooths the musty quilt tucked to his chin as though he's a nursemaid. Christopher wears new clothes, all white, with yellow-tinted aviator glasses. He's done a poor job shaving. Bits of toilet tissue are like bad acne, and none of the wounds have properly clotted.

"You look like a Third World cult leader," Miller says. And he also looks older, deep wrinkles have appeared, and he's gone from skinny to nearly skeletal. The head cold has turned into something worse. Something like cancer, Miller hopes. A fast-spreading version that is especially painful and makes his dick rot off, would be ideal.

"I've been called worse." Christopher holds out his arms and does a complete turn. "These are some digs, huh?"

The bed faces French doors and a Juliet balcony. Beyond is water that melts into a foggy horizon. It was once a grand master suite, a lofty ceiling with ornate crown molding now cracked and missing strips. Cobwebs soften upper corners, and faded cabbage rose wallpaper peels away in tight rolls. White sheets cover all the furniture except the bed. The ghostly mounds are sharp contrast to the dark wood floor. There's a dim light in the adjoining bathroom that's decorated in salmon color tiles.

"Quite a find, if I say so myself." Christopher is again inspecting the hidden furnishings.

"Where are we?"

"Somebody posted a condemned sign on the front door," he says, then laughs maniacally until he's overrun by a coughing fit. He covers his face with his hands, rubbing hard, sunglasses askew. Miller catches a glimpse of bloody gums when the hands lower. And there's something out of sync with his movements, not all pistons firing correctly. "Get it? It's a home for the condemned. A fitting place for you and me, kid!"

Miller reaches from under the quilt to touch his forehead. There's a bump, but no abrasion. He turns his palm to examine the skin. It's soft and pink, with unbroken creases. His life and heart lines are intact, and his fate line runs clear and deep toward a middle finger. The only plausible explanation for the missing damage is that he's been asleep for days. No, make that weeks. The cuts had been severe. Blood poured from his head. He left most of the skin from his palms on the road. He reaches back under the quilt and strokes his right hip, reimagines the car's impact that sent him careening. With a full twist, lest we forget. Judges would have added points for acrobatics, but the landing was sketchy at best. He slides a hand over naked skin and presses, then rolls slightly to touch his buttocks. Nothing. No lumps, and not a hint of discomfort. Only smooth skin on a once flabby ass. He makes a fist and raps his hip bone, braces for pain that doesn't come.

"Jesus, take it easy." Christopher comes to sit at the end of the bed. He shakes his head, touches Miller's leg through the quilt, squeezes just above the spot where the twine snared him as a kid. "You were in rough shape when I found you. Looked like you'd been dragged under a city bus."

"But I'm fine now. All healed up like nothing ever happened. Right as fucking rain, and ready to jump back in the game."

Christopher props the sunglasses on his forehead to rub the bridge of his nose. He's showing his patience is being tested. "You're fine, I'm fine, we're all fine." The tone is mocking, but then turns cheerful. "Come, Mr. Fine, let me show you the new rumpus room. I promise it'll lift you out of these nasty doldrums. You won't believe how much I've gotten done."

Christopher stands, grasps the end of the quilt with both hands and pulls hard and fast. It's the magic trick where dishes are left behind when a tablecloth is whisked from underneath. "O come all ye faithful," Christopher sings. "Joyless and no trumpet!"

Miller cringes when the man's long fingers close over his wrist. He's led naked from the room, down a steep flight of stairs covered in a faded runner, each step groaning under their weight. But the entryway is bright, and the crystal chandelier reflects diamond patterns all around. Through an archway is surely the home's most stately room, now jammed with boxes, tables, and odd equipment. Maggot curls in a dog bed in one corner, tail thumping twice when he sees them. There are work benches with iron vises, sinister masks hanging from welding tanks, and a pyramid of metal pipes and other plumbing gizmos. It's a helter-skelter workshop, with a milk crate full of cell phones, jars of screws, hoops of colored wire, and card tables piled with electronics.

But the walls are the most disconcerting feature. They at first appear graffiti-covered, sweeping spray-painted lines of roller coaster tracks running up and down faded wallpaper. But it's not a random composition. It's in fact some kind of map. Torn newspaper pages are pinned along the way, black and white photos of ribbon cuttings and grand openings. Below each clipping is more paint, block letters that read EXPLODING HOSPITAL WOODS, BURNING THEATER FOREST, FLAMING TRAIN CASTLE, OLD FOLKS SWAMP, and on and on.

Each destination has pen marks representing fire and curling smoke coming from the paper edges. The artwork has been produced by a manic hand, hours of work to create a lunatic's mural.

"Pretty neat, huh?" Christopher stands proud, arms folded and a big smile.

"I don't understand."

"Did that car run over your head?" Christopher makes a fist and taps knuckles to his own skull, knocking his sunglasses to the floor. He sneezes a bloody spray, and casually wipes with the back of his hand. "It's the game you told me about. The one you played with your sweet little girls."

He stares at Christopher, who raises his eyebrows and lowers his chin, as if waiting for Miller to find something lost on the tip of the tongue.

"Candy Land," Miller whispers.

"Isn't it the most awesome thing in the world?" Christopher holds out his arms, palms up, turns another slow circle and accidentally crushes his sunglasses.

"No."

"Look!" Christopher brushes past Miller to shove boxes out

of the way, glass breaking inside. Maggot barks, then whines from his corner bed. Christopher drops to his knees along the wall, points to stick figure drawings of three people, one holding what looks like a baseball bat. "Remember this goober? Gimme back my fish before I knock you out of the park. Had me pissing my pants! This is cool, huh?"

"No," Miller repeats.

Christopher looks up with a dismissive frown, then returns to his artwork. He's leaving bloody handprints. "I dabbled in watercolors, but never had a lesson. Interesting how we all find different sources of inspiration. Did you know the word inspiration literally means to breathe into? This just flowed out of me once I got started."

Miller's eyes follow the track away from the stick figures. It passes next to a double-wide mobile home at the end of a long driveway, moves on to the sketch of a town with the obituary photo of a local police chief. Another stop is at a circus, with a clipping of an arrival announcement and half-off admission coupon. There's a grainy crime scene photo of a police detective squatting over a small victim's chalk outline. The detective's right hand touches the ground, his other covers his face as though hiding tears. The background is an ugly brick structure Miller knows is fourteen stories and contains further atrocities.

"Oh, wait. Stupid old me." Christopher pulls out a pen while scooting forward on his knees. He stops to consider the tracks, seems to measure a phantom distance, then draws a large hollow arrow a few inches from what must be the outline of Lake Erie. The arrow is also next to a photo of the mayor and city council lined up behind a wide ribbon. The mayor holds comically oversized scissors matching his politician's smile. It is the photo Christopher has captioned EXPLODING HOSPITAL WOODS. Inside the arrow he writes YOU ARE HERE. "Good to have perspective," Christopher says and laughs. He gets to his feet and brushes dirt from his knees, gore from his nose befouling the material.

"Your nose is bleeding," Miller says, watching several drops stain the front of his shirt.

Wiping a sleeve across his face, Christopher looks at the mess and clucks. "Getting old is a bitch." And as if to demonstrate, he pinches his left middle fingernail with the thumb and index fingers of

191

his other hand. The pointed nail wiggles free to leave exposed skin that's pink and raw. He flicks the fingernail over the spilled boxes and shrugs.

Miller is disgusted and elated. "Jesus."

"The fucking sands of time," Christopher says. "You should see the color of my piss. Speaking of which, pick through those bags before your pecker snags on something sharp. There's jeans your size."

Miller rips open a black garbage bag and dumps the contents. He slides on a pair one size too big and rolls the waistband. "You know I'm not helping with this shit. Not in a million years."

Christopher pulls a shirt from the pile to blow his nose and wipe his hands. He goes to the table with cell phones, tosses aside the shirt to rummage through the crate. He turns to Miller, phone in hand, then struggles to lift his butt onto the table.

"You know how this works?" He holds out the small black device to Miller. "I mean how it works as a detonator."

Miller shakes his head, watches Christopher's unsteady hands.

"The secret is in here." Christopher taps the phone's bottom corner. "You open it up and grind a hole through this piece. Attach two wires to the vibrator mechanism, running one directly to a battery pack. Any alkaline set is fine. The other end goes to a low amp wire that's also connected to the batteries. When a call or text comes in, the circuit completes to incinerate the wire. Bingo, bango, you have a detonator that essentially lights the fuse."

Miller peers at the wall. "How many bombs are in the hospital?"

Christopher's head lolls and he nearly falls backward, grabbing the table with one hand for support. He smiles and rocks from side to side. "A thousand." His voice is low and conspiratorial, a drunk in a bar telling a whopper.

"The truth."

Christopher purses his lips and rolls his eyes. Purple half-circles have formed in each socket. His trickling nostrils create a sanguine goatee. "You caught me, smarty pants. Bombs, bombs, how many bombs? I wore sunglasses and nobody suspected a thing. I'm a stealthy bastard when required. And before I forget, I need you to raise the limit on your credit card. I'm done arguing with those suspicious buggers."

"You're dying."

"No shit, Sherlock, we're all dying. Every recent graduate of Miss Manners third grade class is dying. Even Oprah is dying."

"Yes, but you're also bleeding on the inside," Miller says. "You need me to take over in order to maintain the balance."

Christopher lifts his head, snorts and spits a red glob. "You, my skeptical friend, have an unhealthy amount of negativity. My pappy had a saying when it came to motivation. He'd put me on his knee and say, sonny boy, dangle a sweet carrot and even a stubborn donkey will come around to your way of thinking. Hand to God, those were his very words."

Miller steps back when Christopher drops to his feet and charges back to where he'd last drawn, moving with surprising agility. Christopher slaps the wall, and Miller is distracted by white hair flying loose and wafting to the floor. "Here we are. You and me. Right on this spot." There's now a bloody palm print over the arrow.

"You're coming apart," Miller quietly says.

Christopher whirls sideways and goose steps along the wall. One hand is flat against the tracks, boxes kicked away as he marches the room's perimeter. "A little boom here, and a little boom there. A little boom-boom everywhere. You getting the picture?"

"You expect me to blow up those buildings."

"Not without a carrot!" Christopher traces his way to the end of the tracks, and turns toward him. "You were supposed to ask *but what's in it for me.* Swear to God, that car really did run over your fucking head."

"There's nothing you could say or do. Nothing."

"Well, now, that's not true, my friend," Christopher says. "Not true at all." He whips out his pen and begins doodling where the tracks leave off. Miller watches him draw three coffins. "Your inner voice was about to spill the beans, so I shut him up. Notice how quiet it's gotten in there? And you're welcome, by the way. Anyhow, you and I go way back. I've always had a talent for recognizing potential."

"You killed my family."

"That's just like you. Always jumping to conclusions." Christopher continues his child-like artwork. Next to the coffins goes a house with a tall tree in the backyard, and a dog with a jagged line across its throat. The dog is Petey.

"Stop."

"Mary was sick," Christopher says over his shoulder. "She had the C word, and it had snuck into some tricky places for the doctors. She'd started feeling it. Sharp stomach pains woke her up nights, and then awful, awful rounds of vomiting. Didn't want to worry you, though. She was a real trooper."

Miller is unable to speak. He watches Christopher's long fingers at work. They are dappled with blood and now missing most nails. Miller vaguely hears the rain that beat against the window, the roll of distant thunder and flashes of lightning that showed a stop action movie of his family being murdered. He can feel those impossibly strong fingers snake around his neck, choking and holding him back while everything he loves is destroyed.

"Your girls were collateral damage." Christopher's voice is suddenly tender. "Sometimes it's unavoidable. But it can be fixed, my friend. Maybe not all the way, but finishing the work will bring enough balance. And the really delicious part? Come on, I know you're dying to hear about your yummy carrot."

Miller shakes his head, doesn't want to know.

"You choose which daughter comes back." Christopher begins drawing a face, and the cartoonish scribbling transforms into elegant strokes, with blended shadowing and depth. He works fast, as though the image in his mind will at any moment disappear. He finishes one, and then a second. He completes the portrait of Miller's dead children with a flourish, signing his name across the bottom with flair. He steps back, extends an arm with an upturned thumb to regard his artwork, head nodding agreeably.

Christopher tucks the pen back into the front pocket of his bloodstained pants and turns with a satisfied grin that is missing a front tooth. "Your carrot," he says with a wink, and then bows.

THIRTY-FIVE

They sit in a diner not eating. Christopher is surrounded by plates of meatloaf and scrambled eggs, sides of mashed potatoes and double gravy, all gone cold. Miller's toast never comes, but he leaves the waitress alone. She's suffered enough, deserves a great big shiny medal for coming by their booth twice. It was Christopher's idea to venture outside during one of his rare flurries of vitality. But his juice ran out, and he's reverting back into one of his drooling idiot phases.

"You want me to cut that?"

"No, I'm fine." Missing teeth slur Christopher's words. His cheeks are fallen caverns, his voice nasal from the toilet paper stuffed up each nostril to dam the flow. He wears blue rubber dish gloves and a wool cap to conceal some of what's happening. But there's nothing to contain what radiates from his haggard body, the malignant heat emanating from a breached core. Miller imagines it's the same sensation as when walking past an overworked torture chamber.

The diner is a ten minute walk, and looks to have had a lake view before apartment buildings went up.

"We should ask for a doggy bag," Miller says.

"That's a good idea." And then Christopher frowns, confused, leans back to check under the table. "Maggot's gone. I need to find him."

"We left him home, remember? He's not doing so hot."

"Oh, he's home." Christopher's voice is wistful. He rests his rubber encased hands on the table, several blue fingers dipping in gravy. There's an ebb and flow to his ambition, and Miller knows he'll have to wait for the next tide to get him back to the house.

Miller is refreshed by the excursion, despite the company. He hadn't realized how rancid the old mansion's air had turned until stepping out the front door. While Miller has been constructing rudimentary bombs, Maggot has spent days curled in his dog bed, occasionally fouling himself. Miller gave up cleaning, instead throwing towels over bloody stools. He slipped in it once, nearly blowing them all to smithereens when he hit the floor cradling a live pipe bomb. He sat spitting splashed shit morsels from the back of his tongue, but was also smiling from the memory of an old Pee Wee Herman movie he'd rented for the girls.

"I meant to do that," Miller said, then laughed.

In their bomb factory, Christopher has his own unique set of smells, working up a sour sweat to go with the other rotten things brewing within. He'd found a yardstick to use like a crazed professor, slapping tables for emphasis, and stomping around the room to point out inventory necessary for each type of explosion. Some would kill directly, while others targeted support beams. You wanted it right the first time. Measure twice, blow up once.

Miller comes around to slide onto the diner's vinyl bench next to Christopher. He tells him to lift his arm out of the way, wanting to touch him as little as possible. He fishes inside Christopher's pants pocket for cash, something he should have done back at the house. The pocket is soaked and the bills are in a balled clump at the bottom. He's wet himself, and there's a strong ammonia smell when Miller pulls out the money. Pets and their owners really do end up alike.

"Please go away."

Miller looks up to see the back of the waitress's uniform as she hurries off to safety. On the table is the torn up check for their meal.

THIRTY-SIX

Miller adjusts the shoulder pack crammed with the fruits of a month's labor. He takes extra care because he's still a wiring novice, fearing connections might wiggle loose. He's confident none will accidentally detonate, but he's never been good with his hands. Replacing the cord from a flea market lamp had been his crowning achievement for household projects. And these wires are miniature by comparison, wanting to come undone no matter how perfect his solder work appears. He occasionally glances at Christopher's signed portrait of the girls.

You choose which girl comes back.

Christopher is no longer any help. They'd been assembling side by side, teacher and student, organizing calamitous material into a workable production line. Pipes to be cut were stacked next to the vise used for pinching off ends. Then came the black powder and jars of shrapnel. The wood background boards and electronics table were last. Christopher began lecturing on more complex devices, had unwrapped a block of tan clay he called Semtex. He molded a piece into the shape of a hotdog and pretended to take a bite.

"This is the size that took down the Pan Am flight over Lockerbie." He then hoisted a full brick. "Imagine the hullaballoo from this little baby."

But Christopher is nowhere to be found, and Maggot is in no condition to talk. It's the faded carpet runner that leads Miller up the stairs and down the long hall. There's a faint blood trail, and bits of skin with white hair attached. He creaks open the closet door at the end of the passageway and finds Christopher in the shadowy back corner, as if hiding from light. And it could very well be that he's become light sensitive, considering his skin has peeled away. A skinless purple grape, he looks like he's been turned inside out. The only remaining hair is a ponytail tuft in back. He seems to shift toward Miller, gums parted, tongue bared because his lips and teeth are gone. Air sucks in and out in quick pants. It's hard to be sure he's even conscious because of his missing eyelids.

Miller's head cocks to one side, pausing for any emotional response that might come. But he feels nothing. He does not hate the monster who turned his daughters into collateral damage, doesn't find any particular satisfaction that Christopher is dissolving alone in a dusty closet. He steps back and closes the door with only a brief thought of dragging him out into the front yard's sunshine.

There is balance to consider. And there is work finish.

Miller sets out to complete another mission after nightfall. He's almost cheerful enough to whistle. It's a short walk, and the backpack is full and ready on his shoulders. He pulls open the rear door of a one-story building. Guide rails are everywhere, down hallways, into the smallest alcoves, and in every bathroom stall. It brings a nervous smile thinking how the importance of balance increases as you age. How losing it can cause so much damage in a flash. One minute you're unloading the week's groceries, the next you're in a cruddy joint like this, a hip full of screws and the Angel of Death impatiently tapping his wristwatch.

There's a cloying disinfectant odor, and the sound of televisions despite residents having succumbed to nightly meds. He visited this place two days earlier for reconnaissance. Childlike artwork stapled to omnipresent corkboards gives it a Kindergarten feel, and there are errant balloons trapped in out of reach spots. In the daytime, wheelchairs lined the walls, elderly residents backed up as if awaiting a parade. A few had lifted their eyes, and he was certain some recognized who he was, who he has become. He'd been able to stroll past the front desk without signing the clipboard, and nobody questioned where he went. He was mostly invisible to staff carting plastic trays with miniature food portions to hushed rooms. There was little sadness or joy, only the impression of people settling in for a long wait. If there was a sense of foreboding, it was well masked. Perhaps anxiety of what was next to come had faded away.

In the dark halls, he follows the mental notes he'd made of the crucial spots to position each bomb. His load lightens with every carefully placed device. If night staff discovers him roaming the halls, he'll be Sheila's grandson from Room 147, having slipped back to retrieve his coat and wallet. He'll be terrible sorry, embarrassed for startling anyone and causing a ruckus.

In fact, room 147 is the final stop on his U-shaped route. During his scouting work he'd peeked in on the elderly woman napping in the window bed, committed to memory the name printed across get-well cards propped on the nightstand.

He delivers his last terrible package, leaving the six-inch pipe and cell phone detonator on the tile floor behind the toilet. Inside the wall is the water supply line for this wing's emergency sprinkler system. He looks back in on Sheila before making his escape. She is awake in the glow of a reading light.

"I know who you are." Her voice is resigned.

The bed between them is empty and inviting, despite having been made with sharply tucked corners. The sheets would be cool at first.

"I don't think so," he says, dismayed she isn't much older. Better to find her languishing with a withered thumb to the nurse's call button, pressing and pressing for more pills, his acquittal delivered by a diseased heart or respiratory infection. But this woman is merely old and tired. Sheila is a tired old woman lying alone in bed, clearly not ready for death.

"It's too soon," she says, making a statement and not a plea.

Collateral damage, he thinks, his back touching the cold wall. He is dealing with what Christopher experienced a thousand or a million times. The Grim Reaper is easily recognized when approaching from a dim hallway instead of a screeching car crash. The doomed know they are looking at the face of a devil. His own precarious balance is jeopardized by those with time to affirm their impending death and then respond.

"I'm sorry," he says.

The woman sighs, and then reaches for one of the cards on her nightstand. She puts it flat on her chest and folds her hands over top. Sheila smiles toward him and closes her eyes. "It's all right," she says. "You are who you are."

He slips out of the room, and then away from the building. He begins dialing the cell phones.

THIRTY-SEVEN

Killing is easy as pie, the planning a game. Miller feels like a natural, sauntering about the work room with honeybee resolve.

One of Christopher's articles taped to the wall features an esteemed obstetrician. Miller read it three times before finding a hint to its purpose. Not that he required an explanation; he was only satisfying curiosity. It was just another stop along Christopher's demented version of Candy Land.

The doctor is employed at a prestigious hospital, has an adoring family, a penchant for Wednesday golf, and volunteers a monthly shift at a family planning center. Miller assumes this service work involves abortions, which gives relevance to the adjacent clipping for a Minnesota gun store. It's all part of the change that effortlessly puts two and two together. Cuts from wires and sharp pipe edges heal in minutes, just as he knows a Minneapolis man has purchased a handgun, completed the paperwork, and endured the required waiting period. The man will proudly own up to his deed, despite the fallout for his wife and grown kids. Miller heard God speak to the man, or at least a voice the man believed was God. The man's plan includes surrendering to police a few days after the assassination, enough time for clinics across the region to stew in the terror of uncertainty. Miller takes no joy from preempting the holy mission because the man will someday find a new target.

Abortionists do not upset Miller, nor do their killers. He hums while applying his magically acquired knowledge to the creation of a package bomb. The explosive is a chunk of Semtex carefully molded into the likeness of a human fetus. He uses a tiny extra piece to make it a boy. There's no need to look up the doctor's home address because Miller simply knows what to write on the brown paper. He has a photographic memory without having taken a picture. Probably how Santa keeps things straight among all those

200

naughty and nice girls and boys, ho ho ho.

Being busy keeps him from obsessing over the carrot. Who knows, maybe the carrot isn't real. Maybe it was only a desperate lie from a dying monster. The lectures about balance could have been more of Christopher's bullshit, with Miller's sanity being collateral damage. And the carrot? Celia had commenced the battle for independence, while Lizzy possessed her mother's quiet melancholy. He suspected Mary shared some of her secret poems and paintings with their younger daughter, while Celia was lost in her iPhone and school friends.

He will probably leave Celia dead. But it can go either way. If there really is a decision to make, he'll wait until the last minute. Take it down to the wire. Killing is easy, but he suspects bringing life back could be a real stumper. All the hard decisions had been Mary's. Even the Sunday crossword belonged to his wife. He was more of a Wizard of Id savant. Mother Goose and Grimm, too, if he was being honest.

He packs the remaining Semtex back into its Army surplus ammo box, stores the unused cell phones, and uses a brush to clear metal shavings from his main workbench. The last thing to clean up is Maggot, who died curled in his corner bed. He grabs the edge of the corduroy material and slides the soft cushion through a small sitting room and the once grand kitchen. He kicks open the back door and makes his way down the wobbly deck steps, the dog's rigid body thumping on each plank. He leaves Maggot on the lawn at the water's edge, where seagulls immediately come to investigate, and perhaps exact some revenge.

The post office closes soon, but he's compelled by one more task. He grabs a screwdriver to pry an unframed mirror from the entryway hall. The beveled edge cuts into his palms as he carries it to his workbench and props it at a slight downward angle. He attaches an extension cord to a soldering gun and plugs into a wall socket, then pulls off his grimy shirt. For as strong as he feels, even given up needing a vise to bend the pipes, his body is emaciated. He has the torso of a 90-year-old man, brittle bones poking from under sallow skin. His hair has gone completely white.

He rubs his hollow stomach and reaches for the gun once its tip puffs smoke. The pain is excruciating when he makes the first sweeping line from his solar plexus out over his upper ribs. But the pain is also comforting, like going for a long walk, and there's a warm surge through his muscles from the intense heat. Left and then right. Pain and relief. It's easiest to work looking down rather than into the mirror, as he finishes one side of his artwork and then the other. The troubling sections are the thorax and abdomen, which fill with his boiling blood and are difficult to see. The final strokes are the long antennae that end just below each pale nipple. He unplugs the cord and uses the shirt to wipe his stomach.

It's much larger than Mary's butterfly tattoo, but it's even better than he hoped. He gently touches the outline of one wing, the puffy burned skin producing a three-dimensional effect.

"I miss you," he says to Mary, his voice insignificant in a room crowded by so many instruments of destruction.

Staring into the dusty mirror, he is closer to his wife than at any other moment in the last days and weeks. It's impossible not to smile. The bloody tattoo begins to heal and fade, but he vows to make another tomorrow.

THIRTY-EIGHT

The narrow dock sways under Miller's bare feet, bleached and splintered planks showing glimpses of the water beneath. He comes to the last board, toes curled over the edge, hanging ten as they say. A few deep breaths and he lunges, hands slicing the cold water, then forehead and shoulders. It's a shock to his naked body, but a few easy strokes and warm blood floods into his muscles.

He doesn't panic when he hears a second splash somewhere behind. He's had this dream a hundred times, experienced the outcome far too often. Relaxed and strong, he continues swimming away from land, to where the bottom slopes from sight and he is a flesh and blood airplane lifting from a rock and humus tarmac.

It's hundreds of yards to the deeper channels, but he's well practiced for the endeavor. Left and then right. Pain and relief.

He nears the perfect spot when a hand clamps around his ankle, and tugs him backward with superhuman force. He tries to remain calm despite getting a lung full of water. This is new. In prior dreams the arresting grip always misses, sharpened nails leaving marks, but coming up empty. He gags, and attempts treading in place one-legged. He coughs foam, doggy paddling to keep his face above turbulence. He twists his captured leg and finds that although the grip is strong, it's also slippery. From the coppery taste in the water he knows whatever holds him is bleeding. He's tasted plenty of blood in recent months.

"Love me," says a voice intended to sound like a girl, like Lizzy or maybe the young prostitute he'd help murder, but he knows better. He knows Christopher is trying to trick him.

Miller bends his free leg and then kicks with all his might, driving his heel squarely into his subduer's face. The impact is the same satisfaction as stomping an empty soda can that collapses perfectly flat. He doesn't see the result, but knows he's caved in the evil head because the fingers no longer bind him, have slid away and set him free.

He continues swimming in place, gives his heart time to calm, his Zen to reconstitute. Then he rolls onto his back, arms and legs oscillating, until he settles into absolute balance. If he's learned anything from walking alongside Christopher, it's the significance of balance in the world. Tilting even just a little invites chaos. Lose balance and bad things crash through your door on a stormy night. Get the balance correct and perhaps some of the evil will withdraw enough to leave a smidge of goodness.

That's the hope, anyway. It's complicated, Christopher would say.

The water around him quiets as he splays in a reverse dead man's float. Water fills his ears and the sun warms his chest and face. The sky is blue and clear. There are no clouds to sculpt, but that's okay. He's done with clouds. Two small birds flit overhead, bright yellow canaries that dance through the air as though reveling in their own newly found freedom. When they disappear into the horizon, he exhales deeply to make his body dip under the surface. He slides head first into the quiet. Sinking is another version of flying, and he extends his arms—his wings—to soar weightless, the pulse in his ears and temples reminders of his continued life.

Lizzy is lying on the bottom in footy pajamas that have been too small for the better part of a year. The seams in spots are frayed, the elastic stretched and torn. Her stuffed bear is tucked under her chin, framed by billowing locks that are refuge to darting minnows. The scene wavers in bending light, and her body shifts with the deep current. Her eyes are open, alert, and she turns her face slightly as if to better see her approaching father, who must only be an expanding silhouette.

His momentum wanes 10 feet from the murky bottom, and he remembers his grandpa telling him all lakes and ponds were temporary, that nature was always working to fill them in, make them fertile ground for grizzled old farmers like him.

Miller kicks, and pulls twice with cupped hands. Lizzy's pale cheeks are a roadmap of tiny unbroken veins. He marvels at the rows of small white teeth, perfectly spaced by specks of pink gums. She is smiling at him, arms unfolding and reaching, her bear in one balled fist. She mouths the word *Daddy*.

He ignores the awful bruises, the fierce purple scarf left by her killer. She is alive and yearning for him, and he again kicks to close the final distance, his body a hovering storm cloud over a sinless Eden.

"My beautiful girl," he says, silty water washing across his tongue. One hand slides behind her back to separate worn fabric from muck and gravel. The other cradles her head.

She emits feverish heat as she squirms and folds within her father's arms, their salty tears spilling into the cold nebula. Maybe Christopher was the Devil, or maybe just another human soul drafted for its vulnerability. It doesn't matter. Whatever the tall man was, he kept his word, because this foreboding world is more than a dream.

Daddy. Her voice is unchanged by creatures that haunt pinched spaces under beds and shadowy closets with doors ajar. It is the sound of morning light's first lemon ray, or a drop of rain the instant before landing. *Hold me tight.*

Miller's pilgrimage ends in a luxuriant embrace.

ABOUT THE AUTHOR

Cole Alpaugh's newspaper career began in the early 80s, starting with small daily papers in Maryland and Massachusetts, where his stories won national awards. His most recent job was at a large daily in Central New Jersey, where his "true life" essays included award-winning pieces on a traveling rodeo and an in-depth story on an emergency room doctor that was nominated by Gannett News Service for a 1991 Pulitzer Prize. Cole also did work for two Manhattan-based news agencies, covering conflicts in Haiti, Panama, Nicaragua, El Salvador, Thailand and Cambodia. His work has appeared in dozens of magazines, as well as most newspapers in America. Cole's debut novel, *THE BEAR IN A MUDDY TUTU*/Camel Press/2011, was a national bestseller in Canada, and he has authored three other novels, including a finalist for the 2015 International Book Awards. The charity he founded a decade ago has supplied thousands of soccer balls to kids in Haiti. Cole is currently a freelance photographer and writer living in Northeast Pennsylvania, where he spends his afternoons watching his youngest daughter hit fuzzy yellow balls. You can find Cole online at ColeAlpaugh.com.